COUNTRY ROGUES

Antler's reaction to stories in *Country Rogues*

About ***Another Idaho*** by Mike Newman:

A thin stream of pre-come stretching from your lips
to a young cowboy's stallion cock as you pause
in sucking him to look up at his face
in the flickering light of a campfire
in a mountain wilderness miles from anyone....

About ***Spirit of the Pond*** by Frederic Trainor:

Meet the black boy who longs to rub his thang cross
your booboo
up tween dem plump white cheeks and den cornhole
your dookie hole
wit his big black mamba wit de moon shinin bright
and da hogs
a-gruntin in da pen while crickets and bullfrogs
sing da blues....

COUNTRY ROGUES

Short Story Anthology

Edited by

BILL LEE

GLB PUBLISHERS SAN FRANCISCO

FIRST EDITION

Published in the United States by
GLB Publishers
P.O. Box 78212, San Francisco, CA 94107 USA

Cover Design by Timothy Lewis

Number 4 of ROGUES Series

Publisher's Cataloging in Publication
(Prepared by Quality Books Inc.)

Country rogues : short story anthology / edited by Bill Lee.
p. cm. -- (Rogues series ; #4)
ISBN: 1-879194-19-8.

1. Gay men--Fiction. 2. Erotic stories, American. I. Lee, Bill, ed. II. Series: Lee, Bill. Rogues series ; #4.

PS648.H57C68 1995 813'.54
QBI95-20261

First printing, July, 1995
10 9 8 7 6 5 4 3 2 1

PREFACE

Many of us have memories of country experiences, some haunting, some comic, that, acknowledged or not, form the basis for our more urban existences. Some are coming out stories, when "outing" was something one did with one guy rather than in the pages of the tabloids. It wasn't a political statement, it was a welcome acceptance of what we knew to be true, and sometimes the rural setting added spice or familiarity or even danger to a revelation of reality.

Others, accustomed to dark, smoky dungeons or strobe-flashing discos, encountered realignments of priorities, clarified concepts of masculine relationships when relieved of the trappings of urban blight, and were brought back to the basics when the music changed to chirping crickets and the lighting to peaceful moonglow.

So I asked some friends to help put together a collection of short stories celebrating our rural heritage. This fourth in the "Rogues" series ranges across rural U.S., from misty beaches to deserts and plains of tasseled corn, even temporally from colonial times to the age of AIDS, recapturing the impact and accompaniment that nature can impose. We purposely included subjects frequently ignored in anthologies such as this, such as generation gap, black and white lovers, spiritualism, even country musicians. A few of these stories have been previously published in some form, but for the most part we produced them for you from scratch, contemporarily and from recollections of simpler times.

The authors, as usual for this series, are also varied in locales, age, and experience. They bring a spectrum of attitudes and orientations with at least some common denominators: they are masculine and they are gay, and they wouldn't have it any other way.

We hope you like the stories.

TABLE OF CONTENTS

THE FINDING 1

Lee Williams

UNCLE BUD 13

Joseph W. Bean

ANOTHER IDAHO 28

Mike Newman

Adapted from SECRET BUDDIES *(GLB Publishers, 1991)*

SPIRIT OF THE POND 45

Frederic Trainor

Published with permission of The Acolyte Press, Amsterdam, The Netherlands. First published as POND *in* The Ninth Acolyte Reader.

BERDACHE 55

Bart Louis

SEA–BEAT 64

Robert Burdette Sweet

CARLOS 82

Lee Williams

MOLEHILLS AND FORGOTTEN THINGS 90

Frederic Trainor

THE HORSEMEN 125

Bill Lee

COUNTRY CARRYINGS–ON 133

Reid Dennis

CAVE BEAR ! 149

Lee Dennegar

PENDULUM 158

Bill Lee

THE CIRCLE Q 186

Denis Hunter

PICKUP 202

Bart Louis

THE FINDING

Lee Williams

My eyelids were drooping in the heat shimmering above the highway between the cornfields. It was dusk and some of the infrequent cars I met had their lights on, but they only half registered with me in my somnolent state of hypnotic driving. I hadn't bothered to turn on my lights; the rhythmic thudding of tires of the old pickup across the section cracks of the concrete pavement held me spellbound, inhibiting even the casual reach to flip the light switch. I was returning from delivering a small tractor to an account in Arlington. I am in the farm equipment business with my father.

Automatically my eyes registered a group of headlights far behind in my mirror, pale in the twilight, but they also left me unimpressed. Motorcycles, I guessed, because of their irregular spacing and tight clustering.

My gaze caught briefly the terse, reflective sign as I passed and I stirred a little. **REST STOP AHEAD**. I was only about twenty miles from home, but the part of my brain that was still functioning admitted that I needed to stretch the legs and maybe even play with my dick a little. These long, lonely drives tend to do that to me—my cock gets into a semi-hard state that torments me with thoughts of the pleasures I could be having if I weren't tied to the wheel. I almost missed the exit and had to swerve quickly into the narrow lane leading to the solitary bunker-like building hunkered behind the trees on the hill.

There were almost no cars parked between the parking lines, and only a couple of semi's on the other side. Probably the truck drivers were taking an afternoon siesta, preferring the cooler night driving after dark. I climbed down a little stiffly from the cab. The sudden silence around me, except for the evening crickets already starting to sing, was a little startling. The only other sound was a dull, muffled roar from the highway behind me.

I strode into the dimly-lit, empty men's room and dug out my half-hardon at the middle urinal. The stream started strong but tapered off quickly as my dick gave a little lurch of its own and started growing in my fist. Vaguely I heard the roar of the group of motorcycles crescendo in the parking lot outside and then the silence returned as their engines were shut off one by one. Right now my dick was the focus of my attention, and I began to stroke it slowly, my toes curling in my saddle boots with the pleasure I knew I could have. As usual my thoughts flew to Greg, my team buddy from high school, and his hard, muscular body that had plagued my dreams ever since that day a couple of years ago when I walked in on him jerking off in the showers at school. Of course he didn't know I had those sinful thoughts about him—nobody knew—but I had to be careful not to look his way in the Sunday service when I sang praises to the Lord and prayed that I could forget the forbidden thoughts and dreams of holding him, stroking that enormous meat, and maybe even—

My fist started to fly, beating my dick in growing anticipation, especially twisting the head a little to get that ultimate thrill. My balls started to pull up and my breaths shortened, but just then there was a clatter of boots on the tile floor as two guys entered and cut my fantasy short. They quickly took up positions on both sides of me, pulling out their dongs at the other urinals. I could feel them towering over me, and I'm pretty sizable myself. I tried to cover up, but nine inches of rigid rod, red and rampant, is hard to conceal. The almost hypnotic fragrance of their leather jackets and their masculine aura radiated into my brain, although I tried to keep my gaze downward and ignore them. I could feel my face redden. I could feel their eyes drilling into me.

"Hummmm?" One of the guys murmured in a sort of questioning way. "Hummmm!" was the response from the other one. I didn't look up. The first one leaned toward me a little.

"Hey, you don't have to cover that up on our account, you know," his gruff voice almost purred in my ear. I could see his hand moving at his crotch out of the corner of my eye.

"Hell, no, man," the other confirmed. "You might say we appreciate the better things of life, and that includes big hard dicks." They both drew closer and turned toward me. Even with my eyes downcast I could catch glimpses of growing pricks in their leather-gloved hands. My breath caught in my chest.

"Shit, Rod, he's got pretty buns, too, did ya notice?"

"Yeah, but that dick looks good enough to eat. You can plug his ass while I swallow that dick, how about that, Steve?"

"'N maybe pull on his tits a little, too, eh?"

"Sure, why not? There's enough there to go around for some of the other guys, too, don't ya think?"

They were talking about me as if I were a piece of meat, or a stud animal just deposited there for their wicked pleasures. I was horrified and suddenly stiff with fear, but my cock seemed to get even stiffer!

I looked up into the clear blue eyes of the guy on my right (I think his name was Steve) with all the bravado I could muster. "What the hell are you guys talkin' about—" I growled threateningly. But just then the other guy grabbed a fistful of my butt and my voice choked off abruptly.

Steve grabbed my dick in his gloved hand and gave it a wrench. "Well, ya see, sport, we're on our way to a party, and we just invited you along. You wouldn't want to disappoint us now, would you?"

I jerked away but didn't get far. The guy behind me had his arm around my neck in a strangle hold before I moved a foot, and Steve quickly twisted my arm behind my back. I tried to loosen the arms around my neck, but that arm was quickly imprisoned as well in a steely grip. I was in a desperate fight for my life, it seemed, and the fact that they seemed more amused than predatory was even more threatening.

For a moment the three of us struggled back and forth, each with a stiff prick bobbing from our crotches. I wasn't going to give up without a fight–

"Hey, you guys, come on! We got to start the fire and get the show on the road!" The voice came from the door – another black blur in my leather nightmare.

Rod chuckled. "OK, Pres, but there's one more for the rack. Help us get this hayseed trussed and we'll get under way."

"Oh, yeah," Pres breathed softly as he strode over to us, his eyes practically stripping me bare. He whipped a pair of handcuffs from his belt and in a minute my wrists were manacled securely together. "He oughta be fun," Pres chuckled, flipping my stiff dick back and forth a few times appreciatively. I was breathing hard but couldn't see my way out of this dilemma. They just grinned at me as Steve and Rod stowed their dicks in their pants, and then they marched me out to two more of their buddies gathered around the parked bikes. My protruding cock bobbed jerkily as I walked toward them. What can you do when a gang of five strapping leathermen get it in their heads to manhandle you, especially when they all wore supremely confident grins on their faces?

"I saw him first–he rides with me," Rod growled. At first Steve seemed about to argue, but then helped force me to sit behind Rod on the firm leather seat. They used more handcuffs to fasten my ankles to the frame of the bike, and the motors roared into action again with me a helpless passenger.

Rod reached around and positioned my dangling cock up against his leather back, shoving back against me to keep it upright. That leather contact seemed to give it new life, and it throbbed heavily against his back. I gripped the leather seat rim behind me as we began to move.

Steve led the way from the parking lot down a barely discernible path down the hill away from the highway. It was dark by this time, and I hoped they knew where they were going. Their headlights cut narrow paths through the trees. The roar of the engines echoed in the otherwise silent night.

We came out suddenly into a clearing with tall trees surrounding us like sentinels, their dark branches leading into the vagueness of the moonlit sky. When the motors were shut off I could hear the crickets again, added to the creaking of leather when the men dismounted. Even the normal sounds of traffic on the highway, now on the other side of the hill, were stilled. Before all the bike lights were doused I noticed a couple of old picnic tables arranged around a central fire pit, and there seemed to be some strange wooden structures built in and between the trees.

"Build the fire, Rake, while Rod and I get this guy ready," Steve said, apparently the leader of the gang. In a minute my ankles were released and Rod, Steve, and another guy roughly pulled me off the bike, my wrists still manacled. Should I try to break away? Run—where? Without my hands free? The answer came quickly as they practically dragged me a few yards away to a rough wooden **X**-rack between two trees.

"Hold his arms behind the cross, Stan," Steve ordered. "He's a fighter, so be warned."

Stan forced my arms down over the cross and leaned his weight against them. This practically eliminated any hope I had for fighting the bastards off. I could feel his cock bulge against my hands, and figured I would try to grip his jewels in my own choke-hold if things got too rough.

Rod, a tall dude with black eyes and a two-or-three-day growth of dark beard, sneered at my helplessness. He pulled a bowie knife from his belt and showed me the long blade; it glinted in the growing light from the fire being built in the pit nearby. His eyes also carried that steely flash as he brought the knife close to my belly.

"You got a lot to learn, stud," he breathed, "and I'm goin' to enjoy educatin' you."

The blade grew closer. I made up my mind to kick him in the nuts as a last resort when the blade touched me, and I tensed, ready for the worst. But instead of the thrust to the gut that I expected, he expertly clipped off the top button of my shirt with the tip of the blade. Steve was watching closely, his blue eyes never leaving my face. One by one Rod snipped off the buttons of my shirt and Steve pulled my shirt back, leaving me bare chested, pinned against the cross.

"For a blond you got a nice nest of chest fur," Rod almost purred. Steve grinned in agreement, it seemed. "But those tits need work," he commented mysteriously. "Let's get those levi's off before anything else."

Rod bent and literally picked me up by the legs. I sagged back against the cross, Stan still holding me securely. Off came my saddle boots and then the levis, the two guys stripping me expertly from the waist down before putting my boots back on my bare feet and planting them on the ground again. Just as expertly they spread my ankles, tying them to the bottom of the **X** on both sides. They stood back to survey their work.

"He's a beauty, ain't he, Steve?" Rod's gaze lowered to my crotch and he nudged my dangling dick with the tip of his blade. "Won't take much to put some starch back in that, I reckon."

Stan spoke up impatiently. "Come on, you guys. Let's get his arms tied so I can get into the action. You got the key to these cuffs?"

With my ankles tied to the cross I couldn't do much in the way of resistance when they removed the handcuffs and tied my wrists to the upper arms of the cross. What a predicament! Tied up practically nude in the middle of the woods with a crazed, knife-wielding gang ogling me in the flickering light of a camp fire! All the guys grouped themselves around me, each from the vantage point that interested them most, I supposed. Their gruesome anticipation was obvious.

The trouble was, I could feel my prick begin to harden

again with all those leathermen staring at me. If anything, that problem only increased when Pres suddenly grabbed a handful of my butt and Steve bent to nibble on one of my tits. My dick began to point at the dark sky.

Rod bent to the other nipple, his tongue lapping the curly hairs around it and then following the pattern downward. He dove into my button for a minute (which really set my teeth on edge) but then continued downward to my crotch. Meanwhile I could feel at least two hands groping my thighs and ass behind me.

I found my voice at last. "What the fuck you guys doin'?" I gasped, almost preferring the unpredictable violence of the knife-wielding terrorist to the insinuating, blissful sensations of their hands and tongues and teeth. By this time I was starting to tremble but it was not from fear.

And then I felt it, the forbidden thing that I had tried to banish from my thoughts: Rod was taking my stiff cock in his mouth!

At first he twirled his tongue around the head, and then slowly, lapping as he went, worked his way down the shaft. As my cock went deeper and deeper into his throat, I couldn't suppress a groan and must have reached a real yell when he finally hit bottom and I could feel his chin nuzzling my balls. It was just as well that he didn't stay down there long; I think I would have screamed. But then he started moving up and down, first slowly and then speeding up gradually, and my teeth clenched, trying to maintain control.

Stan was shamelessly spreading my butt cheeks and I dimly heard him say, "He's got some of that pretty blond hair around his asshole, too." There seemed to be a smile in his voice, but I forgot all that when I felt his tongue, lapping its way down my crease and making its way right into my hole!

And then there were gropes and tongues and lips all over me, up and down my spread legs, on my balls, both nipples, and of course my cock and asshole that received the most attention. It seemed like I was the main course for those five guys, all feeding on me in their frenzy.

I didn't even know it was going to happen, but then it did; I started spurting into that hot, twisting mouth that was swallowing my dick so deliciously. I roared my joy to the silent sky above, and the other guys grunted and murmured in unison. I wondered fleetingly if maybe they were also playing with themselves. I thought I felt some liquid splashing on my leg, but I wasn't sure. I was thrashing and jerking like a convulsing bull.

Eventually my brain steadied and my overstretched muscles relaxed; I sagged on my cross and only vaguely felt the lips on my skin and the caresses of the guys. My attackers had somehow become my lovers, it seemed.

When I raised my head the first thing I saw was Rod wiping his lips, obviously relishing my load. I'm sure I flushed again, but I couldn't truthfully regret what had happened. The truth was that I wondered why it hadn't happened sooner, somewhere, somehow.

"Shall we take him down, Steve?" he asked hesitantly.

Steve was buttoning his fly. "Naah," he answered briefly. "He might just get it into his head to run and get lost in the woods. Best to leave him there until—" He left the rest unsaid.

The guys reassembled around the fire and soon the aroma of broiling hamburgers filled the air. At this point I was content to sag into my bonds, my breath recovering slowly and my thoughts more confused than ever. Then Rod came over and fed me a hamburger under the trees. He fiddled with my tits a little while I was chewing. I never knew guys liked to to have their tits played with before. Without asking permission, he lowered my tethered wrists, restoring the circulation before returning to the fire.

After the guys had had their fill, I again became the center of attention. This time they took me bodily to one of the picnic tables and lay me face-up, again tying my wrists and ankles in a spread-eagle position. I must confess I don't think I struggled much that time.

At once they began their tantalizing tonguing, five of them staking out parts of my body as their territory, it seemed, and every touch a searing, searching symbol of their power over me as my prick soared upward again in demonic demand. In the background I was vaguely aware of another motorcycle picking its way through the trees and settling its metal talons into our island of lust and virility. I was too busy reacting to pay much notice, especially when a hot mouth descended again on my engorged cock, focusing my entire being in my tallest part. My eyes stared blankly at the dark sky above, at visions of naked men in all kinds of satyristic acts.

"Bill."

The voice was soft and loving and intimate, and I knew it well. My eyes shifted back to earth.

"Greg!"

He looked down at me from a terrific height, his dark eyes and mustache etched silver in the flickering firelight. His tightly-curly hair had been mashed flat by the helmet he was removing, and he ran his fingers through it absentmindedly as he studied my face. Steve stood by his side with a shit-eating grin on his face, one hand on his leather-clad shoulder.

"As you can see, we started without you."

Still searching my eyes with his, Greg smiled. "Can't say that I blame you," he said with a grin. His gaze shifted to scan my naked form as the other men pulled back, leaving moist trails cooling in the slight breeze and my cock lurching. I could feel my body melting, sinking into the rough table, spread out like some sort of willing, pagan feast for his covetous gaze. But my cock didn't melt—it surged stronger than ever.

"Have I finally found you?" he asked huskily.

"Found me?" I gasped. "Do you know these guys?"

Instead of answering, Greg shucked off his leather jacket,

followed by his T-shirt and levi's. When he next appeared in my line of vision, his huge prick stood out like the branch of one of the trees surrounding us, even larger than I remembered. One hand cradled his heavy balls while the other pinched a brown nipple almost hidden by the dark thatch of his chest hair. I couldn't take my eyes off him.

I felt him grasp my throbbing dick; his grip was tight and hard, possessive, just like I wanted it to be. He looked into my eyes again, this time imperiously, knowing I could not resist him. Then he moved down and took my cock into his mouth.

All my dreams, all the fantasies of my masturbations for several years came flooding back in a mélange of incredible complexity that left me quivering and yet aggressive and assertive. This was it – the moment I had been waiting for during the last two years of confusion. As his tongue flickered over my cockhead and engulfed my entirety, everything fitted into place. Almost immediately my balls signalled their need, and I groaned in trepidation that it would be too soon. His lips kissed every inch, his tongue lashed every crevice, and my muscles snapped to full rigidity as he consumed me. Up and down, around and under and over, he set his stamp on me from that day on.

And then he pulled up and looked into my eyes again. His face was determined, and so I was not surprised when he calmly climbed onto the table and straddled my chest, his throbbing tool in his hand. I was ready. I nodded silently.

He moved forward and tipped his cockhead downward. I opened my mouth without further thought, and it entered slowly, steadily, the sweet head and thick stalk spreading my lips and fulfilling many of my fantasies. He leveraged himself above me and conquered me in the most complete way possible. His cock in my mouth, his spirit in my body, our beings fusing in total harmony.

Gradually he fed me more and more of that masculine meat, and I took whatever he wanted to give. Knowing I was inexperienced, he was considerate but still demanding, and I gave him the best I could give. I was quickly convinced that I would never again be complete without his cock in my mouth. I could hear his gasping breaths as he moved slowly, rhythmically, in and out of my throat.

But then he also pulled up and back, his body trembling, his eyes glazed. Without further hesitation he moved backward, raised himself, and poised above me, my cockhead at his asshole. I had never even imagined that! With one hand on my still slick prick, he guided it to the opening and slowly descended, taking my entire tool into his grasping recesses, swallowing me whole, until I could feel my balls pressed against his body.

The heat, the grip, the intensity of the union was enough to tumble my brain to incoherency. I twisted and thrust and cried out repeatedly as he began to move up and down, demanding my surrender, and I needed that surrender as my commitment to him. His eyes closed and his fist began to stroke his cock as he fucked himself on my pole. I wanted his prick in me, too, but that would have to wait for another time. This was Greg's moment as well as mine. I also realized that there was no actual surrender involved; we were both victors from this time on.

I couldn't stop. I thrust upward once and there was no return. My juices bathed his channel and my dick throbbed violently against its walls; my throat let out a war whoop that echoed through the woods and probably frightened the night animals. But my cry was matched by Greg's as he spurted hot cum over my belly and chest in long ropes of white, streaking my entire body with his love for me. Sweat glistened on his straining body, bronze in the firelight, as he took all I could give and gave as much in return. I vaguely heard the other men climaxing in their own way, unable to resist the passion being played out in their view.

Finally Greg sagged to rest on me, chest to chest, and we

kissed for the first time. I don't remember much after that, except he explained that he had asked his friends to keep an eye out for me (he knew approximately when I would be on that highway) and bring me to the campsite. We made love again, more deliberately that time, and then slept together in his sleeping bag.

And that explains why Greg and I are back on the road this morning but with his bike in the back of the pickup. We have a lot of catching up to do, but right now he's got my dick out, stroking it slowly as he is doing with his own, and I know that I've really got to concentrate on my driving as he leans down, his lips heading for my crotch. . .

UNCLE BUD

Joseph W. Bean

You'd probably have trouble believing it if you saw me at the opera, jotting notes on the perfect and less than perfect sailors of the high C's for the city's biggest paper, but I was raised in the Missouri Ozarks. I lived my first 18 years there, far enough back in the "hollers" that we didn't have electricity till I was seven or eight, and the family house still didn't have indoor plumbing when I moved away.

We were a big family of pretty ordinary folks. Ma'am and Pa, my grandparents, presided over a household of four of their adult children and nine of their grandchildren. We raised chickens and sold eggs and milk. We made whittled-wood chains, crepe paper flowers, and quilt-top paper cutouts for an Ozark crafts store up in Joplin. And my uncle Bud did art work for a couple of stores in Kansas City.

I always thought my uncle Bud was amazing. I could sit and watch him for hours on end. Whether he was drawing, which he did very well, tooling leather for wallets and purses, which he did a lot, or working on the farm—stringing fence wire, clearing fields, or whatever—I was always enthralled. My grandmother said he was vain, but I thought he was beautiful. I appreciated the perfection of his clean-shaven, chiseled features, and was glad he used plenty of Fitch's Rose Oil to keep his dark, wavy hair in sculpted curves all day. My grandfather said Bud was lazy, but I thought Pa just didn't understand what hard work it was to draw so wonderfully or hammer such intricate designs into thick, brown leather.

Sometime while we were still in the chicken and egg business, I must have been 15 or 16 at the time, Bud noticed how I watched him. He began asking all the time, "What're y'doin', boy? Y'waitin' fer me t'mess up?"

I never had much of an answer, but I didn't want him to

think *that*. "No, Bud, I just like to watch," I'd answer. That always got a chuckle, a mysterious chuckle as I recall it now. Sometimes he'd say something about how that would change in time, or he'd concede that I was doing him no harm.

One day—I must have been 17 or 18 by this time—as I was coming out of the outhouse, I ran smack into Bud. I guess I was busy buttoning my fly—I don't know—but, suddenly, I was flat up against him. One of my hands was against his big silver belt buckle, the other was between his legs. I was shocked and embarrassed, but I didn't pull away. I mumbled something and turned my eyes up to meet his. Just as our eyes met, I felt something warm on my arm. He'd already flipped his cock out before reaching for the outhouse door. The warm something was his meat on my forearm. I closed my eyes and froze.

"What's a matter, boy," Bud asked, almost laughing. "Hey, ease up, Joey. Cat gotcher tongue?" I opened my eyes, and tried to relax, but my arm wouldn't move.

Bud reached down between our bodies and clasped a hand around his cock, pinching his fingertips into my arm, holding his now-hot meat against my thin, trembling arm. With the thumb of his other hand, he began gently rubbing up and down on my chest, pushing my T-shirt into the valley between my pecs. After a few strokes, I knew I should do something. I ought to pull away or run away or stop him somehow. Instead, I leaned into his touch, ever so slightly. Then, hardly aware I was doing it, I turned my torso very slowly. Bud didn't move with me. Instead, he let his thumb trail across till it stopped on one of my nipples. He pushed in sharply. I moaned. I couldn't help it. And I sounded awful, girlish and submissive.

"Looks like we ought to do a little talkin', boy," Bud said. I was still frozen. "I'm gonna just take a leak, then we're goin' out there past the milkin' barn to chew some stored-up fat." He reached over my shoulder for the top edge of the outhouse door, and I turned away from him, toward the outhouse. He had let his cock slip off of my arm which was now behind my back. He nudged me with his knee, bumping me forward as the door swung open.

Inside it was pretty dark, but Bud shuffled around a bit so the streak of sunlight coming in through the round hole high on the wall fell right across his cock. "Wanna watch?" he asked. "You allus say you like watchin'."

I was watching, transfixed, but I said nothing. "The show won't start till y'say y'watchin' or lookin' away."

My throat was tight and dry. I had to try two or three times before I got the words out clear enough to suit Bud. "I'm watching, Uncle Bud," I said, almost afraid I'd be heard back at the house, nearly 100 yards away.

"Y'don' hafta whisper," Bud said in a whisper. Then, in a very loud voice he added, "'S no crime to be curious." Then he pissed. I couldn't believe my eyes. He spurted out a stream as broad and loud as a bull's, and it just kept coming. I don't know why, or where I got the courage, but I reached out and put the index finger of my left hand into the stream of Bud's hot piss.

"Play if'n y'wanna," he said very casually, "but don' splash any a my wet on me." I pulled my finger back and looked up. I watched his face, not clear at all about what he was thinking. When his attention went to the buttoning of his fly, I drew an invisible moustache on my still-hairless upper lip with my wet finger. A moment later my tongue was testing the moustache, teasing itself with the very slight salty taste.

"Now, young man, march y'sef out to the root cellar door behind the barn, and wait for me there." Bud's voice was suddenly stern and adult, not his usual tone of acceptance or inclusion, but one of authority like most people use when telling me (and other kids) what to do. I never disobeyed that or-else voice.

When I got to the cellar door, I noticed my cock was sore. It had been rubbing "wrong" in my jeans, sticking out of the leg of my briefs. I also noticed a lot of cigarette butts in a semicircle on the ground. They were store-bought ones, not the roll-your-owns Pa and my other uncles smoked, so they had to be Bud's. I decided to sit where he must always sit when he smoked here, right against the middle of the low outer edge of the cellar door frame.

I was pushing the butts into some kind of pattern on the ground when, after several minutes delay, Bud arrived. "Hop y'sef up ont' the door there," he said, and I did. Sitting Indian-style on the cellar door, I felt like a tiny kid gazing up at the perfect adult male.

Bud had taken off his shirt and tucked the end of it into a back pocket of his jeans. The tracery of dark hair on the sweaty mounds of his chest seemed to me as perfect as it would be on one of the men in his drawings. I felt myself holding my breath, but I couldn't *make* myself breathe. "Yer gonna plum faint if'n y'don' start suckin' air, boy."

I breathed. Too loudly.

"Do y'have any idey what you were doin' back there, Joey? Do you think at all? For land's sake, boy, you'll learn t'think, or you'll find out what the quaint old custom of lynchin' feels like first hand, I sw'on!"

"No," I whispered. My mouth was dry, my mind blank, my body hot and trembling, and my cock was poking up against a fold in my jeans again, but I seriously didn't want to be adjusting it just then. "No," I finally managed to say clearly. Then I wondered if my "no" sounded wrong, if Bud might think I was turning him away or saying I didn't want to think or believe I ever would learn to do it. So, past a stiff tongue, through a crackling-dry mouth, I continued. "I don't know what *that* was, and I'd be beholdin' to you for any light you could shed on any of it." I thought I'd finished, then I heard myself go on. "I've been wanting to touch you any way I could for a long, long time. I've been hoping you'd go into the crick again like you did last summer so I could see you. . ." I stopped. I couldn't make myself say "naked." After a moment of silence, I continued, haltingly, "wet. . . like that. . . all. . . *all* over."

"Well, boy," Bud said in a voice that made it sound like he had a long story to tell, "I 'spect I know better'n you do y'sef what yer feeling and what yer wantin'. I'm sure I know better'n you the passel of trouble y'ken get into goin' the way y'will and bein' the way y'are. So, like a real friend—the only one yer like to find in these here hills—I'll give y'a bit of advice. Get away f'm here. Go soon an' go far, an' don' be too careful about keepin' in touch with yer kin er tellin' too much the truth if'n y'feel like y'hafta write at all."

For a long time neither of us said anything. The cows dragged past us one by one, making their way into the barn to be relieved of their milk, but neither of us was expected to help with the milking that day. Pa'd do that with Jimmy, my brother, and Elery, Bud's brother. The sun cooled noticeably as I sat there mostly looking at the ground, wishing I could just say "thanks for the advice" and slip away.

I heard Bud light a cigarette and take several loud, throaty drags on it. A smoke ring drifted over and broke up on my face. I thrilled to it. Bud's rich, warm smoke, sailing off in rings, was as much a part of his mysterious spell over me as his clean, black cowboy boots, his clinging-tight jeans, and his shiny, wavy hair. He dropped the cigarette, half-smoked. It landed in my view, just off the edge of the cellar door. I reached to crush it out, but brought it up close to my face instead. Coming in swirls from the cigarette in my own hand was Bud's store-bought smoke. One breath of it brought tears to my eyes for a second. The next made my head swim. Or, maybe the smoke had nothing to do with what I was feeling.

"Y'know, we can't really talk here," Bud said. "And sure 'nuff, we can't do n'more'n talk." He turned and walked away. I watched the low, soft sun make a glittering triangle of light appear and disappear on the ass of his jeans with each step. Twenty paces away, Bud kicked the ground with one boot toe the way I'd seen him do when he was frustrated, like when Ma'am would call him useless or Pa'd say (as he did nearly every day), "Yer here an' yer my son, but that don' mean I hafta *like* what y've made a y'sef."

Every time I saw him kick the ground like that and wander off with his head down, I wanted to run after him and. . . . I never knew what I'd do, but I wanted him to know that I liked him, as if my liking him might make him feel better. This time it seemed I was the cause of his frustration. This time I would run after him, and I'd do anything I could to make him feel better. Anything.

I trotted up behind him, my head still swimming. "Bud," I said, still searching for words, "if I did anything or said something wrong, I'm sorry."

He turned suddenly. He had lit another cigarette, and smoke was blowing out his nose. His eyes were wild, and his jaw was set, square and hard. "Just come," he said in a voice that rumbled through me.

He strode off fast toward a line of sassafras trees at the east side of the close pasture. I followed, half-running to keep pace with his long-legged stride. He ducked through the sassafras and jumped down into the deep irrigation ditch beyond. He was sitting on a big, round rock by the time I caught up.

"Git ova here!" he snapped, pointing to the thick mud between the toes of his boots. I stepped into place, putting the toes of both my shoes right on the spot he had pointed to. "Open yer pants, an' let 'em drop," he ordered. I did it, then froze again. He slapped my shorts down past my knees till they were against my dropped jeans.

My cock was hard and it was wet at the end. Bud's huge, hard hands began to rub at my belly, my legs, and my ass cheeks. He ran his thumb back and forth between my asshole and my balls, his hard thumbnail scraping a raw stripe in my skin. I was suddenly burning up, panting, shivering as the cool, sunset breeze lingered on my skin. And my nose was running.

I pulled up my T-shirt and blew my nose on the front tail of it. Bud grabbed the shirt tail as I dropped it, and pulled it over my head, leaving my face covered and my arms pushed up and back by the tight cotton. He kept fingering and rubbing my body. From my belly to my knees, my skin was hot with his rubbing and touching, but he wasn't touching my cock or balls, except by accident, now and then, usually with a wrist or the back of his hand. A few times, as he reached between my legs to squeeze my ass, the wiry hair of his forearm brushed my balls and slipped back and forth on the scraped stripe behind them. Each time, the touch of his prickly arm hair made my knees weak.

The rubbing was soon mixed with slapping, and the touches turned to pinching, but he still didn't touch my cock. I wanted to touch it myself, to put it in his hand if I had to, but if I moved my arms down I'd pull the T-shirt off my face, and I was sure he didn't want that to happen.

There was just enough sun light making its way down into the ditch for me to see silhouettes and highlights of Bud's hands and arms. My cock looked huge, bigger than it had ever been, but still puny next to Bud's wide, square hands.

He kept pinching and slapping, harder and harder, boring each pinch into me with a thumb, crushing in each slap with the heel of his palm. Then, just when I thought I was going to scream or piss or pass out—or maybe do all three at once—he jerked back, sat up straight, and gave my cock a really hard slap on the side. I caught a deep breath and threw my head back. I didn't scream or pass out, but I thought I *did* piss.

The T-shirt popped off my face and stuck to my sweaty body, across my chest. I looked down. I wasn't pissing at all. My cock was jerking around wildly, and it was spitting out little dabs of white jizz with every jerk.

Bud was catching my jizz in his hand. Somewhere along the line, he had wrapped his other hand around my balls. Now he was milking me. He'd roll his fingers down in milking order, then tug, and my cock would respond by jumping and squirting.

After an eternity of this milking, I was suddenly chilled, trembling with cold, covered with goose-bumps, and crying. No, not crying, and not laughing either, but I was shaking with something between the two.

Bud brought his hand up near his face, and breathed a few wide-open breaths on the lumpy white pool in his palm. Then he stood up and put his hand under my nose. The smell was amazing. It was horrible, but I wanted more of it. It was ugly, but perfect. My eyes half closed as I breathed slowly and deeply, so I barely noticed when Bud started scooping the jizz into my mouth with his fingertip. I didn't swallow. I couldn't. My mouth and throat were as dry as old barn wood and just as splintery.

When all the little wads were on my tongue, my mouth hanging open, I just stood there feeling the impossible wads growing cold against the warmth of my mouth and breath. Bud took out his own hard cock and washed the sticky hand with a sudden splash of piss. He put his wet hand over my mouth, stepping behind me as he did. Immediately, his other hand was also on my face, and he was pulling my head back against his chest.

"Lick my pissy hand," he hissed, as he squeezed my nose shut with his other hand.

I started licking instantly, but I couldn't breathe. He kept my nose clamped shut and my mouth covered long after I stopped licking. Soon, I felt myself beginning to slide down Bud's body, and he let my face slide free of his hands. When my bare knees squished into the cold mud, I came to.

"Come see me after supper," Bud said with a gentleness I'd never heard in his voice. "Come and see me in my tooling room."

I was scared to go back to the house. Everyone would *know*, wouldn't they? The mud on my jeans, mostly between the legs, would tell the story. I could wash the salty stiffness off my face at the pump, but something would show still. I knew it would.

After a while, I got the idea of setting my clothes to rights and hopping into the pond, clothes and all. I'd claim I rode the bull in. I wasn't supposed to be riding the bull at all, but everyone knew he'd try to get into the water to get me off if I did.

All evening I knew that Ma'am and Pa knew what had happened, but they played along with the bull-riding story like they believed me. Pa even scolded me very realistically for riding the bull, and I played along with them, promising never to do it again. But mine was a half-hearted promise. After all, I might just need to blame the bull again. Soon, I hoped, maybe even right after supper in Uncle Bud's leather tooling room over the tractor shed.

Supper was uneventful except for Pa imagining aloud what I must have looked like dragging myself out of the slimy pond after the bull threw me in the water. I felt like I was in for trouble when Ma'am was amazed that I didn't come out smelling of the green pond water, but no one picked up on the hole in my story. Bud didn't come to supper, but no one mentioned that either. It wasn't unusual for him to stay at a drawing or a piece of leather through dinner, just sitting at his work drinking beers and smoking.

I was inevitably honored with the opportunity to clear the dishes into the kitchen, but just clear them. Boys were never expected to wash or dry dishes in a house with so many girls and women. By the time I had the tables cleared, Ma'am and Pa had gone up front to their room, so I was able to slip out the back door and get to Bud's tooling room without having to explain that I was being allowed where no one ever got to go.

Ordinarily I could only watch Bud work on leather if he was at the dining table—cold weather sometimes chased him in, and very little else could entice him to risk the abuses Ma'am and Pa always had ready for him. My heart stopped as I climbed the rickety, outdoor stairs to the tooling room. What was I expecting? What did I *want*? Did I even want to be here? At least I knew that if I didn't see Bud tonight, it was going to be hard to face him again when I did see him, and I wasn't willing to have anything come between me and my "god."

As I reached for the door knob, the door swung open in front of me. It almost felt like I was being dragged or blown into the room. In any case, I stumbled.

Bud was there, standing just inside the door, and he caught me. I don't think for a moment that I'd have actually fallen if he hadn't caught me, but he dipped his knees as he pulled me toward himself, giving the impression that he had swooped down and saved me from smashing into the floor. The gesture was just silly enough to make me laugh as I struggled to get my balance. Bud was laughing, too.

The next thing I knew, Bud's arms were around me, holding me tightly. His teeth were grazing on my neck, nipping and pinching slightly, not really hurting me, but putting the brakes on my laughter nonetheless. I definitely didn't know what to expect, but I didn't expect *this*!

Uncle Bud never really let me get my feet under me. He swayed a bit, stepped back a time or two, and turned away from the still-open door, and each movement was timed to keep me always trying to line my legs up under myself. Then, in one powerful move, he lifted me off the floor altogether and, kicking the door shut as he turned, deposited me—butt first—on one of his two waist-high work benches. I guess I must have found the speedy moves and unfamiliar actions of the next minute or two fascinating at some level. If I'd had my wits about me, I'd have protested, but I didn't twitch or squeak.

When Bud stood up over me, his shiny curls lolling low over his eyes, my wrists and ankles had been buckled into beautifully tooled belts of brown leather which were securely nailed to the corners of the work bench. I was still dazed from the realization of my situation, and almost equally stunned by Bud's sweaty magnificence, when he was at it again. This time he held the belt he intended to use above my face. It was the most intricate and detailed tooling I had ever seen. Tiny musclemen were climbing and crawling on one another's bodies along the entire length of the belt. They were touching and using each other in ways that I understood so little at the time that I didn't even recognize the scene for the orgy I now know it was.

After he was sure I'd had time to examine the belt—but probably not suspecting how little I actually saw in the tooled picture—Bud slapped the five inch wide center section of the belt against my belly, then ducked under the table where he noisily buckled the belt tightly around me and the table together.

The feeling of being pinned to the table by both ankles, both wrists, and my waist was terrifying. . . and I knew, instantly, that I liked it. More important, I understood immediately that I was meant to like it, so the sense of the terror shifted. I knew I was not going to be hurt. Uncle Bud would not hurt me. But I could hurt him. That is, I could disappoint him. I could fail to understand what he wanted. I could do or say the wrong thing. I could turn out not to be worthy of the special attention he was lavishing on me.

While I was worrying about living up to whatever Bud had in store for me, he was moving ahead with. . . his plan? He put a collar on me, something like a dog collar, but even though I didn't see it, I suspected it was as intricately tooled as the rest of the leather equipment he was using. He attached something—a little belt, I think—to the back of the collar, and pulled it down and attached it somewhere over the edge of the bench above my head. Once my head was immobile, he unbuckled my wrists and pulled my T-shirt up, over my head, and tucked it away. He must have left the shirt hanging on the little belt, then he rebuckled the belts on my wrists. My hands had fallen right back into the embrace of the belts, and I hadn't thought to move them. Next, Bud opened my jeans and pulled them down as far as my spread-eagle position would allow.

Suddenly, and for the first time, I noticed that my cock was hard, bobbing up and down against my lower belly.

Bud disappeared under the table again, and reappeared with a canvas bucket which he dropped between my legs. I couldn't tip my head down enough to see the bucket once it was on the bench, beyond my crumpled jeans.

Bud began dipping into the bucket, pulling out handfuls of spring wire clips, and placing them carefully here and there on my body. Just placing them, not opening them and clipping them to my skin. "If I toldja I was gonna pinch every one of these lacing clips onto y'right where it's layin' now, would that be like a threat or a promise to you?"

The question sounded dead serious, but I couldn't think what answer he wanted to hear. I wanted to give him the right answer as if my final grade in the Class of Life depended on it. "I'd leave that to you, Uncle Bud. If you said you were threatening me, I'd be scared; if you said that was a promise, I'd be countin' minutes till you did it." That sounded flat-out stupid as I heard myself say it, but it's what I said.

Bud turned away for a moment, then swung back toward me with a short, dark brown mule quirt in his hand. "S'pose you'd leave it t'me to decide about this little gem too?"

"Yes," I answered, feeling fear building in my chest and throat. Bud stretched the whip out along the center line of my body, the handle under my throbbing cock, the tails barely tickling my chin just above the collar. He patted it, bent over and kissed it. I was getting really scared. Maybe he wasn't vain or lazy. Maybe he was *crazy*.

Just as that thought took shape, Bud said, "I'm fuckin' crazy. We can't be doin' this, 'specially not here at home." Then, without another word, he clapped his hands down on my chest, and held on tight as he sidled around so he was reaching up from the end of the table, his chest resting on my jeans, his face against my cock. He turned his face, rubbing his stiff whiskers across my balls several times, then sucked my cock into his mouth in one gulp.

Suddenly his head was thrashing wildly, his forehead pounding into my belly, his whiskers still sanding my balls at the bottom of every stroke. Before long, I was squealing, biting my tongue to keep from screaming out loud, then crying and crying hard.

I spurted my jizz into Bud's mouth, whispering louder and louder as I did, "I'm sorry, I'm sorry, I'm sorry."

When Bud finally let go of my tits, and squeezed my cock out of his mouth, he stood up where he was at the foot of the bench. He was glowing, grinning like I'd never seen him do before. "What the hell you sorry *for*, boy?" he asked, putting on a silly looking, quizzical face with his eyebrows all scrunched together.

"Why, for what I just did, there," I said, trying to nod in a way that would indicate that *there* was in my crotch.

"Hush that kind of talk," Bud said, suddenly serious, "hush it this minute. *You* did nothin' at all. I took advantage of you. That's what happened. . . ."

He let his voice trail off, and I was at a loss for anything to say. I just wanted to feel all the things I was feeling, to swim in the waves of happiness that were washing over me. I'd forgotten all about being belted down to the table till Bud started taking the belts off. Then I had something to say, "When you do think of when and where you can keep your promises about those lacing clips and the mule quirt, will you have a bench like this and belts to keep me still while you use those things on me?" I moved as I spoke, and the wire clips began clattering on the bench.

"That," Bud said hesitantly, "that or something better." Then, after turning away to light a cigarette, he turned again, looked me straight in the eye, and said, "I've promised you more than you know here tonight. Yeah, a lot more than you know, but it's nothin' you wouldn't a come to one day on y'own."

When my head was finally freed, I sat up. Bud was right there against the edge of the bench, and I tried to reach my arms around him. "That part, though," he said, "that's the part that bothers me." He caught my wrists in his huge hands, put the two of them together, and lifted straight up till I had to slide off the bench and stand to keep my arms from tearing off. Clips crashed to the floor.

"Better get in the house now, boy," Bud said. I started toward the door, straightening my clothes and searching for a reason not to leave. "Say, don't try to blame that ol' bull f'the bruises on yer tits. It won't wash if you do. Just remember you got marks, and keep 'em covered up."

"I will," I said, pulling up my shirt to look at the angry red finger prints on my chest. Turning back to Uncle Bud, hoping I sounded calm, I said, "I promise."

"So, now we both of us have promises to keep, don't we?"

I nodded, finally feeling the confusion clear away, and a big grin spread over my face. "So, git!" Bud shooed me away with the backs of his hands, and I went, dragging my feet and hoping to be called back. As I tiptoed into the dark, silent house, I wondered about Uncle Bud. If his advice to me was that I should get away, why had he not gotten away already? That, I knew, would have to be answered before I'd go anywhere. Maybe the answer would be long in coming, and we could find lots of promises to make and keep in the meantime.

ANOTHER IDAHO

Mike Newman

This story is adapted from Mike's best-selling romantic novel, SECRET BUDDIES *(GLB Publishers, 1992).*

At lunch break I sat under the tree by the parking lot with the rest of the guys in my crew, only off to one side by myself, as usual. I wanted time to think about what had happened the night before. Every time I heard the others call each other "cocksucker" I tried not to cringe or turn red.

Then I saw Donnie moving toward us through the parked cars, slouching along with that slow, sexy, deliberate, give-a-shit attitude he had at work. Even from far off, I could make out the line of his dick curving down his right pants leg.

There were two dozen of us living together out in the boondocks of Idaho that summer, working for the Forest Service, most of us 18 or 19 and all of us pretty obsessed with sex (or the lack of it). But nobody else in camp did what Donnie did with all that bottled-up sexuality. Donnie had a sort of greasy swivel to his walk that only tall, lanky guys like him can pull off without looking feminine. With his bushy mustache and hairy forearms and that wiry patch of curls twisting out from the neck of his workshirt, he could twitch his hips that way and come off looking like a cat instead of a fag.

And I had found out the night before that he was a cat on the prowl. I stared at the way his hips seemed to rotate around what was hanging between his legs, remembering the feel of it in my hand. . . and then laughter from behind me woke me from my dream. I realized I was frozen with my sandwich halfway to my mouth, staring at Donnie way too hard.

He came over and nodded to everyone, but it was me he sat beside to open his lunch sack. "'Lo, Bill," he said. My mouth got so dry I couldn't answer. All I could think about was what I'd let him do to me the night before, sitting in his car out in the parking lot, drinking beer. Too many beers.

We couldn't talk much with everyone around. "How's it going in the office?" I mumbled, trying to sound nonchalant around the other guys.

"Pretty boring," he said with his mouth full. "Rather be out here." After he finished his sandwich, Donnie leaned toward me. Very casually, he threw his elbow around my neck, just horsing around in front of the guys. He held his hand beside my cheek and lifted his index finger like he was shooting me a bird.

"Sniff it," he said under his breath. I turned my nose to it, and his finger still smelled of my butt. Donnie laughed and slapped my back.

Walking back to work I asked him, "Isn't anything too gross for you?"

"Aw, it's not so gross. It's just your crapper. You wash it out in the shower every night, don't you? I'm just playing a little stinkfinger with you. You liked it plenty last night."

"Well," I said, "it's unsanitary. You might get some disease or something."

He shook his head. "Not me. I never catch anything. Anyway, I don't do it with just any old body, you know."

Looking behind us quickly, Donnie took my arm and guided me off between two buildings. I backed up against a wall, and Donnie got up so close to me I could feel heat from his body. He put his mouth to my ear and whispered, "Buddies got to take care of each other's, uh, special needs, you know what I mean?"

He looked around. Putting his hand on the front of my pants, he said, "I mean the need to get raunchy, real raunchy." He fingered my crotch. We both looked down our fronts, and Donnie's cock was jutting at an angle under his pocket instead of hanging down like before. "First interesting thing that's happened to me all day," he said.

Then he looked me in the eye. "I ain't your little girlfriend back home," he growled. "We'll take the car out someplace tonight where we won't get interrupted this time." My dick was curled up tight and hard inside my Jockeys, and his fingers were moving all around between my legs. "Are you with me, sport?"

I squirmed against the wall, nodding "Uh-huh."

He gave the pouch of my underwear a squeeze. "You save that for me, okay, big fella? Work up a good load of spunk down there, and save it for me. I already got some ready for you. This time, I want us to have a real hot session. I wanna go all the way tonight."

Donnie patted the hard-on I'd gotten as soon as he'd touched me, turned and disappeared around the corner. I was left panting against the wall.

"Aren't men fun?" a voice from behind startled me. It was Stanley, the little sissy. He'd come around the back side of the barn just as Donnie had left. He put his hand on his hip, looked down at my pants and arched his eyebrows. "If you can't be one, the next best thing is to have one." He smirked the way he knows gives me the creeps. "Huh?" he breathed at me, tilting his head back and fluttering his eyelids.

"Don't do that, I've told you," I whispered, trying to tuck myself between my legs. "Don't start acting like a girl every time you're around me."

He made a prissy face. "Oh, don't worry, I understand. It's perfectly obvious. Now that Donnie's back, you want to be the girl, that's all."

"Oh, fuck you, man," I snarled. "This has nothing to do with anybody wanting to be a girl, believe me." I added, "Man."

"I told you to stop calling me 'man.' You ought to be glad

I'm around. I'm the only one in camp who's a bigger sissy than you are. I make you look good, stupid." He spun on his heel and left me hating his skinny ass.

After dinner, we didn't even wait for dark. Donnie and I walked back to the cabin quickly, grabbed jackets, and headed for the car. Donnie had brought his little jar of Vaseline jelly from his locker. He set it on the dashboard and started the motor.

"I know a place where we can have us some privacy," he said.

"Put the top down," I suggested. He unhooked the clamps and we both lowered the ragged top into the well behind the back seat. It wouldn't go all the way, so we just left it there without putting the cover over it.

I listened to the tires crunch on gravel as we pulled out of camp and followed the dirt road into the woods, the first time I'd gotten away since I arrived in camp. I tried to find some music on the radio, but got only static. I stared at the blue Vaseline label and imagined what he wanted to do with that stuff.

This must be what it's like to be the girl on a date, I thought, and the guy shows you he has a rubber. Stanley had said that about me, that I wanted to be Donnie's girl. I squirmed in my seat. Was it true? I'd never thought about being a girl before.

No, actually this was more like going for a ride after school with one of the kids my mother didn't want me to hang around with. It was like sneaking off with one of the bad boys for the afternoon. My mother wouldn't approve of Donnie's looks for one hot minute. Not with those sideburns. Especially not with that mustache running all the way from the corners of his mouth to down below his chin. He didn't have anything on under his shirt, and I could see chest hair at his neck. He whistled, steering with one hand, stroking his pants leg with the other. I watched him until our eyes met, and he grinned at me.

"How do you like being a cocksucker, now that you've had a day to think about it?" he asked me.

"I like it," I said. "With you."

"Me too. We're gonna have us some fun."

The wind blew our hair the wrong way and I threw my head back and laughed, watching the tall trees pinwheel above us. He turned off onto a freshly-scraped side road, following a creek. We bounced into the shade under a grove of cedars. Around the bend it got so dark he switched on the headlights, and then beyond the next bend a muddy, yellow bulldozer glowed in the headlight beams. We circled it and parked, headed back the way we came in.

"If anybody pulls in behind us, we'll see their lights before they see us," he said, killing the motor. "Won't be anybody, though."

We finished our beers in the silence of the big woods, breathing cedar scents as night air drifted through the open car. Wordlessly, we got out together and stood side-by-side to pee on the treads of the giant dirt-moving machine, making two dark streaks in the caked mud, and then crossing streams to make one big streak together.

Donnie climbed up to the seat. "*Brmm, brmm, brmm,*" he said, pulling control levers and stomping pedals. I clambered up behind him and watched him play and make motor noises. When he bent his head back to smile up at me upside-down, I leaned over him, and this time when our eyes met I kissed him quickly, just barely touching my lips to his and then backing off.

"Hey, I didn't think you'd want to do that," he said.

"Why not?" I asked, looking away, then back at him. "Actually, I wanted to last night."

"Some guys just don't kiss," he said. "You act sort of straight, you know. Sometimes I can't tell exactly what it is you are."

I shrugged. "I don't know what I am yet, either. Until I met you, I thought I was straight."

He swivelled the seat around to face me. "Well," he said with smile, "if we're gonna make out, let's do it like this." He reached up and pulled me down onto him. I stretched myself over his body and put my hands on his shoulders, feeling the solid muscles even through the thick, rough leather. This time he raised up and kissed back, and I got a mouthful of mustache. My heart thumped. My dick surged. I tried to lean all of myself against him, and the chair squeaked as it rocked back under the weight of two men.

Donnie was as eager for it as I was. He wrapped his arms around me and licked at my mouth, sucking at my lips, wetting my whole face. I put my arms around his big shoulders and chewed at the hairs on his upper lip. His beard scratched my cheek, giving me the shivers as he kissed his way down my neck. He pulled my butt to him, pressing our hips together.

When we looked at each other again, I was breathing so hard I could barely speak. "Damn," I said, "you sure aren't."

"Aren't what?" he asked, licking my chin.

"My little girlfriend back home," I panted. I put my hand up underneath his coat and felt the curve of his chest muscles under my palm. The white woolly fur inside rubbed on the back of my hand, and smelled like a mixture of male sweat and leather and wet dog hair. "Damn," I whispered again. "It was sure never like this with her." I was so excited my voice trembled, but I didn't care.

Donnie gripped the cheeks of my butt and rubbed my crotch against his. My hard-on bumped against his through our pants. "Let's go get in the car," he said. "We can run the heater and get nekkid. Come on."

We grabbed the top and flipped it forward. Inside, he took off his jacket and made a wad against the door on his side. Leaning back, he pulled me on top of him again. I popped open the pearl snaps on his shirt, kissing the hairy nipples underneath, nuzzling my way down his belly, all the way to the rearing horse buckle on his belt. The thick lump underneath it went halfway to his knee.

He held a beer in one hand on the back of the seat, and draped his other arm across the steering wheel.

"Go for it, cowboy," he whispered, grinning down at me. "Ride your buddy's pony some."

I unhooked the brass buckle on his belt and opened the buttons on his frayed Levis. I snuggled my face against his warm underwear, feeling the bristly hairs curling out of his fly. When I reached inside his boxer shorts with my fingers, his dick was so hard I couldn't bend it. He moved his hips so I could get it out, and then the proud, stiff cock I'd wanted so long stood up like an Idaho tree, tall and straight in front of my crossed eyes.

He made it bounce in my face, going "*BRMM, BRMM, BRMM,*" and then I went for it, went all the way down over it. "Ye-a-a-h," he breathed, settling back. "Show your buddy how good a cocksucker's mouth can feel." Dusk came while I sighted up his belly and watched him drink his beer and smile down at me, at me sucking his cock. "Watch the teeth," he instructed me. "Little wider." I loved it. "Play with my nuts some." I was in heaven, giving my guy what he wanted.

There's this funny sort of reversal that happens when you suck another man's dick. You get a wonderful sexual rush of your own from giving him what he likes so much. He goes, "Yeah, feels good," and your dick tingles. His cockhead hardens up, and you think you're about to come. His juices start to flow, and you wet your pants. How come, if I'm the one blowing him, I feel like my whole body is one giant orgasm? I mean, I didn't even have my dick out yet.

He groaned and put his hand on the back of my head, stopping me for a moment. "Go slow," he said. "Don't make me come. Make it last. I'm so full of spunk I can't hardly hold it in." I found I could keep his entire erection in my throat for minutes at a time without gagging, just holding my breath, suspended in time, wrapped around his sex.

He whimpered with pleasure. I felt the head of his cock throb against my tongue, and then he grabbed my hair and pulled me back until only the tip was between my lips. "Hold up," he whispered. "Don't move, oh, oh, shit, yeah, I got to let some out, UNH-H-H. . ."

A burst of cum spewed around my teeth and dripped from my lower lip. Donnie moaned, still holding my head motionless, as my mouth filled with his thick juice, not in spurts, but in a quick flow that lasted for two or three seconds, then stopped.

"Don't swallow, or I'll shoot off all the way," Donnie told me, and I held the slightly salty wad of his semen in my mouth. "Don't move," he said. "Don't do anything." I waited and felt another short squirt against my tongue. Donnie shuddered, then began to relax back against the seat.

"Uh-huh. Right there, that's right," Donnie said at last, and took a deep breath. "That's right where I want to be. I love it when I can stop in the middle of shooting my load, and hold it half in and half out."

He moved my head with his hands, up and down over his dick, slowly masturbating himself with my mouth. "Ah-h-h, yeah, that's what I call ridin' the high trail, yeah, just clip-clopping along on my pony, up there on the top of the ridge. I can go forever now without actually shooting off. I just have to leak some out now and then, sorta let the pressure off. Wups, here comes one more." He pulled my lips away, and I could see a new dribble of milky jism drooling from the tip of dick. His hard-on twitched once, then held stiff.

"Don't swallow it, buddy." He took my arms and raised me up. "Bring it up here for me. I wanna lick it out of your mouth. Come here, sport. I wanna eat my own jism."

I was limp in his hands as he lifted my face to his. I opened my mouth and Donnie kissed me hard, running his tongue in between my lips, licking at my teeth, sucking his own cum out of my mouth and swallowing it. He ran his hand up under my shirt, pinching both my nipples, and then worked his hand inside my zipper, rolling my hard-on around inside my Jockey shorts. I could feel sticky wetness, and when Donnie put his hand inside my shorts and pulled on my dick, it was already slick and dripping.

"Uh-h-HUH," he said, cranking me around. "Pretty juicy down there, fella. You really like this queer shit, don't you?"

"God, Donnie, you turn me on so much," I moaned, "I'm just crazy for your dick." My voice was husky and hoarse. "You stretched my vocal cords," I told him as we sat up for a while and ran the motor for heat. We giggled as I tried to clear my throat and couldn't. "Next thing, I'll be losing my voice. Or maybe it will just get higher," I said, coughing. "I'll be swishing around in a dress, like Stanley."

"Ah, Stanley doesn't wear a dress."

"Not yet. Give him time. He'll be our maid."

Donnie didn't laugh. After a moment, he said, "You put him down too much. Ought to keep in mind that he's one of our brothers."

"Sisters."

"Whatever. We're all faggots, Bill."

"Don't say that."

"Better get used to it."

"You're not. You're a man. That's why you turn me on."

He sat back and stared ahead without saying anything, and I thought he was mad about something, but then he started a story.

"My buddy back home, my jack-off buddy, he used to mail-order sexy underwear, girls' stuff, you know, with the hole in front so you can fuck your girlfriend while she's got them on. From L.A., Hollywood.

"He had boxes of them, and he'd take them with him on weekends and give them to girls and come back and tell me how it looked to stick his dick into them, with the girl's cunt inside all that red lace.

"I wasn't even in high school then, and I just ate that shit up. He lived out back in a bunkhouse, by himself most of the year. I'd go back and hang out with him.

"I woke him up one day, and he had 'em on in bed. Turns out he liked to see his dick sticking out of them better than he liked to see it go into them. He wore girls' panties all the time, under his jeans, and this is an ugly fucker who never shaves and wears chaps when he's herding cattle and all that good shit."

He paused, and I told him, "I don't quite get it."

"It's just that you shouldn't, you know, judge people. Especially about their sex habits. Some rough-tough cowboys wear lace panties. And some real pansies are tigers in the sack. That's what being queer is all about, being different from the bozos. All the pussy hounds know about is how to make babies in the dark. Nothing wrong with guys who act a little bit like girls. They're just being what they are. Nothing wrong with that. Turns me on, in fact. They're even queerer than me, and I like that."

He took a long pull on his beer, swallowed hard, and let out a long burp. "'Course, I like anything with a dick hung on it," he said. "Including Stanley."

I didn't want to talk about Stanley. Sliding back next to him, I ran my fingers under his open shirt, feeling the hard muscles of his chest, plucking at the hairs. He turned up his beer can, gulped, and crumpled it. I leaned over to rub my cheek against his sideburns, and he hooked his elbow behind my neck.

When I turned my face up to him, he kissed me, gently, and I closed my eyes and leaned toward him. I was beginning to get the hang of making out with another guy. I chewed at his mustache, and then opened my mouth for him, but this time instead of his tongue he gave me a mouthful of cold beer that leaked out and dribbled down our chins.

"Heh," he chuckled, wiping his neck. "Guess I ain't much good at being romantic. Whyn't you take your clothes off for me? Let me watch you strip."

He tugged my teeshirt up over my arms and then used it to dry my chin as I took off my sneakers.

"Socks, too," he told me. "Get buck nekkid. And help me get my boots off, okay?" I did it all, pulling his cowboy boots loose, then balancing on my knees on the seat as I dropped my pants. "Keep your shorts on for a minute," he told me. I pulled my pants down and tossed them onto the floor.

He pulled his cock out and put his hand on my Jockey shorts, feeling my behind. "You got a sexy butt. Anybody ever tell you that? No? Hmm, yeah, cute ass." Donnie ran one hand all over my backside, squeezing the cheeks of my ass and calling me "Sexy Billy," over and over. Me, he called me that! I was dizzy with excitement as he rubbed my bare back and felt my legs and wrapped his fingers around my arm and pressed his thumb against the muscles.

His dick waved from his pants as he peeled off his shirt and moved over on the seat. Still on my knees, I could feel my erection pushing my Jockeys out in front. Donnie stuck his fingers in under the leg holes and tickled my nuts.

"Lemme get a good look at this thing," he whispered, hooking my hard-on with a finger and tugging it out so the head of it was aimed down beside my leg, sticking half out.

"Nothing I like better than a big ol' dick pokin' out like that, pokin' out from the side of a guy's undershorts."

"Aw, mine's not nearly as big as yours."

"Don't matter, when two guys are fucking around with each other, big dick is one word."

He worked it all the way out, and it was so hard it ached. When he let go, it flipped straight up. "Big ol' ball bag you got on you, man," he said, pulling those out, too.

He tugged down on my nuts until it made my dick drop down level to his face, and then Donnie leaned forward and spread his lips around it, and my dick glided easily into his mouth. It seemed like such a natural place for it to go, like it belonged right there. He made a long, slow slide all the way down to the hilt, twisting my briefs all out of shape as he sucked my cock. I had to hold onto the seat back as he worked me over with his tongue and his lips and his throat, swallowing and sucking and fingering my balls until I had to warn him I was close to coming. When Donnie moved back, a thin string of my pre-cum stretched from me to his mouth.

He licked it off and looked up at me with his eyes narrowed. "Now, pull your shorts off, big guy," he said, still jacking off as he watched me. I sat down and kicked my underwear off. I was totally naked. Kneeling on the floor-board, pushing my legs apart, Donnie had complete control of me, and I closed my eyes and let him handle me like a toy. He licked my thighs. He kissed all around the base of my cock. He sucked my balls. I put one foot on the steering wheel column and braced the other on the dash. I was wide open, utterly open to him.

Donnie pushed my knees up and spread the cheeks of my ass. I expected his finger again, but this time I felt the rough scrape of his beard instead. He was licking me back there, Donnie was licking my ass! Yielding to the obscene and the sublime, I closed my eyes and groaned at the maddeningly sweet, warm slide of his tongue over the slot of my butt. He pushed my knees up higher and spread my crotch open wider, and then I felt the tip of his tongue press against the hole.

Gasping, whimpering, rocking my head from side to side, I let go down there, let myself go completely loose. Donnie never lost an advantage when he was close to getting what he wanted. Pressing up, higher still, he wedged his tongue in and darted it all the way up inside me, right up inside my asshole. My reflex was to bear down, and I squeezed him back out of me, but it had been too good, what I'd felt. I got control of myself and relaxed my ass again, and sure enough, I felt Donnie's tongue push up, and up, and then he held it there, held his hard, wet tongue right in the center of my butt, right up inside the hole between my legs.

Hanging there in ecstasy, I made a little squeak in my throat. He swirled his tongue around inside my asshole. My dick swelled up, throbbed, and dripped pre-cum onto my stomach.

Donnie backed off. I went limp. He wiped his mouth and burped.

"Find that Vaseline for me," he ordered from between my knees.

I held it while he dipped a finger into the goo and then prodded under my legs, back up between the cheeks of my ass, and once again he fingered me where I'd never been touched before, except by a few doctors. Well, okay, my mom got a thermometer up there a few times when I was a kid. But Donnie was whispering, "How'd you like to feel this end get stretched like your throat did?" and I knew he wasn't thinking about taking my temperature.

He stuck his finger up my asshole. It made me squinch my eyes shut and gasp out loud, "Ah! Donnie! Oh! Mmmh!"

It stung at first. Donnie purred in my ear. "Can you remember back when you were real little? Back to when you were in diapers? I can," he said.

He put more goo on his finger, and I squirmed when it went back in me. "I can remember crapping in my diapers, and feeling the hot turd back there sliding out of my asshole. I'd squeeze my butt on it, and it felt real good. That's why babies cry when you change their diapers. They're pissed off. They don't know it's shit, they just know it feels good, having something big and warm back there. Very sensitive spot."

He twisted his finger, and it felt slick, and delicious. I groaned.

He whispered, "Open it up, Billy. Make like you're gonna shit in my hand. Nothing will come out. I already checked. Maybe one little old fart up there, that's all."

Dirty talk, shitty talk, floated up from the floorboard. I thrashed and slumped down over his hand, feeling my cock thump stiffly against his arm, and Donnie whispered, "That's one." Then he did something with his fingers that made me gasp for breath. "That's two," he said. His fingers moved up, and then popped out. The next time, the pressure brought tears to my eyes, but I took it, and Donnie said, "That's three, old buddy."

I heard a high squeal and realized it was coming from my nose, but all I could think about was the feeling of his three fingers wedged up my rear end, and I was sure he was going to force his whole hand up my ass. It hurt and it felt so good all at once, and I threw back my head and went "GAH-H-H-H-H-AH!"

Then he was out of me again. I was straddling him as he knelt on the floor. He leaned forward, looming over me like a bear. "You're gonna like this," he said, and chuckled. I felt the real thing, Donnie's hard dick, slick with Vaseline jelly, sliding up between my legs, between my cheeks, poking at my butt, tunneling up my asshole, and I wasn't ready for what I felt then.

He jabbed upward but my ass didn't want to stretch that far. I pulled back, "Ouch, wait."

But he didn't stop. He reached under us to aim it, feeding the big tube through his fist and up my ass. The pain made my jaw drop. When it popped inside, I tried to part myself for him, but he was splitting me open.

"Wait, you're so big." I put my hand on his chest. He backed off, trembling.

My big mistake was reaching for him, wrapping my arms around his muscular body. Chest hair rubbed between us, and his beard rasped on my neck. I felt his urgency, his male potency, and I couldn't help telling him, "Fuck me, Donnie. I want to take it inside me."

He leaned forward and pushed, and the next time it got halfway in he went wild, lunging at me, growling, kissing my mouth, and then he raised his hips hard and just impaled me all the way down on his dick. The pain made me dizzy, but there's no stopping a man halfway through a fuck. As it sank into me, my guts seemed to turn inside out. I let him do it as long as I could, hanging onto his neck, but when he started to thrust at me, roaring in my ear, it hurt so much I had to twist away. I reached down and pulled his cock out and pointed it up under my balls instead.

"Oh-h-h, shi-i-i-it," he groaned, and slippery warmth shot up between my legs as Donnie fucked my fist, pumping his load out into my hand instead of my ass. His dick stabbed at me, squirting cum up under my nuts, flooding my crotch. I hugged him and rubbed him, trying to make it good for him while he got off, even if it was only between my legs.

The big guy was crazy on top of me, grabbing and humping and shoving his hips at me, and when he laid a line of his cum up between us, his hairy belly was scratchy and slippery against my dick at the same time, and I felt myself unloading with him, coming at last, making a big messy glop of cum between our bellies that trickled down my side as we lay there panting together.

My asshole ached. The cum on my belly was turning cold. Everything that had built up between us seemed to be slipping away. Without knowing why, I blurted out, "I'm sorry."

After a long moment, Donnie mumbled, "What for?"

"I couldn't take it. . . you know. . . all the way."

Donnie sighed. He turned his face to mine and slowly raised his arm, clenching his fist. His biceps muscle bulged in my face. "Feel that," he ordered me.

I put my hand on the rock-hard knot in his arm.

"Push my hand down," he whispered.

I took hold of his fist and pushed down. He held it steady. "Now, listen up, Bill," still whispering, "If I wanted to fuck a girl, I'd have some chick from town in the back seat squealing her tits off right now." I put both hands on his fist and pulled down, but couldn't move his arm. "And if I wanted to fuck Stanley," he continued, staring into my eyes, "I'd have Stanley buck nekkid in my car right now instead of you." His arm began to tremble under my pressure. I threw my weight into pulling down on his fist, to no effect at all. He narrowed his eyes and put his face right in mine. "And if it was real important for me to shoot my load up your ass," he purred, "there's nothing you could have done. . ." The tendons on his neck stood out as he pulled his clenched fist up to his chest, lifting me out of my seat and dragging me over on top of him. ". . .to stop me," he hissed. My naked body was draped over his powerful, hard arm, and I realized that he was strong enough to make his cum shoot out of my nose if that's what he set his mind to do.

I hadn't stopped him. He'd let me stop him. I felt myself melting down over Donnie's furry chest. I snaked my arm around his shoulder and pressed my cheek to his. He took my other hand and guided it down between our bellies. "So forget about girls," he told me. "You know what you really want, and it's not pussy. It's never been pussy and it never will be. Has it?"

I touched his soft cock and instantly wrapped my hand around it, shaking my head. "And forget about Stanley," he continued, pulling his sheepskin coat over my bare back. "Forget all that shit about fags and sissies and what's queer and what's straight. Who fucking cares what anybody else thinks?"

He reached down beside my hand and pushed my own cock up next to his. I opened my hand and then closed my palm around both our dicks, slippery now with the mixture of my cum with his.

"And, no 'sorry's,' buddy," he whispered. "When you get it on with me, it's all just man-to-man fucking. Ain't gonna be no need for 'sorry's' when we're both getting what we want."

We watched the moon edge up over the treeline on the jagged Idaho ridge beyond the windshield. "Man-to-man fucking," I repeated. "I like the sound of that." I snuggled closer to Donnie's naked body. "It's crazy. I just got fucked, and I never felt more like a man."

"Yeah," Donnie smiled. "Queer world, ain't it?"

SPIRIT OF THE POND

Frederic Trainor

I stood there by it—that murky, kidney-shaped pool of brackish, brown, putrid water—swatting relentless insects absently as the woods around me chirped and hissed and crackled with the sounds of spring.

The glare of the late morning sun reflected off the water in bright, jagged ripples. It wasn't even noon yet, and already I was wiping beads of sweat from the back of my neck and forehead. The nervous flutters in my belly didn't help much, either.

He would come. He promised.

Or was I just crazy? Drunk from the toxic vapors of Daddy Mo's corn mash whiskey and my own buck-wild imagination? You crazy, Bobby, the chiding voice scolded in my head. Believin' in spooks and haints and mystery promises; in pop-go-the-weasel niggah boys who rise up unannounced from Jesus knows where, quiet and sure and more than a little bit. . .

"Scared you came?"

I jumped, my head whipping around as if snatched by an invisible hook. His bewitching, lazy brown eyes hooked mine for a second, then swung out across the pond in awkward silence. He'd kept his promise.

"No," I answered, lying. "W. . .wouldn't be here if I wuz." He said nothing, stooping down in one fluid movement to pick up a rock, tossing it with practiced ease across the pond. Three skips and it was gone, leaving a trail of shimmering ripples in its wake. Still crouched, he gave me a strange, sidelong glance over his shoulder, one that made me feel like he knew something I didn't and had no intention of sharing it.

"Promises made to be kep'," he said in that Mississippi Delta Negro drawl that conjured lost and brutal eras of Amerikkkan history in my tender, young mind.

Ante-bellum spirituals and lively banjo strumming.

Smoldering hatred and blood-fueled passions.

Opulent wealth and dismal poverty.

He turned slightly and the oil in his short, nappy hair made it glisten and shine as if his dark scalp was saturated with tiny, sparkling diamonds, each move of his head producing a lustrous shimmer.

He was taller than me by three or four inches, his T-shirt sleeveless and torn, coarse sackcloth trousers cut off at the knees with sloppy thread tendrils hanging raggedly. I had guessed his age as about fifteen. He had a track-runner's body, lean and greyhoundish, his skin the golden brown of peanut butter. The ugly criss-cross scars on his thighs and neck disturbed me, but I hadn't the courage to inquire. Something about those eyes restrained me.

Eyes of mint-green, boot-black and scarlet-red.

The colors of Mother Africa.

Not actually, but *beneath*.

"What day dis be?" he queried as he moved up toward the trees out of direct, relentless sunlight.

I looked at him, confused. "Don't you know?"

He stared back, almost like a startled person would, blinking twice to clear his vision of its cobwebs. Then his expression seemed to waver between embarrassment and irritation. "Jus. . . jus' tell me what day dis be, lil' niggah."

"Tuesday." My answer only irritated him more, slipping beneath his skin like the heat and anxiety of the moment. He fidgeted as if about to pee on himself, shook his head from side to side in a quick, definitive way, then blurted out, "Don't mean *dat*. Ah mean, what year?"

I started to burst out laughing but wisely checked myself when some inner warning told me he wasn't playing games. He really, truly was ignorant of what he claimed. When I told him the year was nineteen ninety-three, a vague shadow, a *pall,* seemed to pass over his handsome face. He peered up toward the sky and sighed, a weary, overburdened sound, then closed his eyes as one would in prayer to the Lord, his full, slightly-chapped lips moving unintelligibly.

"'Tis da devil done claimed mah soul," I heard him mumble as I unconsciously moved a few steps back into the shade of an overgrown, knurled pine tree. I didn't understand, and the fact that I didn't was beginning to nudge me on to a dull but sharpening fear.

There was a *wrongness* here.

Essentially out-of-whack but functioning.

A paradox.

I suddenly thought of my sister, Rochelle, and her boyfriend, Dwayne. Yo, Dwayne. What up, Dwayne. My sister, forever in love with love, worshipping the very ground on which the dude stepped, sporting his signet ring on her finger with cocky pride, her hot, vulgar mouth frothing with over-blown platitudes and puppy-love predictions of having a litter of Dwayne's babies someday. Silly-assed girl.

She didn't know boys – no more than I knew *this* one.

A chance meeting a week before when I'd come to the pond to be alone, to escape Mama's shrill complaints and Daddy Mo's whisky-breathed obscenities, the boy a wraith-gift from the archives of my bitter loneliness. I didn't even know his name.

"Say what?" I asked.

"Don't matter none," he answered, then let loose with a self-satisfied chuckle-snicker, air whistling through his clenched teeth, shoulders jerking up and down rhythmically. The gesture reminded me of that snickering dog on the old Hanna-Barbara cartoons, Smudley or Snidely or whatever his name was. The image it conjured in my mind was absurd and made me laugh. After a moment we stopped laughing and looked at each other, unsure of what to say.

It was like this our last time. . . that pivotal point between *deciding* to Do It and Doing It, both of us seeming to be waiting for the other to initiate. My hormones and conscience were busy waging quiet battle.

To mask my tension, I turned around and began picking strips of bark off the pine tree's trunk, absenting humming the melody to some old soul song that had been running through my mind all morning, trying hard to ignore my bass drum heartbeat, the anxious flutters in my belly.

"Cain't go back," I heard him whisper. "Ain't nuttin' but col' black sleep back yonder."

Deeper mystery. "Huh?"

"Back yonder," he said behind me, crunching leaves underfoot. "Massah Dupree and dem white folks. Dey gots it in fo' me 'cause uh what I done to Massah' boy, Charles. He be yo' age, I reckon. Thereabouts. Keeps him in da big house 'round all dem high-class wimmen folk. Spoilt bad like rotted catfish." I started to turn around, having absolutely no idea what he was talking about, but he wasn't through. "Yeah," he went on in that low, reflective voice, its sound soothing, hypnotic. "Spoilt *dirty* bad. Boy come 'round by the slave shack when da moon done rose up. Massah don't know, right? Done been in da Missus' wimmen thangs, his eyes and lips all colored up, silk britches tight as sin 'round his fat backside, dark curls fallin' down 'round his perty face like his sister, Miss Audrey. White boy call fo' me, talkin' 'bout Massah Dupree send him to fetch me. I follows him out past da hoss stable. It be *real* hot dat night, right? I's barefoot, ain't got no shirt on, wearin' deez heah britches.

"We gets out by da ol' shithouse in backuh da big house, and Massah boy say, 'I lied. Massah don't want you. But you tell, niggah, and I'll tell mah Daddy you been eyeballin' mah sister, and he'll whip you somethin' good.'

"Den da boy tell me to lean 'gainst the shithouse. I do it

and he reach down and start feelin' 'tween mah legs, rubbin' mah thang, makin' it stand up hard in mah britches. I lets him undo mah britches and take it out, all black and long and hard like Mama's skillet handle, and he wiggle down his silk britches and tell me to rub mah thang 'cross his booboo, up 'tween dem fat, white cheeksuh his, and den I fucks him, wit' da moon shinin' bright and da hogs a-gruntin' and a-snortin' in da pens out yonder. . ."

I felt his presence directly behind me, peering over my shoulder. A light breeze whistled through the woods, rustling leaves and overhanging branches. The nagging sensation of *wrongness* returned, like a violin tone produced from an off-pitched piano, the stilted English uttered in cheap Kung Fu Movies, unsynchronized with the actors' lips. Out of place, out of time. Or like. . . like a wish that had stumbled into being without a clue as to why or how. . .

"What choo doin', lil' niggah?" His voice was hushed, husky.

"Nuttin'," I answered. And then he was pressed up against me, palpable proof this was no dream, his groin snugly fitting against my behind. Automatically I pushed back, rubbing my ass from side to side against his crotch, feeling the heat of his arousal spread like a fungus across the seat of my rear. He let out a deep moaning sound, one of his long arms encircling my waist while the other crept its way down my groin.

I had a scorching erection.

He deftly massaged it through my trousers, a thousand and one little explosions detonating inside my head.

"Da devil be damned, Bobby," he breathed lustfully, causing me to wonder if and when I had told him my name. "Yo' thang hard as mine."

Yo' thang. My thang.

You know: Wiener. Cock. Dick. Worm. Wee-wee.

Dirty, vulgar words we learned when we were in grammar

school, timeless and universal and naughty enough to get you a good ass-whipping if you used them around the wrong set of grown-ups.

That 'thang' you peed with.

And his 'thang'. It *was* as hard as mine.

I could feel it back there. It was like a warm length of lead pipe, trapped inside those ancient cut-offs, digging and rubbing into me, giving me that hot, twisted thrill I'd come to yearn for.

Yeah, I was a sissy. A faggot. A 'gump.'

I'd known I was since the third grade when me and this little high yellow niggah, Reginald Colfax, used to sneak off behind the tool shed in his backyard, drop our pants, and rub our wee-wees against each other's bodies. Reginald always greased his dookie hole and crack with Vaseline, ever ready for some lewd action.

Confess yo' sins unto da Lawwwd, bruthahs and sistahs, and all thangs shall be fo'given.

So sayeth the Good Reverend James W. Reid at Sunday morning services. And I did confess unto Him, each and every night, but no sooner had the guilt retreated than the desire reasserted its prowess, proving to me its knowledge of those filthy secrets I was trying so desperately to hide from God and everybody. . .

"Bend over."

I hugged the tree trunk, my trousers and underwear pulled down, my breath escaping in labored spurts. My *thang*, chocolate-colored and stiff as a death sentence, swooped upward from my smooth crotch fork like a throbbing sword, pointing fearlessly toward the bright, azure sky.

I was afraid to touch it.

I shut my eyes and purred as he slipped It between my buttocks, making them clench and squeeze around It possessively. I wanted It up my boodie and told him so.

That long, greasy, black mamba.

He didn't speak.

I heard knees pop and felt him slip away as he hunkered down. Strong hands gripped my thighs. His entire face pushed its way up into my ass. I groaned in alarm, trying to pull away. No one had ever done that to me. He held fast, pleading in a rushed whisper, "No, no. Lemme do dis. You'll like it. It feel good. Feel *real* good."

A buzz saw noise close to my ear.

I swatted away its perpetrator, then clutched the tree tighter.

His efforts were crude and ardent, burrowing with a ravenous abandon, his hot tongue stabbing its way past my anus, up into that dark, unclean place.

The feeling was base. Animal nasty.

I let go and rode him, working my boodie around on his face in a lewd gyration, supplying him with all the access he needed to get to whatever it was he was after.

I could hear Rochelle's pesty, grating voice now if she was here: Oooooo, you *dirrrrrty*, Bobby. Lettin' that niggah lick all up in yo' booboo like that. His tongue all up in yo' dookie hole!

Yeah, man.

In my dookie hole.

Makin' sweet, obscene love to it with those wet, suction-cup lips, my bubble-round, Hershey butt doing the mojo hump and roll in broad daylight, in the woods, my wee-wee jumping up and down like a nervous spring lever.

Feel good. Feel *real* good.

In my dookie hole.

My pleasure increased, my hands reaching back to pull my rump cushions apart for him. Everything felt relaxed and nasty-slimy back there.

Ready.

A questioning caw, then another, resounding through the trees as he stopped and rose to his feet. His breath was ragged, urgent.

"Ah eats Massah' boy booboo real good 'fo ah fucks him," he revealed without shame, his hands gripping me firmly about the hips. "Dat's why dey hang me. Say a niggah burn in Hell fo' his sin. T'rew mah body in de pond fo' good measure."

Before my thoughts could organize themselves over what I'd just heard, make sense from the senseless, he pulled me back onto his blood-filled need, nudging the head past my willing bull's eye. I grunted, gritted my teeth. "Oooo, *goddamn*," I gasped, reaching behind me to steer his hips. "Yo' dick *big*, man!"

"Yo' booboo tight, Bobby," he breathed excitedly, pushing more of himself up my back region. "Lawd have *mercy*, yo' booboo tight!" I grimaced from the pain, my stubborn sphincter refusing to yield easily, the wrath of da Lawd blocking the road to unholy sacrilege. But soon the sweet numbness took over, the road clearing, the path yielding. My eyes drooped shut as a whirlwind of memories which weren't my own thrust their way to the surface of visceral awareness; the chattering of cicadas and nesting fowl interlaced with the rhythmic clip-clopping of horses hooves and rickety carriages; rich, spirited harmonies sung in bassoon baritones and magnificent tenors about hope and liberation from the iron shackles of servitude; the sharp, merciless crack of whips across sweat-sleek, ebony skin; cruel, imperious laughter; soul-wrenching screams.

Ohhh, fuck me.

Make that fucker sing the St. Louis Blues in the key of B-flat, you bad motherfucker.

I bucked and jerked my hips with each ramming stroke, giving him all of what he wanted, taking all of what he gave. We took from each other, two immoral black boys, bridging the gap between dream and reality, need and escape, time Present and time Long Forgotten. Our pact was bonded, sealed, consummated with the eternal lust god, immersed in the musical choir and the vistas of Mother Nature.

A dozen plunges later up my back-route love canal and I was groaning, clenching my buttocks and spurting all over the tree in front of me. "You doin' it, lil' niggah?" he asked me several times. "Huh? You doin' it?" The fact that I was seemed to fuel his ardor even more, causing his haunches to twitch and hunch with increasing speed until he was literally slamming his cock in and out of my ass, his hard pelvis slapping loudly against my boodie, my body shuddering from impact.

And then, before I knew it, he was pulling out entirely and splashing warm semen all over my ass, down the backs of my wobbly legs.

The fever cloud began to dissipate.

Slowly, I bent down to pull up my shorts and trousers, afraid to turn around, afraid to look into his eyes and see the same cesspool of spent emotion, dark satisfaction and confusion that I was feeling reflected back at me. I was suddenly aware of the serenity of my surroundings once more.

The chittering of insects.

The garbling of birds.

The crackling, rustling leaves.

Nature's symphony blending unevenly with the rattling of his belt buckle, his hard cough, crude hack, spitting.

Dat's why dey hang me. Say a niggah burn in hell fo' his sin.

Burn in hell fo' his sin. Burn in. . .

The chill descended then. A choking, bone-freezing coldness that made my very soul shiver. Incongruent pieces abruptly fell into place: his neck and leg scars; the archaic mode of his speech; the ragged sack cloth he wore; his bewilderment over time and place.

From beyond the cold, bleak grave he'd come.

A slave boy from a time preceding that of my great grandmother, perhaps even her mother's mother. Irrepressible yearning for love and breath of life, miraculously defying fate's untimely decree of a cruel and unjust death at the ruthless hands of cultured savages. *Fuck you, Massah. Niggahs don't die, they jus' move on.*

My gift. My strange, beautiful, frightening, inexplicable gift. I wanted badly to say something, anything, to let him know I thought I understood—understood the cancer of loneliness, how it spoke to its captives in a deep, esoteric tongue which sometimes leaped across the conventions of space and time. So desperate its pitch. So hollow its echo. But words eluded me, like the shadows of specters.

I turned then, but there were only dead branches and pine cones that had been trampled where he'd been standing. An echo, so thin, chimeric. . .

The gift was gone.

Only the woods and the still, kidney-shaped pond remained, its murky, dark water a giant mirror for the hot, glaring sun above me. . .

BERDACHE

Bart Louis

The canoe paddle dipped in and out of the placid water with barely a whisper. My shoulders and back continued the repetitive motions without conscious thought, leaving my mind free to remember and fantasize and dream as I wished. Only the untarnished sun dipping low, temporarily blinding me around a curve in the river, reminded me of time passing, of details of living. But I was still left with the dark burden on my shoulders, the black, oppressive, mental cloud.

It seemed good to use my legs again, I realized, as I beached the craft on a sandy spit under drooping willows and unpacked enough for the night. Now that I was no longer a part of it, I could hear the river's voice reflecting off the sand and pebbles at its bottom. It had been days since I had heard human voices, including my own. I had no wish to break that spell.

But try as I might, my thoughts went over and over the past few weeks of increasing pain. Perhaps when I am older, I thought, this separation won't seem as tragic as it did to me then at age nineteen, in boundless love with the most handsome man in the territory, Hector Forsman of Boston and St. Louis. Of course I always knew that Hector had been married and a family man back East, but when we met that fateful day in the muddy main street of Montrose Falls and our eyes met—no, collided like some sort of celestial genesis, my world became focused on serving his needs in every way.

Every task he gave me was further proof that he valued me, needed me as house and body servant in his important affairs which I never really understood. Washing his clothes, cleaning his house, cooking his meals became my points of honor, my only source of pride in my accomplishments. I shone in his approval and as a reflection of his accomplishments.

Sometimes he was cruel, everyone said that, but each time when his anger had dissipated and his arm grew too tired to raise the lash again, he would take me in his violent mood and send my senses soaring ever higher, and I knew there could be no other for me. For more than a year our love blossomed and we were a respected couple in the community, even by those whose sexual appetites were very different. But then Roberta appeared and the dream began to shatter.

At first I thought they were too much alike, it would never last. Both were tall and with dark, almost black eyes that seemed imperious, even suspicious. Roberta's hair was raven black and long, tied together and hanging nearly to the waist in a luxurious fall. Hadn't Hector, innumerable times, confessed to me his love for my short, blond curls and the fine, pale fuzz that almost covers my chest and legs? And my violet-blue eyes–hadn't he claimed that they spoke poetic intimacies to him and him alone? And when we made love, in our bed or under tall sycamores or beside the thundering falls, his huge cock towered high and thick and plundered me so deliciously that I was convinced there could be no other. I knew his beatings were manifestations of his love, and they became sources of gratification in themselves. But one day he made it clear that he had chosen Roberta as his mate. Some of the other businessmen had called him "squaw man" behind his back, but he hadn't seemed to care.

As I unpacked enough supplies for my evening meal, I wondered how far west I had come from Montrose Falls, situated at the edge of the wilderness. Twenty, thirty miles? Trappers had been in this region before, but never stayed longer than necessary, and never in summer when the dangers were greatest. I didn't care; it was vital that I be by myself, the solitude therapeutic and undisturbed. Sitting quietly on the fallen log in my new campsite, I could hear only the distant cry of the loon and the whisper of the river.

Suddenly I rose and stripped off my buckskins, needing the river's embrace before the sun was gone and the night breeze picked up. I waded in and swam long and hard, to the other side of the river and back, splashing and listening to sounds that only I was making. When I returned to the campsite dripping, my cock arched forward by my balls pulled up tight, my body hair glistening golden in the slanting light, I felt lighter somehow, washed free of soils of the past. I also began to shiver from the evening coolness, and realized that I needed to forage for firewood before the light was gone.

I replaced only my boots—I would dry as I gathered the fuel. I set off into the woods where there should be dry limbs and perhaps even a short log if I decided to watch the night pass in the light of the campfire. I decided to explore at right angles to the river so there would be no difficulty in retracing my steps.

I had only gathered a half dozen small branches when I heard a soft sound, a sound I instinctively knew was not from a woods creature. Was it a moan? A groan? I stopped and listened, but all was silent. When I started forward again, my footsteps rustling through dry leaves and twigs, I heard it again, directly ahead. The sun was gone and the night was arriving rapidly. Then I saw a break in the forest, a small clearing ahead, and moved forward cautiously. I saw him almost immediately.

Between two trees was a man, a young native, tied with vines in a spread-eagle position, his long, naked limbs bronze but streaked with red marks that were familiar to me. After one of Hector's rages, my body must have looked like that. I shrank back, not wanting to face this apparition, this reminder of what I had left behind, and yet I was drawn forward irrevocably, slowly approaching the beauty of what I had been and the horror it must have seemed to some others.

He was also lean and sinewed, about my age, and his

sculptured muscles cast shadows emphasized by the fading light. When I appeared at the edge of the clearing his sounds stopped, and I realized that they had been hummings of song rather than groans. His eyes, dark and intense under dark brows, were fixed on me, first on my face in concentrated gaze, and then roving over my naked body emerging from the brush. It seemed that all the evening sounds of the forest had stilled, waiting for our next move, our relationship to become manifest.

Except for a thick mane of black hair shrouding his shoulders, his body was nearly hairless. In the crotch of his spread legs another thick patch of black hair framed a long cock, its foreskin neatly concealing the head. The long, thick shaft was pushed outward by large balls that seemed to attest to his potency. As I watched, the organ moved and stirred, thickening slowly as his eyes bore into mine.

I knew I should cut him down, release him from his bonds and tend his wounds, ease his discomfort, but I didn't. Instead my cock began to rise and I drew closer, experiencing vicariously his plight but unwilling to change it. His cock throbbed upward and I recognized my power over him, a power that I relished like a fresh peach picked ripe from the tree. His handsome face remained expressionless, waiting for his new master to reveal his desires.

I dropped to my knees and took his burgeoning limb into my mouth. I engulfed it and felt the head emerge from its sheath, moving deeper, deeper into my throat, a shaft fitting into a socket tailored for it by nature and the gods. There it throbbed and swelled, imparting its sweetness while signalling its surrender. I knew I could extract its heart, its lifeblood, and my own prick rose tightly against my belly with my newfound power. Each time I moved or flicked my tongue there was an answering throb, and I could hear, dimly above, the humming beginning again in the Indian's throat.

I caressed his leg columns and felt the long, tapered muscles tense and move under my fingers. His toes curled in the leafy moss under his feet, especially when I came up for air and again consumed the thick rod. His humming was replaced by short gasps. I refused to give him release.

Pulling back, I rose to move to his rear. As I expected, the taut, lean muscles of his buttocks were rounded and trim, overshadowed by the broad shoulders and sinewy back. His legs, spread widely, left his hairless asshole exposed to my avid eyes. It was mine to plunder, to plumb the depths; my rigid prick demanded it. Lubricated only with my own saliva, I pressed into him with no preliminaries, the tight heat welcoming me, adding to my own feverish pressure.

Gradually I pushed all the way in, gratified by his groans and gasps, his pain my pleasure. By pulling his slender hips against me, I buried my shaft in his body and thrust deeper and deeper until there was no more to impale. His muscles were strong and tight, so confining that I was able to move the head of my cock in and out of my foreskin deep in his bowels without withdrawing each time. His gut kissed my exposed cockhead hotly each time it emerged.

I had almost forgotten the joy of fucking in my many months with Hector Forsman. He had grown furious if I expressed any suggestion that I needed release myself, and knowing that I was pleasing him, receiving the hot spurts of his love in my ass or my mouth, was generally enough for me. Sometimes I came spontaneously when he did, and occasionally I hurriedly jacked off after he went to sleep, but I always felt very guilty about that. As I fucked the captive in the woods that twilight, my guilt evaporated, the violence of my actions a satisfying antidote.

The Indian began to meet my thrusts and I knew I would soon lose control. His head was thrown back onto my shoulder, the aroma of his long, black hair sweet in my nostrils.

I reached around him to grip his stabbing cock in one hand and his heavy balls in the other. The deeper I thrust the tighter my grip.

I could feel vibrations in his throat, transmitted through his back to my chest, revealing his approaching crisis; the anguish I was producing in him sent me over the edge. At my first spurt assaulted him, I could feel his balls contract in my fist and he began to fill my other hand with his seed.

Our bodies seemed glued together in our mutual love and lust, moving and writhing as one nocturnal, primordial creature in nature. Each had power over the other while sharing power and full understanding with the other, proving again the universality of the human experience. His ass grasped and milked my cock until I was drained, relieved of the heavy pall that had beset me for so long. As I reluctantly pulled back, I brought my cum-filled hand to his mouth and he lapped it up obediently.

For a full minute I stared at his back, my brain slowly returning to the present. He hung from his fetters, his muscles trembling, the vines cutting into his wrists. Finally I strode to my campsite and returned with my knife, cutting him free. He collapsed into my arms for a moment, and my head spun at the unaccustomed tenderness I felt. Then without speaking, I took him by the hand and led him to my campsite.

We sat cross-legged on the ground, shaken and staring at each other. Then he spoke.

"I am called Phillip," he said in perfect English.

I was startled. "You speak English?"

He nodded. "Trappers from St. Louis visit us each winter to buy our pelts. Some are friendly. One is called Solomon—he sleeps with me sometimes. He gave me that name, the name of a king, I believe. He taught me his language. He taught me—many things." For the first time he smiled.

"Who tied you to the trees?" I had to ask.

"My brothers, others of my people. They know that I – need – enjoy it sometimes. They will return when they want more sex."

"You are a slave to them?"

He looked puzzled. "I do not understand the word."

When I only shrugged, he brightened. "Are you hungry? I can catch some fish for us if you wish."

I nodded and he immediately padded to the river, wading in some distance. I wondered how he could see anything in the darkness, but by the time I had a fire going, he returned with two fat, silver fish. He busied himself at the fire, cleaning the fish and frying them in my pan, as I watched him move with liquid grace. His bronze skin glistened in the firelight, and his bright eyes caught mine frequently as if asking for approval. We ate ravenously but for the most part in silence. After we finished he spoke again haltingly.

"Your beautiful hair –" he began. "A golden god –" His eyes dropped to my cock and settled there, knowing it would respond.

He was a lord of the forest, the curator of nature, his tawny skin draping perfect muscles, the blackness of his hair matching the night. Sparks from the fire drifted upward in the lazy breeze but some seemed trapped in his eyes. My cock reared high and his cock raced with mine for supremacy. After a moment I spread my buckskins next to the fire and lowered myself on them face down. I spread my legs and turned my head to look at him, my message clear.

Gravely he moved to me, his lips touching my neck, his tongue searching for the fine, fair hair he seemed to admire. Slowly he moved downward, lapping my skin and hairs as he went, eventually into the slope of my ass groove. I could not remain still; I moaned and spread my legs even further. When I felt his tongue enter me there I thrust upward against his face, eager for the next, inevitable step. And when he entered me, his cock rigid and conquering, it was right.

He was gentle at first, and I felt a twinge of guilt for my earlier roughness, but that disappeared when he began to thrust heavily, spreading me wide and striking the depths. Again I gloried in submitting, in being the receptacle for the beautiful man to whom I freely relinquished control. My prick grated against my smooth buckskins, and with each thrust I glowed brighter and hotter – for him. His pace quickened and I could feel his cock thicken even more as I entered further into his aura.

Suddenly he stopped in mid-air and I heard a footfall nearby. I looked up from the ground to see two Indians standing only a few feet away, their eyes fixed on us and our coupling. A few guttural words were exchanged between Phillip and the men; they were somewhat older, thicker of body and more heavily muscled. They wore some sort of crude leather vests and loincloths. Their black hair was pulled back away from their intent faces.

Phillip resumed his slow fucking, his arms supporting his weight on both sides of my chest, as they watched us in the firelight. After a moment they pushed their loincloths aside and took their hard cocks in their hands, and while we stared at each other, one came close and knelt at my face, his turgid tool extended to me. I took it into my mouth, sucking it sumptuously, greedily; there was no opportunity for subtlety; my role was service.

The other Indian watched for a moment and then took his place at Phillip's rear. I felt his additional weight bear down on me as he entered the ass I had plundered earlier. Phillip groaned and dropped to rest on my back, gripping my shoulders tightly as he adjusted to the new invasion. And when the older man established his rhythm it was also Phillip's rhythm, his cock thrusting deeply in me as he was sandwiched between us. My own cock was ignored, twisted under me and the double weight above.

We grunted and moaned together, each in his manner, guttural, growling, gripped in the shared celebration of our masculinity. Muscles snapped, sweat poured from our overheated torsos, and balls mashed against the man closest to us. Our cocks were our masters, driving us to the brink of the precipice that we all knew so well but that was different each time.

The swelling cock in my mouth was the first to erupt, spewing sweet-salty syrup into my gulping throat. He shoved my head down on the gushing fountain, increasing my delirium. He had not completed his flow when Phillip's fucker stiffened and groaned, driving Phillip's cock deeper into me as he burst through the barriers and merged with his lover/victim. Almost immediately I became aware of Phillip's cock thrusting, jerking deep inside, pressed there by his own need and his lover's. The crackling tension of the moment, three men struggling together with me, loving, needing, sharing their bodies and their minds, exploded any residual restraints, and I gushed silently, semen spurting and seeping along the contours of my belly pressed against the buckskins.

The two men quickly withdrew, stretching out at the edge of the clearing, and were soon snoring. Phillip and I embraced and lay quietly in each other's arms by the fire. There was no pall around me anymore.

Phillip kissed me and drew back, looking at me lovingly. "Now I have a friend again."

I nodded. "Again?" I murmured sleepily.

"Yes, there was another like me in our village. I thought he was a friend but he was not a good man. He sometimes told lies and stole from the others. The Chief threatened to expell him. Recently he left to live in the city. The trappers called him Robert, but I think he calls himself Roberta now."

SEA-BEAT

Robert Burdette Sweet

Lucien Blacker decided not to complete the article he was doing for a trade journal and irresponsibly drove to the beach, for once unimpeded by thoughts of his 'mother-wife and father-sons.' That matters at home had gotten out of hand disturbed him, despite the fact that he and his wife and boys had settled into an easy pattern of mutual dependency, mutual indifference.

Sea birds were standing, hazed by an overhead sun into spectral nuggets a full half mile from cliffs the waves usually beat upon. He wondered if he'd ever felt so exhilarated, so unconfined. He sensed his body as a being separate from himself, raw and prickling. The black, wiry hairs that crawled down his wrists and flecked the joints of his fingers stirred in the wind. His wife called him a hirsute raisin, pronouncing the dark pelt that covered his ass Neanderthal. To which he'd responded with a quiet shame that now, poised on the cliff, squinting into the brightness of the warm fog, seemed inappropriate.

Had it not been for his extraordinary meeting with the young men on the beach that day, there would be little more to tell about Lucien Blacker except that he was a forty year old joke whose disdain for himself was as culturally insisted upon as was his life with his nibbling wife and crueler children. He'd reacted by searching out illicit affairs, struggling to recoup desire and daring for which he recently managed to reap only laughter at himself and growing impotence.

Part way down his descent of the cliff he took off his shoes and socks, stuffed them in his knapsack. Though the stone outcropping on the narrow path hurt his feet, he liked the hurt. Physical hurt, unlike mental hurt, made Lucien feel alive. Already he questioned the advisability of dragging the red awning chair whose folded legs scraped with an irritating whine across the rocks.

The fine sand the path led onto warmed his feet despite the brisk wind hurling from over the breakers. The beach was so wide there seemed to be few people there: two children playing ball, a pot-bellied man stationed by a pole stuck in the sand, a sun-bonneted woman strolling gigantic dogs. Though a jutting cliff of slate rock usually closed the beach on its northern extreme, the tide had withdrawn from its still gleaming wet base so that a line of sand ran round to what must be a beach unknown to him. Wanting to be free of all people, he proceeded around the rock. The sun began to leak through the fog and sweat ran down his forehead. He removed his shirt, stuffing it along with the shoes and socks in the knapsack. The frail streaks of sun felt like fingers stroking the hair on his chest that spread wild and heavy across his flat stomach, funnelling into a thick coil before plunging into his white shorts.

At first Lucien saw no one, nor could he detect any end to the new beach. Enormous cliffs studded with yellow flowers, intense against the darker sky, barricaded the drifts of sand from the highway and towns he knew to be beyond. Were it not for the birds, mostly pipers and gulls, that rose as Lucien neared them, he'd have felt unnervingly isolated. As he continued along the ocean following the water line of hissing waves circling and sinking far into the mounds of sand, the behavior of the birds began to bother him. They took off in front of him with noisy squawks and snapping wings only to hover above his head and then settle into the tracks he'd just made. He began to feel enclosed, moving warily down the beach in a box of shifting wings, as entombed by solitude as he was by the too-many people who shared his life. When was the last time he'd been alone? He couldn't remember.

He'd wandered perhaps half a mile when, through a sudden rift in the incessant cloud of wings and mournful cries, he noticed a grouping of huge boulders near the cliff. What caught his attention was the incongruous phosphorescent bird-track emblem for peace scrawled in yellow over the rough rock and the word 'love' twice, one blue, one red on either side of what must serve as an entrance into a space the rocks enclosed. He swerved away from the water and curiously approached. Colored cloths fluttered between the rocks and then he became aware of smoke spinning up, lifting sparks and black floaters of charred paper into the sky.

The crashing waves obscured any sound that may come from within and he felt it wasn't right to call out, so Lucien scuffed some twenty paces further, opened his red awning chair near blue ice plants clinging to the rock wall. He'd gone far enough, he decided. Besides, the sun had thoroughly broken through the clouds and he thought he'd just rest there a bit, soak up a few rays. He took off his pants. No one would mind his shorts, he observed to his satisfaction weren't particularly stained, in so empty a place. Besides, this was California in 1973 and though some person or persons were nearby they must all acknowledge the unrestraint nature offered. Matter of fact, it vaguely comforted Lucien that he might not be entirely by himself. Nestling into his red chair, he reached under his shorts and felt himself. He arranged his slightly swollen cock comfortably between the pleasing shag of his balls. As the omnipresent sea birds regrouped about him, a shrieking, mewing, rustling blanket, he succumbed to the sun, the boom of the waves, the faint incense of smoke. And slept.

"Well, I'll be damned!" Lucien heard someone laughing at him.

"What's your sign?" sniffed another more quiet voice. As Lucien Blacker's eyes opened the young man announced in evident disgust, the flaps of his nose pulling in, "A Virgo. The thin lips are a dead give away."

A third fellow knelt and began running his index finger along the arch of Lucien's foot. Lucien pulled his foot back, feeling mauled and pried at. "What are you doing?" Lucien hissed in alarm. He sat up stiffly in his chair.

The three men stood close together, arms over each other's shoulders, curiously regarding him. They were naked and their privates jiggled uneasily as they dug their toes into the sand.

The one who had toyed with Lucien's in-step whispered solemnly, "He's all right. Don't let thin lips fool you. He's a water sign. His arch curves like the Golden Gate." He spat as some wind came up and wiped saliva off his cheek with a sweep of his knuckles.

They all squinted critically at Lucien's severely arched foot. Sensing their approval, even before they smiled, Lucien wriggled his toes in relief. "Matter of fact, I'm an air sign, I guess. That is, when I'm not an earth. . ."

"Bull shit," the one in the middle scratched through red pubic hair. Despite himself, Lucien became aware of the thick cock with its zigzag purple veins feeding into the wide, rosy cap. But then how could he not notice, ensconced as he was in his chair, the young man standing in front of him. Eyes take in what's at eye level, that's all there is to it.

Clearing his throat, Lucien got out of his chair. "Do you guys sort of live back there?" Lucien pointed at the painted rocks.

Arms still twined over each other's shoulders, the men abruptly pivoted as though they were one person and began walking away from him toward the rocks. Their asses moved taut and rhythmically, two glowing with fine light hair, the one in the middle smooth, his heavy balls occasionally visible, dark in the shade between his thighs. That they were naked on so deserted a beach didn't surprise Lucien, yet the beauty of their animal naturalness did. They seemed to float across the sand, linked. One called without turning, "We've got some wine.

Come on."

Lucien looked out over the ocean at the curling white waves, hearing and sensing the smack of them in his belly. He felt threatened. But after a moment he decided he was being thrown off his usual balance only by the unfamiliar. Surely, Lucien Blacker was capable of sharing wine with some boys on the beach without being shaken.

He followed them toward where they had disappeared beneath a flap of cloth stretched across a gap between boulders. The day-glow peace sign pulsed electrically in the sun, and the word 'love' danced off the rock upon which it was painted. Lucien ducked inside as though he wished to avoid the glowing yellow and red warnings. . . wondering, even as he scrambled down on all fours, why he must consider such sensible and universally-approved goals as warning.

A hellish sensation overwhelmed him once inside, because, sun-blind, at first he saw nothing but a fire flickering against the rock walls and canopied roof. The youths were already sprawled on blankets, and Lucien watched them trade back and forth a round, wide-bottomed bottle of wine they eventually, without a word, slipped into his hands as he squatted near the entrance. The floor was littered with other bottles and the warmth of the fire carried with it the acrid smell of their bodies. He could now see them lying with their tousled heads upon various chests and stomachs, their legs brushing together or intertwined. Had he stumbled upon some primitive band relaxing convivially after a foray of hunting? He sensed he'd slipped back in or beyond time. Lucien gulped at the wine and then handed the bottle to the red-haired, thick-cocked fellow with the burnished ass.

Hawk said, his full voice almost drowsy, "It's cool here, man." Hawk swept a long arm about the dark and warm enclosure. "It's safe." He fondled his balls contemplatively. "Well, see, it's that we're hiding out. He's after us." Hawk had half risen in the semi-dark, propped on one elbow, staring at Lucien intently.

Lucien laughed an atrocious guffaw. The quiet atmosphere had suddenly altered and was filled with discomfort. His nervous and explosive chuckle indicated his shock at the sudden switch in mood, especially since he was realizing the menacing presence might be himself. Easy-going, bumbling, Lucien Blacker suspect? At least the look in the boys' eyes, the way their lips parted as though pulling cautiously in upon the smoke-filled air led him to that conclusion.

Lucien whined out defensively, "But why invite me in here if you think I'm the one after you? You just don't know what you're talking about." He wondered if the boys had a good grip on reality.

"Because," said Hawk, "if you was him you'd get us no matter what we did. We've talked about it lots, man." Hawk let his head sink back upon a stomach, closed his eyes exquisitely. "Besides, why were you sitting out there, waiting for us?"

Lucien held his knees tightly with pressing fingers, breathed deeply and coughed from the smoke. "I don't know. I wasn't."

Yet he was. He knew he could have placed his chair anywhere on that long, deserted beach.

Another head rose up silhouetted against the flames, handed the bottle back to Lucien. "My name's Bass. And that's Hawk you been talking to, and this here's Stag." Bass shifted his position so that his nose ground into the red hairs on Hawk's stomach. "If he was the one," Lucien heard him whisper, "he'd not have come in here at all. He'd have waited, day and night, outside."

"I'm so afraid I could puke." This from Stag.

And to Lucien Blacker's chagrin, they all three moved closer against one another, and unless the dim light and the sputtering fire confused his eyes, their thighs trembled, as though Lucien's presence were a kind of affliction. And he discovered that he, too, felt somehow wrong in his stomach, not because he thought they would do him harm – something they apparently felt Lucien capable of – but because the young men were naked and touching each other. Stag, whose long brown hair fell over his high forehead as he leaned to caress Hawk's already growing sex, squinted his almond dark eyes at Lucien. "Your wedding band, take it off. Nobody needs to be owned here." With his other hand he reached to fondle Bass who lay beside him on his back, knees raised, the crack of his ass black in the fire's glow. Lucien watched, holding his breath, as Bass pulled Stag's head to nuzzle with a flicking tongue the skin under his bearded jaw.

Though Lucien should condemn them, he dare not. He was outnumbered, the beach empty. When he got home, then he'd condemn them, when the boom of the sea no longer infested his ears, when their sweat no longer invaded his consciousness. He was about to excuse himself from their presence, thank them politely for the wine, when Hawk crawled over to him and pressed his mouth to the faint piss stains on his shorts. "But I didn't ask you, invite you in any way. . ." Lucien protested.

Hawk opened his mouth over the white cotton. Lucien felt the warm breath surround his cock. He sensed blood rushing, tensing him. Hawk shook his head between Lucien's thighs, "There's things you don't ask. Ever. Whatever, this," he squeezed Lucien's erection, "is an answer. Ain't it!" He smiled. "Feels like a pretty guy you've got there." Hawk squatted between Lucien's legs, a silvery string of natural lubricant swinging from the wide slit of Hawk's stick. "I like that hair all over you, man." He pulled at the thickest wires coiled between Lucien's nipples. "You're a wild one." He pulled and slightly twisted both nipples at once, and the heat of a kind of morphine started in Lucien's toes and swept through the tangles of thigh hair and up to burn the wilding black clusters under his arms. My wife. . . he thought.

As though anticipating him, Hawk muttered, "Your old lady won't know, doesn't want to know. . . "

Someone slipped a hand under his shorts, not Hawk, who ran the fingers of both hands lightly through the darkening stubbles on Lucien's cheeks and jaw. Glancing down he saw it was Stag stroking his own long narrow cock as he bent to rub gently the bunching of circumcised skin under the wetting glans of Lucien's cock where it protruded from his shorts up through his stomach hair. He grabbed for Stag's wrist to wrench it away, but instead, in disobedience of any will he may once have had, covered Stag's hand with his own, watching in wonder as Stag slicked the clear drops of Lucien's own excrescence smooth and incandescent around the burning opening.

The light of the fire was suddenly blocked by Bass who had planted feet on either side of Lucien, Bass' head of spun gold hair pressing against the stretch of canopy, his thick thighs cradling pendant balls swinging in the smoky light above Lucien's head. "It's an ape." He spat on the sandy floor. "He's him who's the fourth we don't want. He'll split us." He spat again. "Hey, man, I'm talking to you," his resounding voice descended upon Lucien who observed the penis flaccid. "Got a house in the 'burbs with a garage and all that? Bet you've got a devil's beard sprouting from the small of your spine."

"Clam up, Bass." But Hawk stood, the purple veins subsiding along the sides of his shaft. Stag tucked Lucien's cock back into his shorts. "Don't listen. We're all one," he whispered.

"So, thanks for the wine," Lucien managed to mumble. To illustrate what presence he could manage, he reached for the wine bottle, wriggled it into an upright position in the sand between blankets and crawled toward the cloth doorway.

The sun hurt Lucien's blinking eyes as the sea birds, apparently alarmed by him now, took off into the sky, screaming. He stood unsteadily watching the sea birds and wondering: Was he really something or someone to escape from? Yet he admitted he did disapprove of what had taken place. He disapproved of the fact the three young men lived outside all Lucien knew to be real, had tricked him into following them and then exiled him from their trust.

He kicked the sand as he neared his red chair, his heart turning in an uncomfortable stab of suspicion regarding himself. As he bent to fold his chair, he was surprised at his fingers that clenched themselves, beyond his conscious will, into fists.

He heard feet scuffling through the sand behind him and he spun around demanding, "What do you want now?"

It was Bass, thrusting a hand toward him. He hung his head shyly and stammered, "I just. . . wanted to know. . . if you'd be back, ever." Bass rolled his eyes.

Lucien suspected Bass was being derisive, sarcastic. "What's it to you?" He shoved his now folded chair under his arm.

Bass glared at him, suddenly bold, with eyes the color of the sea. His glassy hair bristled from the wind and glowed across his chest in the sun. "I wanted to know," he insisted, "if you was him." Bass' eyes squeezed tight and freckles bunched across the bridge of his nose.

Lucien again had the image of himself as someone else's nightmare. And though the wind was cool, he felt sweaty. "Look here," Lucien said, "I wandered onto this beach by accident. I wasn't looking for you or anything else. You don't own this place. I'll come back if I want. And I won't if I don't want."

"Don't knock us, man." Bass sounded calm. He turned sideways to look at the water. His pubic ruff glittered. "We could talk, if you came back," he offered.

Lucien belly-laughed. "We'd have nothing to say!" And he began hurrying down the quiet, transparent line of water margining the still retreating tide. Birds ran frantically before him, then lifted out above the slamming breakers. There's something wrong, he decided, about this long, cliff-bound stretch of beach. If this is paradise, then paradise is a trap. He began dragging his chair when he reached the state recreation area after rounding the stone wall that separated the beaches. He passed openly-necking collegiate couples and the bonnet hat of the waffle-thighed lady still walking her dogs. He had come home.

* * * * * *

Yet there was some cloying reason that Lucien would return. . . Had he need to find out why the boys thought him evil? In truth, he was a liberal, compassionate kind of man. Actually, he never consciously decided to visit the deserted part of the shore again. It was just that, weeks later, he simply found himself near the state beach and decided on impulse to calm the headache he'd had all morning by walking along the ocean. The tide was in, and before descending the dusty path, he realized waves beat hard against the jutting cliff separating the beaches. Even if he'd wanted to go around to that further beach, he'd not be able.

Lucien glanced to his right through the shining mist. A narrow trail bordering the cliff edge caught his attention. He began following it on impulse, his soiled sneakers easily managing the slippery rock. Should the trail continue for at least half a mile, he'd be able to check out the boys, see if they were still there. Mere curiosity on his part. Or, at the most, test himself to rediscover that he was, after all, innocent. With eyes peering brightly down through the haze at the untouched glow of the sand far below, he sensed himself to be like a bird of prey, a cormorant, all eyes that hung from floating wings. He'd never thought of himself that way before and he smiled, amused.

He hesitated in front of a high fence with a barbed top curving over and anchored down the side of the cliff. Though usually sensitive to the exclusiveness of private property, the freshly painted sign **NO TRESPASSING**, in this instance, meant little. He slithered on his stomach, oozed under the wire and proceeded nonchalantly along the path. He was feeling curiously freed from going to and fro in the earth, and from walking up and down in it.

Soon he spotted the boys on the sand below, lying together in front of their rocky hogan. He squatted, jeans stretching tight to his ass. Carefully parting dry mesquite with hands gone suddenly cold, his prying eyes feasted upon their luxuriant closeness. And hated them for it. He watched the lightly haired thigh of the man called Hawk ease its way over the sun-burnt chest of Bass. Stag bent over them both, hair veiling eyes as he touched first one and then the other with his lips.

Lucien was on his feet waving his arms and shouting. Of course, they couldn't hear him over the roar of waves. Stag cupped his hand over Hawk's butt. And Lucien Blacker, with grinding teeth, felt like devising death to all who could know of. . . sin, was that how he saw it? He was as filled with rage as were those holy – eventually to be their description of themselves – men with 'love.' But then Lucien never understood the Biblical tint the young men applied to all their thoughts and actions. They seemed to be from another age entirely.

Lucien slipped down the cliff, threading his way cautiously, grabbing on to blue blooming ice plants until his feet struck sand, and he leaned against ochre rocks, panting, arms folded over where he felt his heart race. Shore birds streaked into the sky. Stag, yards distant, head nuzzling the auburn groin of Hawk, suddenly jerked back. Lucien noticed him squint at the circling birds. Stag's beard cut a triangular shadow across the tensing muscles of his chest as Hawk and Bass gradually pulled themselves to alertness, propped on their elbows. Lucien noticed sand fall away from their ribs.

"Hello there," Lucien bellowed, absurdly laughing at the alarm flooding Hawk's face, his widening eyes, the pinching furrows of the skin above his nose. It was Hawk, of course, who first recognized Lucien pressed against the shadow of his rock. Hawk scrambled to a crouch, his dying tumescence glittering wetly near the heads of Bass and Stag.

"What do you want?" Hawk yelled over the boom of the surf.

Lucien wondered, even then, if it were their composite soul or his own he wanted! Arms still folded across his chest, as though to hold himself together, Lucien kicked through squeaking sand, circling them widely and warily. Hawk came toward him and sat cross-legged at Lucien's feet, slumped, as though suddenly sad and broken. "Want to rap? Or fuck?"

Lucien snickered. "I came down the cliff-way. I didn't mean to surprise you."

Hawk stared up at him incredulously. Then, "I just suppose we need you to be watching us. Bass said we had to have you come back. Bass. . . we'd fall apart was it not for him. You got a cigarette?" Hawk held out his arm, a supplicant.

Lucien handed him one from his shirt pocket and lit the cigarette where Bass had jammed it between shaking lips. As Lucien snapped his lighter, shielding it with his hand from the wind, their eyes came close and he felt like shutting his against the intensity of Hawk's look. "Your eyes. . ." Hawk seemed to shudder.

"It's the sun, the glare," Lucien said. "And I've a headache.

I just want to know. . ." Lucien sprawled on the sand glancing at the heaves of waves. " . . . why is it there are three of you? I can't understand. . . the lack of intimacy, the degree of exposure." Lucien was surprised to hear himself ask that particular question. But then civilization would not be, nor would he, had he not managed to arrow the crime. "Well?"

"Guess it just happened that way. But there's no traps in a three-way, like jealousy and all," Hawk murmured rubbing his toes with long fingers. "Bass said you'd try to wedge us apart. Evil is needing, because you're weak, to see that all the world try not to be what you've already failed at. The Devil feels right only when he's wrong like that. Are you He?"

It felt as though Hawk were looking through Lucien, but naively, openly. The corners of his lips curved in slight insolence. "Is it your desire. . . for us, that brought you back?"

Lucien Blacker's arm lashed out, totally against his will. He struck Hawk hard across the face with the back of his hand. There was something unreasonable about Hawk, irresponsible. Not sane. Isn't dropping out of society merely slang for withdrawing into madness?

Hawk fingered his jaw, moaning, "No, no." Then he laughed. "I was right. I was right!"

Lucien saw Bass and Stag start toward them, sand flying from their sliding heels. Gritting teeth, he bellowed when they stopped behind Hawk, "I don't want you to touch me!"

Lucien presumed he'd be happier had he thought they would approach him with vengeful fists rather than the caresses of which he knew them to be capable.

Stag, gasping for breath but his voice deep, "Plan to hit all of us, mister. It's not possible to treat us as separate."

Lucien noticed both Stag and Bass stroked their chins as if he'd already hit them. Because they obviously intended no harm to him, he spoke slowly, "I have the right. You've given me that right. You've asked for my interference." Through the ensuing silence, Lucien tried to focus on the eyes of all three men, one at a time, and then held his right hand out, palm up toward where the sun had begun to shine weakly. "Help me! What am I doing? You've made me monstrous!"

Bass stepped around Hawk toward Lucien, thrust his face with its unblinking eyes into Lucien's shadow and stated, "You've come back. For the first time in your life, to live, and in the only way you can." He grasped Lucien's head, lowered it toward his groin. "Take this. . ."

Lucien sank to his knees. "In remembrance?" He tried for a laugh.

"Of us," Bass smiled. He edged his swelling cock through Lucien's parting lips.

Lucien couldn't know why he complied. Nothing had led to this aggressive move by Bass. Had it? Besides, it tasted like rubber, neither bad nor good. That he had no apparent choice freed him somewhat. He was, after all, innocent. Lucien shut his eyes, hearing the roll and crash of wave upon wave, the stifled cries of Bass. As the cock slid far down his throat and he felt Bass' entire body wince and buck, he knew who was controlled, who the controller.

His knees ground into the sand. Someone pulled off his pants while he cooperated and the sun so hotly grazed his back that the first gentle pull on his own genitals produced a sensation indistinguishable from the sun-feel and the wafts of salt-heavy sea wind. But as a tongue searched through the hairs on his testicles, he came suddenly to know himself as animal: muscled, hirsute and unaware except for what he did and what was being done to him. It was Stag, it had to be Stag, absorbing the hanging core of him entirely in his mouth, then sucking the wrinkled skin smooth. Eyes wide now, he eased Bass' cock from his mouth and, while slicking his spit over the shining head, opened his lips upon the furry sacks that were no longer parts of Bass but whose faint acrid odor and delicate orbs were the sun, the sea, the beat upon beat of hurling surf.

He heard Bass ordering him, "Spread your knees, wider, wider, man. Yeah, like that." And he felt Bass take in the self he no longer was and knew by the singe and soar that the folds of the man's throat moved warmly around his probing thrusts.

"My God, God. . . shit, shit," the words exploding from Lucien as meaningful and meaningless as any ever forced from him. Before he knew whose fingers stroked his ass – but it had to be Hawk were it not a push of the wind stirring the black hairs that ringed his anus – his own tongue licked behind the balls above him and then forward to where ass-cheeks folded over what he needed to know. His tongue reached to explore the crack as he felt Hawk pulling wide his own and then the tongue slicked round and entered the hole. Lucien experienced no separation between himself, the boys, the sun-heat and wind, the surf-salt and sand. And as he knew the pain that ceased instantly as it began, when Hawk worked his huge insistence into the bowels of him, he also knew himself to be joined for his life's first time to himself, to the triumvirate three of them and earth and air and water.

He gaped his mouth again over the dilated, oozing cock in front of him, felt it jerk from the wrap of his tongue. And as shot after shot of hot lead pelted his throat, released his own cum into the bearded lips below him, jerk upon jerk, his entire body caught in sequential spasms as he felt Hawk expel seething currents through to his heart that welcomed the triumph of oneness with all beasts that were and are.

Lucien sank into the sand, legs toward his chest, arms folded, fetal, unable to move, to think, and barely breathing. Only the soughing ocean echoed through the chambers of his ears. He didn't know what had happened to the youths, he didn't care. The burn of the sun melted him where he lay. Eyes shut, he became aware of the young men talking among themselves, nonsense stuff, such as "We got enough wine? Sure, just knock a rock, see if it drains." And then, "Who we got here, a corpse?" What must be a toe tickled his in-step. Lucien arranged himself torpidly into a yoga posture, squinting at them where they sprawled nearby. They looked skinny, unkempt, were the terms applicable to nude persons. The one called Bass rode a pimple on his butt, orange hairs curled from Hawk's freckled nostrils. What had they done been all about? His sphincter throbbed. Had he been a salmon inappropriately spawning itself to death in some dank but strangely familiar stream bed? He hated them, but maybe himself more. He'd been tricked by ignorance of himself. And the coherent trinity of their joyous inter-connection.

Abruptly, Lucien reached over to cut at Bass' cheek. This time with his fist. It felt surprisingly good to do that. Clean and good!

Bass reeled backwards, stumbled and cried out between gritted teeth, "Yes!"

Hawk scrambled to his feet and with bowed head neared Lucien. "This. . . is for the Father," he grimaced. With index and third finger, he gestured the sign of peace.

Lucien spat upon the curved back of Hawk's neck. The effrontery of him to presume upon his twisted lechery a religion, he raged, assuming himself now to be in complete control. But they were like that, hippies were, medieval mystics out of time, out of place.

Stag said, "Poor mister, you obeyed too much. Kiss me now with your fist, friend." He knelt, bearded chin pointing at the sky. "I am the Son."

Lucien's foot slammed into Stag, clean and brisk. Lucien whispered to himself, satisfied, "I am, I am. . . I, I, I!"

Then Bass advanced, shy, hesitant, the strong pectoral muscles of his chest flickering like a borealis beneath the white ice of his skin. It was as though his spectral flesh sought to resist the chastisement he must demand from Lucien Blacker. He said, "I couldn't of held us together even for awhile was it not for knowing you would come. Thank you."

"Oh, you're welcome," Lucien said, sneering, breathing heavily.

Bass knelt, his blue eyes like chunks of the sky staring in wonder beyond Lucien's head to where a cold wind blew. "Everything falls apart?" he questioned in awe. Then he smiled brilliantly, young, vital, animal. "You could suck my cock again, mister. . . or rip me off with your knuckles. It's all the same. I will accept it the same." Bass bent back his head presenting to Lucien his corded, knotted throat. "Make me a ghost, man. We're holy, all of us. And you can't stand it!"

Lucien glared at the beating arteries in Bass' throat and desired nothing so much as to slash the life out of him. But his arms remained hanging useless at his sides. He backed off, stiff with repulsion. Those whelps tempted him to be worse than they were!

Lucien mewed at Bass softly, politely, "I'm not so easy an enemy. If that's what you want to make of me. I can't end the game." He engagingly held out a sweating palm in gentlemanly fashion for Bass to shake.

Bass refused, his lips firmly pressed into a frown. Lucien watched the three draw their heads together in a panicked, whispering huddle. "Remember this," he called out, "I disapprove of even the me in you."

The youths clung to each other, seized by the sun into a pyre of burning light, a flame. . . of weeping? Were they weeping?

Lucien watched as they interchangeably held each other's heads with their hands, large hands; touched their foreheads gently one against the other. . . And then he saw them slowly walk their separate ways from each other: Hawk to the north, Stag to the south, and Bass to scale the cliff to the east from where Lucien had come.

And to where he knew he must return. It had all of it been a matter of necessity. Things are as they are and so will remain; the cormorant seizes the gull and makes of its flesh its own.

CARLOS

Lee Williams

The fall rains came late that year. The dust lay thick and gray in the courtyard, cushioning our clumsiness and streaking our pubescent skins. Rivulets of sweat turned the dust to mud on my bare chest and legs, but Juan never seemed to sweat.

I knew my parents were divorcing, and that's why we stayed at the hacienda longer that year. Sometimes I came across my mother crying quietly in the shadows of the adobe ranchhouse that belonged to my grandfather. I spent as much time as possible outside, avoiding those wrenching scenes, and Juan was my only real playmate. Even Juan, the son of our housekeeper, was becoming more complicated, it seemed, as the days grew shorter. My mother never completely approved of my playing with him because he was really a servant, she said, but for me that was meaningless, and there were no other boys my age in any case. He also was shy at first, but his hesitation disappeared when he was able to best me in many of our childish pursuits.

Tree climbing and wrestling were our favorite sports, having outgrown the childish toys my mother had thought appropriate. At first our natural competitiveness was spontaneous and balanced, but later there developed a layer of tension in our play that I didn't understand. Sometimes when I was high in the gnarled, dusty apple tree in the corner of the yard, Juan would intentionally position himself on a lower branch. I knew he could have easily climbed beyond me, but I noticed his dark eyes fixed on the gaping leg holes of my tan shorts where I realized that my cock was in clear view. When that happened I could feel a thickening there in my crotch, a stirring that I enjoyed but didn't understand.

Sometimes Juan's younger brother, Carlos, joined us because Juan had to look after him. He was a mere boy, someone to be ignored because he couldn't climb as well and didn't giggle at the same jokes. For the most part he was a silent, somber spectator who adopted our discarded toys but generally seemed engrossed in watching us. We as his superiors took pleasure in excluding him, declaring the tree off-limits to children or slamming the door in his face when bursting into the kitchen at times for tepid lemonade. One time I remember beating him rather severely with a stick, a fallen tree limb, because he had accidentally stepped into a pattern of a fort I had drawn in the dust.

When we tired of tree climbing and mock gunfights and wrestling, we turned to athletic exercises. We had a brief flurry of enthusiasm for pushups and chinning bars and deep-knee bends, and Juan and I competed for the greatest number we could manage of these unproductive efforts. But the lowest tree branch was a little high for chinning, and deep-knee bends without weights grew tiresome without accomplishing anything, so pushups became our standard fare. We started doing them in concert, facing each other in order to detect cheating, of course, and I still remember watching his thin biceps bulging as he lifted and his rump rising and falling, his loose denim shorts (cutoffs previously worn thin by his father, apparently) dragging in the dust. But then Juan began positioning himself closely behind me so I couldn't actually see him without twisting, insisting that he was matching me lift for lift. I could feel his eyes on me, on my straining body, and that mysterious stirring in my crotch would recur. Sometimes when I momentarily rested on the ground, I was aware that my swollen cock was being pressed uncomfortably. Soon I looked forward to my pushups, knowing that he was watching from behind, knowing that my cock was extending stiffly down the loose leg of my dusty shorts. Then one day Juan introduced a new twist - a challenge to see who could maintain the straight back-extended arms posture the longest. We would freeze in this attitude until our arms would quiver and our backs would start to sag, and eventually we would surrender to the forces of nature. We timed our performances with a Mickey Mouse watch I had received at Christmas. Carlos merely watched us stoically, as usual. He never smiled.

One day I assumed this position, determined to maintain it for even longer than previously, as Juan lay prone behind me, his face in the dust to watch for any sagging. As usual, I felt the accustomed reaction between my legs. After a moment I heard Juan call to Carlos and whisper some instructions. To my surprise, Carlos came to my side and wriggled under my middle, his face close to my crotch. I closed my eyes in concentration, determined that Juan could not trick me into failing by this underhanded ploy, but then I felt fingers reaching into the leg of my shorts, grasping my stiffening cock, and extracting it from the loose pants leg. Immediately it was clasped in moist warmth, and I realized that it was in Carlos' mouth! I could feel it pushing into his boyish throat and his tongue curling around it. My arms began to tremble and my back threatened to lose its rigidity, much before I had reached the usual limit of my endurance. My brain whirled and the blistering sun brought beads of sweat to my brow. It seemed only a few seconds before I experienced for the first time a pulsing torrent of liquid heat from my cock, and I succumbed to my weakness, my thin, rigid cock pressed deeply into Carlos' hot receptacle. Quickly he rolled to the side but clasped my body tightly to his mouth until the exquisite feeling passed and I regained my senses.

I slowly sat up, staring about me in confusion, but Juan was merely smiling at me. Carlos' expression remained as stoic as before, but he wiped his mouth as he moved away to lean against the tree trunk. After a few moments of silence interrupted only by my heavy breathing, we resumed our play as if nothing had happened, Juan quickly pulling himself up into the tree and beginning to throw the small, stunted green apples at us on the ground. But after a moment I suddenly attacked Carlos, beating his tough, brown hide with the stick for several minutes.

The next day it happened again, but this time I was expecting it. It took a little longer to reach my climax, but it seemed even more profound. After a few days, Carlos would simply lie in the dust and I, without removing my pants, of course, would pump his mouth a few times before that exhilarating release of pent-up pubescence. His lips wrapped around my stalk and his tongue teasing my tenderness quickly became irresistible. Each time I punished him with the stick, but he remained entirely passive to my outbursts.

It was only a few days later that my mother, after receiving a phone call, declared that we were going home, and we left hurriedly the next day. All I knew was that there was a lot of money involved. I was sent to boarding school and then entered Stanford, so it was over ten years before I revisited the hacienda. In the meantime my grandfather had died and left me the property. Juan met me at the station and we became reacquainted during the ride to the house. He had married and had three children, and was already developing a paunch and a receding hairline. He was diffident at first, reflecting, I suppose, what he thought was the proper attitude for the servant of the new estate owner. I joked him out of it, for the most part. His father had also passed away, but after our talk I felt comfortable in leaving the property in Juan's hands as overseer.

The next day I was in the open courtyard again, remembering the uncomplicated days of childhood; even the smell of the dust seemed familiar. The old apple tree had finally rotted through and I was sitting on the fallen trunk when a tall, strikingly handsome young man appeared from the dusty road outside. For several minutes we looked wordlessly at each other; it was his silent, somber attitude that identified him for me. After a few moments he came over to me and, still without speaking, knelt between my legs. Calmly, methodically, he opened my fly and took out my cock which quickly reared high for him. He sucked it thoroughly and deeply, and for me it was almost earthshattering; perhaps it was the memories of my first experience or the realization that sex had never been as good since that summer many years ago. When the explosion came, all the joys and delights of trouble-free childhood swept through me again and my nascent adult slate was wiped clean.

He savored my shrinking cock in his throat for several minutes, his eyes closed, and then, wiping his mouth with the same childish gesture, silently rose and left as abruptly as he had appeared. Later Juan told me that Carlos had won a scholarship to study at the local college and was doing very well. He was then about twenty-one years old.

Again many years passed, years spent in earning an advanced degree in art and eventually gaining a reputation for meaningful acquisitions for museums around the country. The world became an auction block for me, matching up art pieces available from some personage in one country for a collector in another. There was a summer in Rome, when I bedded Lucia for a few weeks and then her husband, Roberto, and then both at the same time. Germany was a treasure trove of stolen art from the 'forties. I was the piéce de rèsistance for a half-dozen Teutonic noblemen who had inherited these objects; Germans are certainly the best cock-suckers in Europe. I plied a riding crop on the pink skin of a decadent Brit dressed in fringed leather combined with lace tights for a coveted goblet. India was a problem until I discovered that it was necessary that the husband *knew* you were fucking his wife; then he would be agreeable, although he might also want to pump away at my ass with his miniature phallus for a while before parting with his valuables.

When I was at home in New York there were parties and bars and orgy rooms where the choice of partners was almost unlimited. My most difficult decision for an evening was whether I was in the mood for a woman or a man or both. There were also episodes of a year or two each with Jack and Maria and Rocky and Sherry, usually ending when I did not come home for several months at a time.

About a year ago I came home to my empty apartment from a buying trip and resolved never to leave again. There seemed to be no future; I made no calls to acquaintances, no plans. After a few weeks of this isolation I realized that perhaps I needed professional help, but there was no incentive for seeking it. I finally made a few calls but, while still shopping around for a therapist, received word that my mother had died unexpectedly. After her funeral I decided to take on the project of writing a book about my art specialty, a suggestion from some publishing friends that I had been rejecting for years. Before I had gone very far along this thought, I received my yearly report of accounts from Juan on the ranch, all scrupulously hand-written in neat columns and showing a modest surplus as usual. Within a few days I had my reservations to the hacienda in hand, along with my laptop computer, copious notes, and files to be used for the book I would write in the quiet calm of the country.

My plans for coming to the hacienda were so hurried that I forgot that in the summer the rambling house could be stiflingly hot. Juan's mother, grey and shuffling, seemed to find me an obstruction to her usual schedule for rearranging the dust from time to time, and meals were irregular; I was obviously in her way, it seemed. She casually mentioned that Carlos was now teaching in the community college nearby, but I did not respond. I gradually became aware that she was studying me silently. I knew I should appreciate her sincere concern, but it only made me more uncomfortable. So I took to working at a folding table in the courtyard, dressed only in shorts as I had dressed as a child, even though it meant transporting my notes and files each day into the shade of a recently-planted jacaranda that had replaced the old apple tree. Sometimes pale purple petals from its blossoms would drift down to decorate my work. I also added some wooden benches and chairs to make the dusty courtyard less barren. I kept neglecting to write to friends or to give them my new address. They seemed far away. I was suspended in time and place.

It was one thing to make a decision to write a book, and quite another to actually organize myself and start to write. More and more I abandoned my notes and sprawled on the wooden bench, my mind in a fog, watching the white sun move across the sky through the branches of the jacaranda. And it was there that I received my first visitor.

Carlos suddenly appeared in my line of vision, tall, muscular, shining through my mental mists to rival the bright sun above. He was dressed in browns and tans, his western boots rooted in mother earth. His black hair and eyes crowned the whole with undeniable verity. Our eyes held even as he walked toward me, and when he towered over me I knew that my life was changing.

After only a moment of stillness, he opened his fly and slowly extracted his long, thick member. I was hypnotized by its dark bulk and beauty, quickly stiffening to point directly at me. My actions were compelled, inescapable. I leaned forward and took it into my mouth; joy suffused my being for the first time in many years as the firm, velvet manhood entered me. I impaled myself on it, forcing it as deeply as possible, frantic to accept its mastery as the ultimate symbol of him, of nature from which he sprang.

When I was forced to come up for air, I slipped to my knees at his feet where I knew I belonged. Again and again

I gulped him down, and I could feel tension building in his tall frame. And when he unbuckled and removed his thick belt, holding it for a moment at his side, my day began to dawn. His first swing was almost gentle, the belt wrapping itself over my straining, bare back and crouching ass. The second stroke was harder, demanding, commanding obeisance, and it was right. As his cock oozed clear nectar and his blows increased, I struggled to be worthy of his touch. Each whistling stroke increased the reward, the dedication I felt in serving him. What others might call pain I knew as pleasure - evidence of his love which I had denied but needed for so long. A new day was dawning. My senses soared higher and higher as I felt our beings merging, our spirits harmonizing, and when he loosed his essence (a gift I had not dared anticipate) mine also flowed explosively, unattended.

That was the first but not my greatest experience with my Carlos. I do not share the others; they are even more profound but too personal to relate. For months I have gloried in the discoveries that came with each experience in this new existence, and now, sharing each moment with Carlos by my side, I am beginning to regrasp the lines of life. My book is almost finished, and I think it is good. Carlos smiles a lot now. Perhaps one day I will extend my artistic horizons and even contact old friends, but for now I am happy, satisfied to serve my man in any way he allows me. Our courtyard is now sewn with fresh, waving grass as a symbol of our new beginning.

MOLEHILLS AND FORGOTTEN THINGS

Frederic Trainor

The sleek, stretched Lincoln braked to a stop, gritty clouds of dust breezing up like magician smoke around its glinting chartreuse chassis. An unpaved road. Thick clusters of maple, birch, and cedar flanked and all but ceilinged them – jungle-like – straining erratic patches of sunlight down through the breaks in the dense, crooked branches and leaves. Seclusion. Welcomed, startling silence.

The boy beside him in the limo's sumptuous rear jerked up his brown, poodle-like head, groggily disoriented from sleep and the uncharacteristic heat, his cobalt eyes luscious, lost. He snorted, then coughed. "What's here, Mil?" The question came out nasally in that fake British accent that Miller detested. "Washington? This Seattle?" Miller Dungeon's eyes were closed. The tangle of his two-toned, snakey hair lay splashed over his face like a morbid Christ. "No," he answered. "Memories."

"Huh? Wha?" Annoyed, the death rocker glanced distractedly at the boy. A trampish, delicious bauble virtually swallowed in the lush padding of lime-green tuck-and-roll leather, his face at once exquisitely lovely and hopelessly stupid. Why had he brought this kid along, this mindless urchin from the maelstrom of Los Angeles street life? Miller didn't know any longer. Didn't care. Something to do with whim, he supposed. With quenching le beast. Familiarity spawning odd attachments. Odder needs.

"Mem–orr–eeees," he repeated, as if speaking to a deaf mute. "A pit stop, man. We're just outside Deer Creek, Oregon. Little buttfuck town I grew up in." The boy rubbed his nose, tongue swabbed his popsicle lips while peering dully out the tinted window. "The schticks," he observed dryly. Miller, feeling cattish, gave a derisive shake to his mane.

"Myyy, aren't we observant, Dean."

"It's Dream." The youth's voice turned instantly peevish. "Why's that so hard for you to remember?"

"Probably has something to do with me not giving a rusty fuck, Dean-fucking-Dream," the rock singer retorted, his trademark smile dripping with blatant sarcasm. The boy, familiar with Miller Dungeon's callous tongue by now, and perhaps even perversely stimulated by it, darted his hand across the seat toward the singer's leathered lap. Miller firmly pushed it away. "Chill out, geek," he spat. "I'm not in that head space," then pushed the intercom button on his cushioned armrest. A soft baritone responded with, "Yo man." It was Trouble Man, Miller's black body guard /chauffeur from beyond the smoky glass divider. The poodle-haired youth poked his mouth out like a spoiled, petulant child, defiantly scooting over closer to the moody rock star.

"We'll be here for a few, Trouble," Miller said, pointedly ignoring the kid. "Gotta check our some shit, then it's on to Seattle. You cool up there?" Dexterous, youthful fingers began working at the buttons of his shiny black leather trousers, pausing briefly for a vulgar grope, to knead and squeeze the bulging lump there whether he approved or not. Impulsively, he backhanded the boy across the face.

"Oww! You dick," exclaimed the kid, his eyes watering from the impact. Then inexplicably, he giggled, his expression turning sultry, darkly flushed. His fingers resumed their work.

"Need some poontang, Cool Breeze," answered the bodyguard over the sound system. Miller smirked, cocked his legs vagrantly.

"There'll be plenty of that up in Seatown, m'man. That lily-white high school stuff that'll get you twenty years." He flipped off the intercom and glanced over at the portable Zenith thirteen-inch perched over the VCR on the mounted console. A porno video, the sound down. The screen cloudy with muted sleaze: three girls and a blond bodybuilder in a sauna of ghostly steam.

Poontang. Maybe for the sake of variety he might. . .?

A brief interlude to reassure that meteoric success at age twenty-two hadn't totally warped his values, turned him into a hopeless deviant?

The boy was saying something close to his crotch, something meaningless and gushy. Leather squeaked softly. The kid's purple PRIMUS T-shirt was dotted with dried cum stains, his black 501s tight as elastic gloves around his delectably rotund thighs and buttocks. No doubt the boy's rectum was still sloshy and sore from the beastly fucking Miller had administered the night before on their way up from Los Angeles, bending the boy over the soft, luxurious back seat and pile-driving his bubble backside through a convenient rip in the delicate pink panties he sported. The back interior still reeked of amyl fumes, flatulence, and tai stick residue.

Sickus Unbelievabus. That's what Rat Tail, the band's droll, junked-out bass player had christened him. Killer-looking babes flocking like lust-dazed seagulls to every sell-out concert Ravaged Soul performed around the globe, and here was their deified vanguard in all his tragically-charismatic splendor, rutting around in a virtual smorgasbord of illicit teenaged peckers and asses.

The victims were the lost sons of corporate Middle America, the suburban misfits in androgynous paint and post-nuclear hairdos seeking a purpose for existence.

A reason to Be.

It was to these angst-afflicted males of limbo adolescence that Miller Dungeon's quirky, gloom-shrouded lyrics had the most poignant impact. He was their spiritual spearhead, their gothic beacon of twisted hope. These were the boys who draped themselves right up next to the stage of Ravaged Soul Concerts, possessively pushing the females back, hanging rapt and mesmeric on every intoned word. And Miller Dungeon gave them all five feet eight inches of himself during shows, offering them glimpses of his pretzel mind, his pitch-black soul, his floppy genitals and grease-painted buttocks, expertly manipulating the repressed lusts of their tormented spirits. Boys who had never entertained the notion of sucking a penis before clamored to suck Miller's, to commune with its phallic perfection, coaxing it rigid and omnipotent while lodged in their mouths, feeling the silky plumpness of his balls rubbing against their chins.

As he performed – at once reverent and obscene, mystic and animal-carnal – boys, most with nubile nymphs clutching at their arms, boldly flirted and teased him from the audience, flashing their privates at him without shame, baring their ripe, pliant buttcheeks, hoping against all odds for that one chance in several thousand to be deemed worthy of backstage attention.

Good, hot brown eye.

Ain't no eye like hot brown eye.

Pottsy had said that an eternity ago. Right here in Deer Creek. How old were they then? Thirteen? Fourteen? Yeah. Juniors at James Madison. Buried, forgotten things.

Maybe it was true. Maybe he was a hopeless perv after all. Maybe those buried, forgotten things, those childhood molehills that with time and repeated denial festered into mountains, maybe those stubborn, lingering specters were the rudiments of it all, the root of all you were, are and ever will be.

Travel the breadth of this bubble we call Earth and go nowhere but back from where you started. The thought unsettled Miller. He felt vaguely trapped. Doomed. Three homes, a bevy of cars, and over two-and-a-half million in the bank notwithstanding.

Outside the limousine window: past, present, and possible looming future, one indecipherable from the other. Settle it, dude. Settle it in the Now. Today. Before you. . .

Reluctantly, his head tilts downward.

Dream is there, sprawled on his knees before him. Miller's leather trousers are open, the flaps splayed, no shorts in sight.

Stale amyl aroma in the air.

Poontang and cocks on the VCR.

His cock, pulsing and pumped with blood, is bloated to three times its normal size and stuffed into the boy's contorted mouth. Why does cocksucking look so perverted, the way it distorts the features? Lusty, enchanted blue eyes gaze up lovingly at him. Drool drips messily from the kid's chin. Filthy little rodsucker. A soft hand gently courses circles beneath Miller's shirt, over his belly, up to his chest and back down. The boy's zipper is down, a turgid, pale boner protruding obscene and lovely from his open fly. Something moist and gossamer dripping from its tip. Those eyes. Miller can't stand it. He leans to one side, reaches down, tugs and pops the boy's top button. The kid grunts softly and arches his back. Fat, humpy buttocks ease into view. He wiggles them, smiles around the meat in his mouth. His jeans slip down a notch. Heart-shaped love pillows. Miller longs to beat them red and tender first. Would Trouble Man hear? Care? Then break out the grease and fistfuck the little cocksucker. Fist him through the sheer stretch panty hose, his thick, shapely legs tossed east and west.

"Suck my nuts," ordered the death rocker, slouching further in his seat. "And spread your knees wider on the floor. That buttcrack, bitch. I wanna see that crack." A crude, slurpy pop sounded as the kid released Miller's bloated dick. It slapped wetly against his shirt, glistening like a sheen of buffed polish. The boy rested his forearms on Miller's upper thighs. His lips had a vulgar, moist swell to them. They deserved gloss. Whore red. Or Black.

"Like this? Hmm?" Eyes glinting intently, drunk with

licentiousness. Dream stretched and strained his legs to accommodate, pushing to the limits of his droopy pants. A tearing noise. His back dipped, making his buttocks rise and split open like a sliced melon. Obscene grovel. Shameless offering.

Rape it. Whip it. Eat it. Fuck it.

"Yeah. . . Now suck those balls, you kinky fuck-boy." A dirty, teasing giggle. "Can I tickle my turds while I do it, Daddy? Hmmm?" Loose, distended lips descended to Miller's bulky pouch, mashing gently. Languid, puppy-dog eyes peered up from the warm intersection of his splayed legs. Dream hummed his balls, one arm reaching back, fingers seeking. The boy's hand disappeared inside the wide expanse of his rear end.

Entry was achieved.

A throaty grunt.

"Schlurp 'em, cocksucker."

"Mmm. Mmmm. . ."

"Shove another finger up your fat, stinkin' ass."

"Mmmmmm!" Miller reached for his cigarettes, his lighter. The boy was noisy and deliberately crude. Juicy, crackling sounds emitted from his hefty, writhing buns, merging with those his rapacious mouth made around the singer's scrotum. His free hand tugged at Miller's leather pants. Casually, the rocker raised his buttocks, finished lighting his cigarette. Acrid smoke curled in a thick cloud over his head. He watched the kid with a clinical detachment.

Frankfurt came to mind. The boy had been very German, gorgeous, bow-mouthed, with a wild mane of curly black hair. Nothing Miller attempted had produced an erection for the youth. Then, peremptorily, came the revelation: "I eat you een thee ahss, ja? I get hard. You see. I eat guten."

The boy's special passion. The filthiest Miller ever had. A real pigmeister. The result was an erection from the pits of hell.

He thought of it now. And Pottsy. Fucking Pottsy. Forgotten, distant thing. Miller slid lower in his seat, allowing his butt moons to hang unfettered over the edge. Lazily inhaling his cigarette, the death rocker firmly pushed the boy's curly head down and out of sight. "Pig around down there, bitch. In my ass. In Daddy's ass. Yeah. . . Yeah. Just like that."

The faint strains of an old Ramones tune could be heard. Front seat. Trouble Man. Checkerboard shadows dancing crazily through the tinted windows, over leather, shag carpet, bronze and gold trimming. Miller's buttocks grinding slowly, carelessly. He grunted, closed his eyes. The tongue felt wondrous. His hole flowered open. Sinful little butt-licker. Ain't no eye like good brown eye, Mil. Pottsy. Bonafide pervert even way back then.

That smirky, chipped-tooth grin coupled with those beady, all-seeing hazel eyes. Pottsy idolized Harleys and old Clint Eastwood movies; had a quirky penchant for vulgar irony, embarrassing unsuspecting girls with his selective crudeness.

Pottsy had done juvie time for breaking and entering and was winding down a year's probation for the county when he and Miller met. Their animosity for one another was immediate and mutual. Rufus Potts considered Miller Breiding a freaky-looking, city-bred wimp in desperate need of an attitude adjustment. Miller viewed Pottsy as a prime example of incestuous breeding; gawky, dumb as a rock, oddly built, horsey-faced, crass and malicious.

Miller was ten years old when his parents were killed in a plane crash over Baja California. There were no close relatives, so the orphan was sent to Oregon to live with a foster family in Deer Creek. The icy bitterness and disillusionment began to settle in. The youth rejected all established symbols of social order and moral principle: religion, school, lawful authority. It was all bullshit, all deserving of his righteous scorn.

Small, self-absorbed, by the age of twelve, Miller Breiding wore his hair as freaky and shocking as he wanted, multi-pierced both ears, tie-dyed and thrashed his clothes, spiced his speech with an eclectic blend of profanity, black urban jive, and southern California dudespeak, and worshipped underground punk heroes like the Ramones, Black Flag, Fear and Bad Brains. His foster parents, well-intentioned but inept, couldn't control him. The meager farm community he lived in – Deer Creek, population four hundred fifty-three, boasting one elementary school, middle school, and high school, two churches, one general store, a cannery, and wood pulp mill – could barely contain him.

Local kids sneeringly referred to Miller as "that weirdo kid that talks like a nigger" and "the vampire queer." Not that any of them knew anything certifiable about Miller's sexuality one way or the other – he wasn't sure himself at that point – but, hell. Any guy that dressed the way he did with all those earrings and eyes bordered with black eyeliner and hair a black and purple catastrophe that seemed to hiss and sneer at a comb. . . hell, he *had* to be fruiter.

Pottsy, freshly pumped from his brief stint in juvenile hall, zeroed in on this conspicuous anomaly, arrogantly pushing for advantage. It started as a curiosity on his part, an amused but honest interest in the new boy with the weird ways. Pottsy, in his tactless, droll way, had made a joke about Miller's hair by way of greeting, soliciting a burst of snickers and chuckles from a group of kids standing in front of James Madison Middle School. Miller, smiling sweetly, locked eyes with Pottsy and picked his nose with his middle finger, then walked on. The war had been declared.

It came to dramatic climax one day during lunch break, outside the school cafeteria in the open sitting area. It was

Miller's habit to sit apart from the other kids, usually on an unoccupied, shaded bench where he could play his guitar without being bothered. Lost in his music, the raucous voices around him fading to distant buzzes of insignificance, his head jerked up, startled, as a hand from nowhere reached down and gripped the neck of his guitar. Miller held it tight, glaring.

"Let the fuck go, man."

"Queers and wusses play guitars," Pottsy spat, grinning malevolently. "Which one are you? Huh? Queer or wuss?" He loomed over Miller, his grip firm around the guitar neck, tugging. Miller tugged back. A cluster of boys on the adjacent bench looked on. "I said, let the fuck go, you brain-dead–"

"What? What'd you say?" Pottsy's face flushed ugly. "Queer punk cocksucker!" His free hand joined his first, gripping the guitar like a bat and pulling back. "You don't know who you're messin' with. I'll take this fuckin' piece-a-shit guitar and bust it on the wall. You think I'm playin'? Huh?"

A vicious yank, bringing Miller to his feet. They struggled, tugging back and forth on the guitar, breathing hard, glaring hatefully at each other. Pottsy chuckled derisively, took his open palm and spread it over Miller's face, roughly pushing the smaller boy backward. Miller lost his grip on the guitar and stumbled, falling against the hard wooden bench. Some girls squealed with malicious laughter, drawing the attention of a teacher by the cafeteria. Still chuckling, Pottsy snatched the guitar, strummed it clumsily a couple of times, then held it out with both hands toward the flustered, embarrassed Miller in mock offering. "Want it back, wuss boy?" he taunted, cocking an eyebrow, displaying his crooked, chipped teeth in a baleful grin. "Huh? I'm talkin' to you, dick. Want it back? No?" Fixing his mouth in a feigned expression of surprise, Pottsy let the instrument slip from his hands. It fell to the tarmac with a rude, noisy clang. "Ohhh, damn. Sorry 'bout that, wuss boy. It fall down, go boom." Hunching his shoulders and turning, Pottsy smirked at some grinning boys sitting close by, then prepared to lose himself in the crowd of lunching youngsters before the approaching teacher could confront him. What he hadn't bargained on was Miller's reaction.

Shaking from head to toe with a fury that frightened him, the smaller boy scooped up his nicked and dented guitar and, wielding it like a club over his shoulder, barreled toward Pottsy with his teeth clenched. Only the warning shout of a boy behind them saved Rufus Potts. Pottsy turned his head just in time to see a possessed, crazed-looking Miller taking a furious swing at him with the guitar, aiming straight for his head. His arms flew up at the same instant he jerked his face back. The edge of the instrument deflected off Pottsy's shoulder, then exploded against the side of the brick concession stand, wooden shrapnel, strings, and pegs flying in all directions. Kids howled and leaped out of the way. Teachers ran toward them. Miller, eyes insanely glinting, wild, punkish hair everywhere at once on his head, advanced toward a shocked and shaken Pottsy with slow, skulking single-mindedness, one hand clutching the jagged remains of his guitar like some primitive warrior, his intention quite clear.

Their eyes bore into each other's. Above the ensuing clamor, Miller issued his quiet warning: "Mess with me or anything that belongs to me again, you dumb, country cretin, and I'll kill you. Not fight you. Kill you." The murderous calm in Miller's dark eyes spoke volumes.

Pottsy knew this kid was different from the rest. He would do what he said. A wary, dawning respect grew for the skinny, antisocial boy, even more so when the two of them were suspended over the incident and Miller chose to remain silent, stubbornly resisting the efforts of his foster parents and teachers to induce him to tell what really happened.

When the school accepted them back on probation, warning

them both that any future altercations would result in immediate expulsion, the boys made a conscious effort to avoid one another. It was Pottsy who eventually broke the ice, happening upon Miller one day in the boys' lavatory. The smaller youth was hovered over a urinal when Pottsy walked up, positioning himself next to him.

"You're a nutty little fucker. Know that?" Pottsy said.

"I am what I am," muttered Miller, not looking up. "You are what you are."

"I'm still tryin' to figure what I am. But you're certified, Clyde." At that, Miller glanced up, looking the horse-faced boy in the eyes. Pottsy was smiling lopsidedly, his beady eyes mischievous, unchallenging. Recognizing the gesture for what it was, Miller managed a weak smile and shifted his gaze back to the urinal.

"I don't make friends easy," he said, idly shaking his sex free of moisture.

Pottsy snickered, unzipping his fly. "Easy enough to see why. They're either scared you'll suck blood from their necks or rearrange their features with a guitar." There was no malice in the words. Miller laughed, a boyish, bubbly sound that was contagious. Unconsciously, his eyes strayed to Pottsy's long, cowled cock, then quickly away. He put his own away, zipped his fly, and turned toward the taller youth. Someone coughed in a toilet stall. Pottsy offered his outstretched hand. Miller started to take it, hesitated, smiling apologetically. "Been holding my wiener with the right one." Pottsy chuckled, cut his eyes toward the toilets, then reached down and clutched the punk rocker's groin, briefly shaking it. "Hey, man," laughed Miller, jerking back embarrassed.

"Pleased to meet you," said Pottsy, his eyes swimming with mischief.

As they left the rest room and headed back to class, Pottsy admitted, "I'm a dick for what I did to your guitar, Mil. I'll get you another one, a better one. My word." Not wanting to remember, to rekindle dying ashes, Miller shrugged. "Whatever, man. Whatever." A week later, Pottsy gave Miller a close-to-new rosewood Martin twelve-string, complete with carrying case. Miller was speechless. The bigger youth beamed with pride. "My word's gold, Mil. We square?" All Miller could do was smile dumbly. It was obvious the guitar was stolen, but he didn't care. No one had ever given him anything of such personal value. He cherished the instrument as if his dead parents had given it to him.

As their friendship blossomed, Miller adjusted his entire view of Rufus Potts. He wasn't the doltish country hick Miller had originally presumed. He learned that Pottsy liked to play the fool, to throw others off guard, to get them to lower their defenses, expose themselves. The boy had a sharp, crass wit and a love for daring, transgressive behavior. He was precocious and vulgar, sometimes to a fault, deriving pleasure from shocking and disgusting people.

Early in their relationship Miller recognized Pottsy's aberrant tendencies in reference to sex. He was forever touching other boys on their behinds, laughing bawdily when someone deliberately or accidentally broke wind, debasing conversations into smutfest tournaments of phallic comparisons and lewd anal musings.

Pottsy seldom discussed girls, unless by extension of his dick-and-ass commentaries, the female anatomy assuming the character of an amorphous backdrop. He shared with Miller his recollections of those summer months he'd spent at his Uncle Paul's farm in Goshen, Oregon, his erotic experiences with the Mexican immigrants who came to pick vegetables there. Pottsy told Miller about his uncle's hay barn, a favorite gathering spot. Seldom used for anything other than storing old, rusty, inoperable equipment, Pottsy and certain Mexican boys would slip in there to steal drags from hot-boxed cigarettes and fight each other, the Mexicans curious to see what the gringo Americano's heart was made of. Other times they would grab-ass and wrestle around on bales of damp hay, lustfully nosing around in one another's asses, groping and straining in a frenzied tumble. Groups would play with each other, finger-probing butts and sucking one another's cocks. They were rough and clumsy, often mashing their behinds into each other's faces and breaking wind with uninhibited abandon, grunting and laughing gleefully. Pottsy ejaculated in his pants more times than he could remember during those bouts.

The day his Uncle Paul walked in and caught them, Pottsy was entangled with three other boys, his pants and shorts lowered, one boy furiously humping his mouth, another tonguing his ass while the third sucked his cock. It was the last time that Pottsy was invited to his uncle's farm for the summer. . .

Miller never forgot those lurid tales, replaying them over and over in his mind during the course of the day. This was, of course, after the moody, iconoclastic youth had decided his hormones didn't have the required patience necessary to endure the double-signaled fickleness of females. One minute girls were gung-ho to let you feel around under their skirts and squeeze their spongy breasts, the next day they were squealing murder, hotly deriding you for your insensitive, heathen ways. It confused Miller, angered him.

"Wha's wrong? Don't you wanna. . . want me to get you off?"

"No. Later, later. On the way to Seattle." Miller abruptly sat up and pulled up his pants, irritably staring out the limousine's tinted window as he rearranged his softening erection into a more comfortable position. His head jerked toward Dream. He sneered. "Wipe your fuckin' face, dude," he snapped. "There's slobber drippin' off your chin. And change clothes. We'll be staying at Seattle's best and I don't want you embarrassing me and the band." Before the hurt in the boy's expression could pierce him, Miller opened the door and crawled out into layered shade and sunlight teasing one another in the lushness of verdant green, into his past.

So damn long.

Even the air smelled the same. Pungent. Clean. He closed his eyes and stretched, shaking off the slight stiffness of extended travel. He knocked on the front window and told Trouble Man he'd be back in a few minutes.

His bullhide cowboy boots scrunching through gravel and dirt, Miller walked up the jagged road until he came to a narrow, leaf-strewn path to his right, leading gradually down into a dense copse of birch trees and shrubbery. Instinct came to his aid before memory kicked in, guiding him through the correct turns and short cuts, under thick, treacherous, low-hanging, thorny branches, his brain functioning on some subconscious level, telling him what he had to do, how he had to do it, to get where he was going. Never could really escape this shit, could you? he thought grimly. Half way around the world it still calls to you like some fucking persistent, nagging beast you left locked in a cage. . .

Before long Miller came to a wide clearing surrounded by moss-covered boulders on one side, cedar trees on the other. The clearing dropped at an angle to a burbling creek, slabs of beige, loose rock flanking it on both sides. The steady, trickling sound of water came to his ears. Subtly unnerving.

In the confusion of trees to the singer's left, a brief cacophony of birdsong lanced the relative still, followed by a sudden flutter of wings and rustling leaves. He took a seat on a large, sunbaked rock, peering down wistfully into the familiar creek. Reaching into his coin pocket, Miller extracted a joint, straightened it out, and then dug around for his lighter. The creek Mob – Pottsy, Freddie Longheimer, and Miller – used to come here. Others too. But Miller and company came here with their ill-gotten gains: stolen tape decks from the cars they had burglarized, cameras, radios, TVs, VCRs. Packed away in waterproofed boxes and stashed in the various cave-like rock enclosures above the creek until such time Freddie's brother, Michael, could secure buyers in Portland and Eugene. As wild and delinquent as they were back then, it's a wonder they all didn't wind up in reform school or prison. Michael did, Miller recalled, for some idiotic rape charge or something. But Pottsy and Freddie. . .

The memories, like an unchecked reservoir, came flooding back to Miller as he slowly puffed the joint, his eyelids drooping to torpid half-mast.

Thirteen. Weird. Hella-skinny.

He dreamt of stardom even back in those days, envisioning himself the outrageous front man in a punk rock band, the new Joey Ramone or Sid Vicious, neurotic and visionary, an artistic anarchist of the first order. "When you make your first million," Pottsy used to tell him offhandedly, "you can buy this town and turn it into a nuke waste dump. Or better yet, nuke it, then buy it. We can raise glow fruit and sell it to the freaks down in California. Make a fortune." Pottsy would say this sort of thing with a detached expression on his misleadingly dumb face, then, without warning, let you off the hook with a ludicrous bird squawk or dog howl.

Out of nowhere he might ask Miller off-the-wall questions like how do fish fuck. Had he ever heard a girl fart? Watched a girl pee? Trivial questions Miller had occasionally wondered himself in silly, idle moments.

The first time the two of them got drunk together happened at the creek, consuming two six packs of Budweiser between them which they had conned some trucker into buying on their behalf. In the seclusion of rustic vegetation and shaded rocks, Miller let Pottsy wrestle his trousers and underpants down and suck him off. It was Miller's maiden experience with queer sex. He liked it, even better than groping giggly girls, though it left him with a slightly soiled, guilty feeling. They had done it in the dirt. Sloppy. Nasty. Rufus Potts was a vivacious cocksucker. By his account Miller had blown him, too, though the punk rocker didn't recall it. All he remembered was the cool breeze against his smooth, bare legs as he lay sprawled on his back on the ground, his head dreamy with alcohol, slowly pumping his pelvis up into Pottsy's burrowing face and moaning, "Yeah, man. Do me. Do me. Do me. Do me gooood."

After that first time it became clear to Pottsy that this was something his friend enjoyed doing, but not talking about. Any efforts at discussing the topic would be met by uncomfortable, guarded expressions from Miller, abrupt shifts in conversation. So Pottsy learned to keep reference to their ruttings out of his lustful tales, instead focusing exclusively on the immoral doings of other boys and himself to keep Miller's gutter meter ticking.

"Wanna hear about juvie, Mil?" he'd ask nonchalantly as they languished by the creek, sharing beer and joints of pot.

"Maaan, screw juvie," Miller would say, feigning disinterest. "Nothing in juvie but a bunch of fruiters and losers."

"I ever tell you about the time I buttfucked this little Mexican queer in the shower? It happened right after. . ." One glance at the lewd sparkle in Miller's eyes would give him away. By the time Pottsy finished telling his story the punk rocker's pants would be sporting a healthy protrusion at the front. Miller seldom initiated anything, but would casually spread his legs and gaze off thoughtfully in the distance, passively awaiting his buddy's desperate caresses and fumblings.

A boy named Freddie Longheimer started hanging around with them about the time Miller and Pottsy began burglarizing cars and stores for extra spending cash. Freddie was a blond, baby-faced kid with nervous, blinky eyes and a tongue that seemed to rattle full-speed ahead of the thoughts it was entrusted with articulating. His frame was curiously pear-shaped: slender from the waist up, curvy and plump from the waist down. The boy's behind was so prominent that boys at school called him "Longheinie" and "Thunder Rump," much to Freddie's chagrin and embarrassment.

When Pottsy discovered that Freddie's older brother had biker connections which could fence hot merchandise, he started to nurture a friendship with him. "This guy's brother can help us get rid of stuff, Mil. Freddie? This is my buddy, Miller. Miller – Freddie Longheimer." Pottsy had brought the kid over to Miller's house to introduce them, the three of them standing on the front porch away from the heavy, pouring rain, Miller's foster parents inside preparing supper. Freddie's hair was rain-plastered to his scalp. His round, effeminate face was flushed bright pink. His nervous eagerness gave Miller the impression he'd just robbed a bank or something.

"Got any pot, Mil?" Pottsy asked in a hissy whisper.

"A little." Miller glanced at Freddie. "So what's your brother do?"

The blond boy shook water from his thick, down jacket, darting his light blue eyes to the front door, then to Miller, hunching his shoulders. "Mechanic stuff. He works on bikes and cars and stuff. Knows some Renegades in Portland and Seattle. You guys got stuff to sell, my brother can get rid of it for ya." The boy's expression changed. "You into music? You write songs?" Miller cut a glance over at Pottsy who stood just behind Freddie making silly, suggestive faces.

"Yeah," he nodded, catching the blond youth's erratic gaze brush over his crotch, then rise. "My music's cutting edge, man. I'm into hard-core mostly. Some metal."

"Miller's gonna go to Hollyweird and be a big, faggy rock

star," Pottsy teased, rolling his beady eyes meaningfully and smirking. Freddie giggled, looking down at his sneakers. Winking at Miller, Pottsy reached out with both arms and locked the blond boy in a bear hug, growling and grinding his hips into Freddie's capacious pants seat in a show of possession. "Ain't that right, Freddie?" He cooed vulgarly. "Ooooo. Ahhhh. Ain't that right? He's got the softest ass in town, Mil."

"Hey, man," complained Freddie weakly, laughing. "Quit, Pottsy, you queer bait." The blond boy squirmed and protested, but Miller could see the effort was half-hearted. Freddie kept throwing mixed looks his way as Pottsy humped up against him. Miller immediately understood. Everything. "Man, I'll fart on you," Freddie warned, giggling goofily, thrusting his wide rump back, screwing up his face in a tense grimace. When he did, Pottsy whooped excitedly and released him. Small threat, that. Miller was well aware of his buddy's quirky affinity for that particular crudeness. The conspicuous swelling in the front of his jeans told it all. Pottsy had found the sort of queer that Miller wasn't, finally. The sort who liked things up his butt. The unholy trinity was birthed. . .

Relaxed and mellow-hazy, the musician climbed down the short hill, taking his time because of his slick boot soles on the loose rocks, dusting himself off as he went to the edge of the creek and bent down. The water was cool and unspoiled on his fingers. What a joke that was. Blood had spilled here, at least once, probably more times, be it accident or design, corrupting whatever innocence existed before its advent, mingling in the crystalline wash along with the regret, the guilt, the endless indictments.

Lost innocence, cow shit and Oregon rain.

The death rocker rose, sighed weightily, and then started walking. His feet seemed to possess a will of their own. They took him along the rough rocks, over crushed beer and Pepsi cans, trampled cigarette butts and sharp, poignant memories. Before he knew it he was standing at the spot where his life had forever shifted but remained unchanged.

Where It happened.

Miller peered up through the trees to his right. A wreath of yellow halo encircled the leaves. A trick of sunlight. He shivered without knowing why. His face grew dark, grim. Farther up the creek several people in cut-offs and skimpy T-shirts. Laughter. Playful pushing and shoving. Could've been me, Miller thought pensively. Once upon a time. Luck or misfortune. Random pick of the draw?

"Won't find answers up in them trees, man." The voice startled the singer. He whirled around, annoyance and surprise clear in his face. The guy had walked up on him from the slight incline leading toward the thick patch of birch and cedars. "All they do is stand around and take it all in. Won't tell you what they know, though." He was tall, about six feet even, with sandy, mountainmannish blond hair worn in a long, bushy ponytail, squinty green eyes, a gentle mouth, thin brown beard. He wore a blue Pendleton shirt, faded jeans, hiking boots, and a nylon backpack slung over his shoulder. Miller guessed his age at twenty-three, -four.

He looked the rock star over with a cool, slightly amused expression, no light of recognition in his eyes, then smiled faintly and shifted his gaze toward the creek. "Used to come up here as a kid," he offered in a low, lazy voice. "Cool spot to get away to, reflect and stuff. That was before it turned into the garbage dump it is now." He dropped his backpack, stooped, picked up a rock and tossed it into the water, listening to the soft plunk that followed. His head turned to Miller. "You in a band or something?"

Miller stepped a few paces toward him. "Yeah. I sing for Ravaged Soul. Heard of 'em?"

"No," answered the stranger, returning his attention to the

creek. "I figured you for something like that. Looking like you do." Miller caught the accusatory note in his voice. Dumb hick. Things change but some things never do. "Ain't no radios where you come from?" Miller asked sarcastically.

"I come from right here. Here, Goshen, Eugene," he sidestepped the question. "Wouldn't live anywhere else."

Miller gave a derisive snort, dug around for his cigarettes and lighter. "Yeah, well. . . the smartest move I probably made in my life was hauling ass away from this place as soon as I could. The world's a big playing field, man. Lotsa killer horizons out there." The stranger suddenly turned and stared in the death rocker intently as if searching for some long lost clue to something grave and urgent. Calmly, knowingly, Miller lit a cigarette, inhaled, braced himself for the inevitable "I know you!" exclamation of sudden recognition. It was a common occurrence. And he was not disappointed, but it came in a form the singer was totally unprepared for. The long-haired guy gave a smug little nod as the puzzle unraveled and solved itself in his head. "Been a long time," he said finally. "What drags you back to Deer Creek after all this time, Breiding?"

Miller was briefly off balance. No one had called him by his last name since. . . well, since he left Oregon with his band six or seven years ago. He'd changed it to Dungeon as soon as he hit San Francisco. The sound of it had an alien, unpleasant quality to it, especially on the lips of this guy who Miller sensed immediately had no fond memories of him.

"I know you, man?"

"We went to Madison at the same time. I was a grade above you and that Potts character." The contempt in his voice was clear. He shook his ponytail and peered off toward the trails. "You wouldn't remember me. I was much too home-spun and normal for you deviants. I'm Gaine. Gaine Brooks."

Miller shook his head, hunched his shoulders. "Don't

remember you."

"Didn't think you would. Ohh, but I remember you, Breiding. I thought you were either in jail somewhere or dead like your. . . friends." Miller didn't like the direction of the conversation. Gaine turned and faced him. They stared cooly at each other.

"Not death or jail," Miller responded flatly. "Godhood, Man. Godhood."

Gaine snorted with disdain. "Godhood, huh?"

"Reasonable facsimile thereof. Worshipping fans. Hits on the record charts. Cult loyalty. More bucks that I can fuck off in a lifetime. What would you call it?"

"I call it pretentious, ego-tripping bullshit." The tall blond smiled unexpectedly, shaking his head in a pitying gesture. "I never did like you, Breiding. Never did. You, Potts, Longheimer. I thought you were a bunch of jerk-off perverts with mega-death wishes. Seems I was right about two-thirds of you, wasn't I? Ol' Potts bought his right around here, didn't he?"

Miller, feeling the anger boiling up inside him like a simmering volcano, sat down on a clump of rocks, saying nothing. Who the fuck was this lame to be talking like this to him? All he'd have to do was go back to the limo and fetch Trouble Man and this fucker's whole world would come crashing down. But. . . there had been no Gaine Brooks in L.A., or New York, or London, Frankfurt or Rome, and still the specters had stalked him. Smiling at him. Winking at him.

Settle it, dude. Once and for all.

"I didn't want to come back," he heard himself begin. "Back to all this. . ."

"But you did," Gaine observed drily, his steps lazy and unhurried as he walked closer and sat a few feet away from the death rocker. "Something obviously drew you back – though I can't figure what it might be. Wasn't no great love lost when you left, I'm sorry to say. Deer Creek's still Deer Creek. Old man Tracy still runs Holiday General Market. The mill still stinks to high heaven. Kids still drag up and down Second Street on the weekend, hootin' and hollerin' out their car windows. You expected things would be different?"

"No," Miller said in a distant voice. "I knew it wouldn't. It never is." A sudden chill breezed down from the trees, ruffling the singer's apocalyptic hair. He shuddered involuntarily, glancing over at Gaine. "You believe in setting things right? In squaring things with the past so you can go on with the future?" The hippie country boy stared at Miller's intent face, remaining silent. He scratched his beard thoughtfully, waiting. The death rocker slipped his hands inside the pockets of his leather jacket, momentarily losing himself in the gently ebbing waters of the creek.

"Demons ridin' your back, huh?" Gaine asked, arching his eyebrow sardonically.

"Fuck off, man," Miller spat. "Who died and made you psychoanalyst for the day? Who the fuck are you, anyway? Some dude in the background of life, that's who you are. . . Elevator muzak with a face and beard." Without warning, Gaine burst into genuine laughter, throwing his head back and slapping his knees.

"That's rich," he chuckled, tears welling in his eyes. "That's good. A good one. I've been called a lot of things, but never that."

On impulse Miller asked, "You toke?"

"Cigarettes?"

"Dope."

"'Course. Got some?"

"Noooo. I'm just taking a survey of hillbilly social behavior. Of course I've got some." He pulled a small wrapped baggie from his jacket, tossed it to Gaine. "You gotta roll it, though."

"No problem, Breiding."

"The name's Dungeon now. Had it changed in California about six years ago. New life, new name."

"Same guy. . .?" Again, the arched eyebrow, amused side glance. A sharp, flippant response struggled on the tip of Miller's tongue, anxious for release. He managed to suppress it, inexplicably sensing the wisdom in that decision.

"In some ways," he offered instead, nodding cautiously. "Yeah. In some ways the same dude definitely."

"Uh humm." Gaine lit a match and torched the fat joint he'd rolled, took a good, long hit and then passed it on to Miller. Their fingers touched lightly. The singer relaxed a bit. He came, oddly, to accept the guy's presence as a necessary component in whatever this was, although its definition eluded him. It would come of its own volition, unforced and in due time. Until it happened he would wait, and muse, and savor the moment.

Remembering. . .

He'd peeked then, through the dense clearing, and seen Pottsy about fifty yards in, wiping his brow with a ragged bandanna, his faded Pennsoil T-shirt ringed in sweat around the neck and down the sides, slender arms streaked with dirt, his cut-off jeans dirt-encrusted brown in the rear and hanging loosely around his lean hips. He was facing Wendell Broghan, the retired laborer who Pottsy had said kept a treasure chest of gold coins, silver and foreign currency, stashed in his house somewhere, nodding deferentially and shifting his posture as the tall, stoic-faced man gestured slowly with his large hands, explaining something Miller couldn't quite make out.

"What's happening? What's going on?" asked Freddie beside Miller in a loud, excited whisper.

"Shhh!"

"But what is – "

"Shut the fuck up," warned Miller, glaring at the high-strung blond. "You'll get us busted before Pottsy has a chance to work the guy." There were three large piles of leaves and trash beside Pottsy and the farmer. A couple of rakes and a shovel. The air held a redolent stench of heavy, ripe magnolia blossoms and manure. They were in Wendell Broghan's back yard, the old recluse having commissioned Pottsy to do a little work for him over the weekend. But everyone, including Broghan, had their hidden agendas in place.

As the boys watched, the stoop-shouldered farmer stepped closer to Pottsy and put his arm around the boy's shoulders in a fatherly gesture, resting his weight on one leg and pivoting his large, mastiff-like head this way and that as he talked, the hand on Pottsy's shoulder gently tapping. They were positioned in profile, Miller and Freddie's vantage point partially obscured by a tangle of criss-crossing branches and vines.

Wendell Broghan casually peered around the back yard in a peculiar, distracted sort of way, like he was worried about someone watching him, then pointedly reached down with his other hand to the front of Pottsy's cut-offs, working his arm in a gentle up-and-down motion.

"Fucker's feeling him up," Freddie whispered, the anticipation thick in his voice. Miller nodded, feeling his belly tighten with tension. The farmer's other hand slipped down to Pottsy's dirty pants seat, Vienna sausage-fingers flexing, squeezing slowly, then with increasing greediness, both hands working in lewd counterpoint on the boy's crotch and butt. Pottsy groaned softly and braced his legs in a wider stance, rotating his hips crudely. His cut-offs slipped down in back, just enough for a glimpse of dark crack and creamy humps. Both Miller and Freddie had taut, uncomfortable erections pushing at the fronts of their jeans. They were crouched on their haunches, knees touching, hearts hammering hot blood to their brains, breathless. Miller wasn't sure how much more of this he could watch, with Freddie so close, the sprawl of his rump so taut and warm and pulsating against the fabric of his blue jeans. . .

Pottsy's cut-offs were down around his sneakers now. Broghan was on his knees in the dirt, rabidly sucking, grunting, his cheeks bloating and caving in as the boy's rigid shaft plunged back and forth, in and out, the man's thick fingers clutching Pottsy's lean buttocks, urgently kneading, pulling them apart, then closed, rolling them in lewd circles. The front of the farmer's shabby khaki trousers held an immense, straining bulge. One hand flew to it, gripping it tightly, milking it through his pants, his other hand hungrily digging between Pottsy's ass cheeks.

Their passion intensified. The boy groaned, feet shifting, his bowed legs wobbly. His buttocks quivered and jerked in increasing agitation. A crude sputter of flatulence. Broghan made an earthy noise of surprise and wantonness in his throat, pulled his dripping mouth away from Pottsy's sex and spun the boy around. Without hesitation the rugged farmer shoved his face into Pottsy's squirming, hairless ass, rutting around like a dog mugging a bowl of warm, succulent meat. Pottsy issued a terse grunt and compliantly arched his back, pushing his lips out in a bawdy grimace, his long, springy cock glossy with spit and bobbing obscenely in front of him.

Filtered rays of sunlight. Criss-crossing prisms of luscious haziness beaming through occasional breaks in branches and leaves. Heady smelling blossoms. Swirling, drunken bees, round and round in zigzagged formations. A lapse in time, in being, slowing to dream cadence. The beastly sounds of lust. Pathetic gasps. Wet, slurpy muffled noises like someone suffocating, in league with the surreal. An old reclusive laborer, his movements clumsy, self-indulgent, primitively fluid, greedily rutting in the proffered backside of a morally bankrupt adolescent.

Now was the time. "Let's split," Miller whispered to

Freddie. "Let's do it."

"Wait. . ."

"Wait like fuck. Put your bone back in your pants and let's do it. Now!" Miller didn't linger. He'd seen enough. Had enough. Quickly he rose, leaving the blond youth in his daze of erotic intoxication, heading straight for the farmer's back door. A few moments later Freddie joined him. Within fifteen minutes the two had ransacked the house, finding nothing of significant value. Miller was disgusted. With himself. With Pottsy, Freddie. Pottsy had lied to him. Again. He was growing steadily tired of it – and all the stuff they were doing. He wasn't a cheap criminal. He was a singer, an artist. If he kept this dumb shit up he'd for sure wind up in juvie before the year was out.

Not.

Pottsy could chat the place up like it was fag heaven, but Miller wasn't buying. They were his friends still, but he possessed a unique ingredient they, unfortunately, lacked: vision, ambition.

He could see past his nose. And his dick. He decided it was time to have a heart-to-heart with his buds. It wasn't something he looked forward to, but he couldn't put it off any longer. . .

"So, being the globe-hopping rock star you've become, I'd imagine you can't keep the chicks away with a bludgeon, eh?"

"You imagine a lot, don'tcha?"

Gaine gave Miller an enigmatic, Mona Lisa smile. "Only stands to reason. Your rubber expenses must be ceiling-high."

The singer offered the blond country boy a measured, contemplative look. The sun had begun its gradual descent over the west tree-lined hills, dusk creeping in like a stealthy burglar caped in somber gold and crimson. Gaine had his head propped on his backpack, one leg crossed over the other as the gap between them formed a pyramid. He toyed with the tractioned heel of one boot. His hairy, placid face seemed relaxed, almost serene. Somehow that offended Miller.

The singer cleared his throat. "If you're fishing for info concerning my bone life, man, why don't you just come right out and ask? It ain't like it's some military secret I'm sworn to uphold or some shit. Find your nuts and speak your mind."

"You know, it's funny," said Gaine. "I don't recall you ever being so. . . this. . . combative, I guess would be the word. Deviant, yes. Obnoxious, yes. So what is it? You pissed at the world because it let you become so successful instead of dead or in prison?"

Miller laughed bitterly. "Oh, ye of little brain. What would you know about success or failure? Where the fuck have you been besides nowhere?" He raked his fingers through his hair with agitation. "Yeah. Yeah, I'm still a deviate. Probably more so now than I was then. As we speak there's a kid with a face like Courtney Love's waiting in my limo who'll suck the lining out of my asshole if I tell him to. But why the fuck am I telling you all this?"

"Don't have the faintest. Or why I'm actually listening to it."

"Ain't no lead weights in your back pocket. You could split." Miller gave the hippie a level stare. There was challenge in it. Gaine stared back, a wisp of a smile on his lips. "That what you want, man?" he asked calmly, uncrossing his long legs, fanning them back and forth slowly. "It doesn't matter to me. Is it?"

Miller stared a few seconds longer, then dropped his gaze, frustrated, unsure. What *did* he want? In his soul he knew. His soul had always known. He wanted the blood to wash, once and for all, from his hands.

To bury old, forgotten things.

After a time of mutual silence, the death rocker expelled

a heavy sigh, lit a cigarette, and in a quiet voice, said, "Gonna tell you a little story. Why? I dunno. Probably for the simple reason that you're here, and I'm here, right now at this point in time. Fate. Who knows? I'm tired of guessing at shit." He looked out toward the fading glimmer of the creek, at the flittering mosquitos and gnats hovering over the water in droves, arranging his thoughts carefully.

"I was up here the night Pottsy died," the singer began, not looking at Gaine. "We – Freddie, Pottsy, and I – had come up here to talk, smoke some dope. They were my friends, man. Right or wrong, they were still my friends. But. . . I came to realize how people sometimes grow apart. I was changing, wanting something more than just chump change from doing dumb, petty shit. Pottsy had already been to juvie once and no matter what he said about how cool it was I wasn't trying to find out. It was either do the music thing or do the criminal thing, but no way could I do both."

"Anyway, so we hike up here to kick it around, and Pottsy's been drinking and he's being a real dick, howling like some lunatic, whipping his dick out to piss and splashing it all over Freddie's pants and sneakers, getting some on me. Fucking Freddie was such a follower anyway. All he did was get this stupid look on his face and whine, trying to laugh it off. It pissed me off, though, and I told Pottsy to chill the fuck out. He did – sort of. I mean, he stopped the rowdy screaming and shit and plopped his ass against a tree, his dick and nuts still hanging out of his pants. He looked funny sitting there like that: drunk, slack-lipped, cock hanging out. In the next breath, the fucker cocked his legs wide and told Freddie to blow him, rubbing his stuff like some dirty old man. Freddie told him to fuck off and looked to me for support. I didn't say nothing. This stuff went on all the time with us. It was different this time, though. Pottsy was belligerent about it.

"Glaring at Freddie, he got up and lurched over to him,

grabbing him by the hair, calling him 'fat bitch' and 'fuck boy wuss,' roughly mashing his cock and nuts in his face. Man, Freddie didn't know whether to laugh, cry, or what. He tried pushing Pottsy back, but Pottsy slapped him and sort of fell on top of him with Freddie's face buried underneath the weight of his crotch. The dude's legs were spread out from Freddie's head at an angle, his butt all hiked up and squirming as he tried to force his cock into Freddie's mouth. Freddie was kicking his legs in the dirt and throwing his arms around and farting, making those wild, desperate noises in his throat. I didn't try to stop the shit. Freddie was into rough stuff.

"Sure enough, the next thing I heard was garbled moans and choking sounds and Pottsy grunting, 'Suck it, bitch. Suck that cock,' his buttcheeks humpin' up and down like bugs had invaded his pants. Any other time I would have joined them, but that night my head was somewhere else, man. You still with me?"

"Yeah," Gaine said. "Go on."

Miller diddled with his lighter, absently staring at it. "Anyway, for some reason I got up and walked down by the creek over there – " pointing to his left, " – sat down, trying to get my head together. I couldn't stay here any longer, man. It was squeezing the breath out of me. Pottsy and Freddie would have to understand.

"After about twenty minutes or so I heard movement on the rocks, some cussing, and then Pottsy walked up, standing over me. I looked up and told him to sit down before he fell down. He just stood there, looking down at me with this weird expression on his face. I asked him what was up. After a few seconds of weird looks, he says, 'Freddie can't suck a cock for shit. I don't want a blow job, anyway. I want some ass.' 'So go bone Freddie,' I tell him. His pants were zipped up, dick put away, so I don't think he's all that serious. Besides, he knew I had a real phobia about things up my ass at that time.

No way, Jose. I just wasn't into that. So I'm totally tripped out when the dude steps right up on me and says it's time for me to get 'stump broken.'"

"Stump broken," Gaine snorted with amusement.

"Stump broken," repeated the musician. "Like a bull or a horse. Freddie walked up about that time, standing next to Pottsy with this cheese-eating grin on his face. They looked at each other, then at me. I didn't dig the look. Pottsy said, 'Well, Mill, we've discussed it and Freddie is in agreement with me that you need that tight brown eye de-virginized. So do you give it up willingly, or do we have to take it?' Man, I couldn't believe what I was hearing, didn't think he was actually serious. I told him to eat shit and go roll a doob or something, then got up.

"The next thing I knew Pottsy was tackling me and snorting like a bull, ordering Freddie to hold my legs as we tumbled to the ground. Fucking Freddie actually tried to do it, giggling like an idiot. I was laughing, too, still not convinced. I mean, like, these were my best buds, man. Everything seemed to spiral toward some Twilight Zone episode. Something was choking off my air, yanking my jeans down, trying to flip me over. It was crazy. I went somewhere - my mind, I mean. Just zoned. My fingers dug themselves around something hard. A rock. A fat one. I swung it and connected. I heard a scream of pain. I swung again, missed, swung again and missed. My vision cleared. I saw Pottsy stumbling backward, holding the side of his head, and Freddie standing off to the side with this pale, wide-eyed shock on his face. Pottsy fell face down by the creek. I heard this dull clunking noise, like a fucking softball banging against something hard, and then I. . . we. . ." Miller faltered, chewing his bottom lip, his eyes stinging wetly. "We. . . fuck, man. Fuck."

Gaine stared at him, his eyes compassionate, gentle. "So his death wasn't like they said," he murmured softly. Miller shook his head, the tears flowing unchecked down the sides of his tortured face. Such a long time coming. The well, released. Lost innocence, a friend's blood, and –

"We. . . we panicked," the death rocker mumbled so quietly that Gaine had to lean forward to hear. The light gloom of early evening had slid in around them, the lines and angles of Miller's androgynous face mercurial and unsteady. "When he fell he caved in his forehead on a rock. Blood was gushing out like a spring, man. Fucking drunk, stupid motherfucker. We. . . shit, we didn't know what to do. He was dead, man. Dead. We split. Just split and left him there. Freddie looked like death warmed over. He was really scared, crying and shaking and shit. I was shaking, too, but I had my head more together. I knew I didn't want to spend the rest of my life in prison, so I calmed Freddie down and rehearsed with him what we'd tell the cops if they should come and ask us anything. They never did, strangely enough. Never did."

"Rufus Potts was drunk, went up to the creek by himself, tripped and killed himself," said Gaine, recalling what the local news had reported about the death.

The singer wiped the wetness from his countenance, sniffled loudly, briskly ruffling his hair with both hands. "Ohh, man, oh, man. Crazy, crazy shit. Freddie went real strange after that. Started doing pills, drinking on top of them, talking to himself, messing around with his Dad's gun collection. Blew his brains out two months after Pottsy. I wasn't here for that. I was in Portland, starting to put a band together. I didn't go to his funeral. I. . . I dunno. . ."

Gaine idly scratched his beard as he watched Miller. He'd never seen such inner torment before. The rocker looked like anything but what he was, a celebrated, visionary artist with millions in the bank. The arrogant shell had cracked in the last few minutes, leaving pathos, bare and unshielded and singular, a post-modern heir to the ancient House of Atreides, empty and so frighteningly alone. But somehow, the country boy knew that sympathy, no matter how well intentioned, was not the answer here, the required medicine. The Phoenix had risen from ashes. A purging. Burn first, then you may live. Greater than before.

Gaine hauled himself up, stretched, scratched his crotch. He looked down at Miller without expression. "Get up," he ordered tersely. "Let's go."

Miller looked blank. "Huh? What?"

"Up. Up." The blonde's voice held a note of authority, assuredness. Before the singer had time to consider his response, he found himself rising, his bloodshot eyes glued to Gaine's implacable, direct, unforgiving ones, surrendering the reins of decision to him without protest.

The longhaired man led the way, bushy ponytail gently swaying from side to side, his stride easy, certain, and unhurried. Miller followed closely behind him, his mind in a fog and feather-light, the soles of his cowboy boots crunching noisily on dry twigs and rocks, the purple shadows of the infant night reaching out to whisper its hidden secrets from the towering trees and mammoth boulders high above.

Suddenly Gaine halted, turning. "This where it happened?" he asked pointedly, his eyes weirdly gleaming in the encroaching darkness. Miller blinked uncertainly, glancing about him. He noticed a section by the creek where the surrounding bushes grew thicker, the rocks were larger, more jagged. He moved toward it, then stopped and looked at Gaine.

"Here, I think. What are you – "

"Unfasten your trousers and push them down," said the blond almost gruffly, fumbling around in his backpack. Seeing Miller's hesitation, he gave the musician a piercing, do-as-I-say look and stepped closer to him, dropping the backpack by their feet. "Forgiveness isn't mine to give you, dude, but then – " he hunched his shoulders, scanning the pale face, "you didn't expect it anyhow, did you?" He uncapped a jar of Vaseline, holding it toward the rock star, adding, "Square up with the past so you can go on, Miller. There are other ways, but I wouldn't know them. I'll be the pyre to your Icarus." They stared at each other for a long, intensely silent moment. Then, meekly, Miller nodded and began undoing his pants. Gaine unzipped his and guided his long, flaccid tool out through the slit in his pants. A rubbery snout of veiny flesh, Miller noted, peeling down his leathers. His prick bobbed up full and stretched. His balls ached. He took the Vaseline, dug his fingers in the jar, and handed it back. His butt arched as he lewdly greased himself. His belly churned disagreeably. Thoughts of Pottsy, his smirk, his leer. Freddie. Pottsy's piss splattering his jeans. The kinky, pathetic look on his face. The hazy blur of moonlight that night.

"Turn around." An unnecessary command. One last peek at his executioner/savior's weapon of impalement. Slick with grease. Swollen. Monstrous. Obscene. Ready to go. He shuffled himself around, bending slightly, leathers hugging his knees. A sadistic slap against his perky buttocks, ringing into the night. "Spread 'em." His shaking hands followed orders, parting them wide.

Torture of anticipation. Hard, stilted breathing. A determined nudging at his hole.

Pucker up, buttercup.

Little pig, little pig, let me in.

A forceful forward thrust. Penetration. Another thrust, more brutal than the first.

"Ahhhhh! Shit, man. Hurts!"

"You're shit. Shut up and take it, punk."

"Fuck you! Ahhh! Fuck you!" That night. Again. Freddie giggling like a lunatic, holding his legs. Pottsy, choking him, wheezing, growling, fumbling to undo his pants, yanking them down, forcing him over on his belly, mounting him, piercing his crack, stabbing, seeking, finding, stuffing to the hilt, grunting in his ear, pulling back, pushing forward, pulling, pushing, pumping, Freddie watching and squealing with perverse delight, good, hot brown eye, Mil, hot brown eye, Mil hot –

Tears streaming. "I'm sorry. Ah. Ah. So fucking sorry, Pottsy. Oh, God. . ."

"Spread 'em wider. Wider!"

"I can't, fucker. Hurts! Ohhh, it hurts!" It was vicious, beastly. Miller's legs gave way. He collapsed, whimpering like a distraught child. Gaine fell on top of him, continuing to hump like a rabid bull, an avenging spirit, sinking teeth into his soft neck, clutching the back of his hair tightly, forcing his head back, his mouth open. Past and present fused. The Now. Settle it. Once and for –

Miller came in the dirt. He howled in agony, feeling as though his very soul had flung itself from the head of his dick. In the next instant the fires of Hades slowly departed from his rectum, a wealth of warm spunk splashing over his buttocks and legs.

The mad, echoing giggles and passionate breathing subsided.

Stubborn, lingering specters ceased their lingering.

The weight of Gaine's tall frame pressed heavily against his back. The sound of a horn blowing on the chilled breeze. A car horn, familiar. Warm, musty breath in his hair.

A grunt of brief exertion. Pressure released from his back. Movement close by. Rustling clothing. Shuffling boot soles.

He didn't want to get up. He just wanted to lie there forever, melt like a glob of syrup into the cold bosom of the earth beneath him. Like the chilled blood of past, forgotten things. Of memories that trailed him like a junkie in New York City, desperate and relentless.

He rolled over.

Alone.

Miller rose and pulled up his pants. "Thanks," he murmured, not entirely sure who he was thanking. Perhaps the Now and Tomorrow, for he sensed the Other would rest easier now. A smile emerged from its place of extended banishment. Yeah. Look out, Seattle. The Phoenix is comin'.

THE HORSEMEN

Bill Lee

The first incarnation of the characters in this story was in the novel Bi Ranchers Bi Mates *(GLB Publishers, 1991).*

When the horsemen topped the rise, they could see at least thirty miles in all directions. The California valley was golden in the summer haze, while the rolling lavender hills slanted west in the distance. At the bottom of the valley were green meadows along the banks of the spring-fed stream where horses were grazing. They rested their horses briefly before descending the slope.

"That's the bulk of my stock, Brad. If you're in the market for the best horseflesh," Steve ventured with satisfaction in his voice, "you ought to find some pretty good head among that herd."

"That was damn good head last night," Brad grinned, his blue eyes twinking under blond brows.

Steve's dark eyes grinned back, his dark mustache tilting in recollection. "You're as constantly horny as I am, fucker. Guess that's why we get along so well."

The two ranchers had been friends since their youthful days on the rodeo circuit. Being married and "settled down" with wives hadn't changed their basic personalities, nor diminished their sexual appetites. Ten years had merely made them more comfortable with themselves and each other. And when Brad needed to buy some horses, it was natural that he bring his wife with him on the buying trip.

Steve led the way down the slope to the banks of the cool stream that flowed winter and summer. The other horses snorted at their arrival but continued to feed in the sleepy afternoon sun. The horsemen dismounted and gave their horses rein to drink from the creek.

"That water looks good, Steve – think I'll take a dip." Brad tossed his hat on a rock and stripped to the buff. Steve watched him for a moment without comment, appreciative of the still-youthful, muscular body that still excelled in horse-breaking and calf roping. Then he also stripped and joined him in the creek.

The water was not deep enough to swim, but it was cool and refreshing. Neither man would have denied that some of the enjoyment of the moment was being in the company of a nude, masculine, muscular man, a man who was honest enough to admit to that source of satisfaction. After a few minutes they left the water and stretched out on the grass side by side, their rangy bodies almost touching.

"I remember the first time I met you," Steve mused. "It was at that whorehouse out in the valley. We could see each other ballin' chicks in opposite rooms across the hall, and decided to make it a foursome. The women didn't mind, either. I was kinda new to the man-to-man scene, but you sure were ready for just about anything," he chuckled.

Brad grinned back. "Yeah, I remember. I was never really new to that scene – even as a kid I could never understand why there was some block against men havin' sex with men. My first experiences were with guys, you know, jackin' off and playin' with other boys, but then girls got in the act and it was just natural to go both ways, right from the start."

"That's sure best. I think that's the way my son, Chuck, is developing. I bought the one-way deal for a while, like most of my friends, but those rodeo parties with a group of open-minded guys like you changed that pretty quick. The softness, the roundness of women are great, but there is a special feeling for flat, strong muscles and hard, throbbing cocks."

Brad turned to him with a grin. "Especially when they got huge 'hard, throbbing cocks' like you got, Steve." He rolled closer and took that subject organ in his hand, hefting it and sensing the subtle stirrings he was producing.

Steve smiled dreamily, content to be naked and close, listening to the quietude of the valley and faint burblings of the meandering creek, bathed by the warm sunshine, and with his stiffening cock in the fist of his friend. A hawk circled the slopes lazily, looking for unwary mice. Steve automatically scanned the hilltops and then grunted. "Horseman on the hill over there. Looks like he's headed this way."

"Oh, yeah?" Brad was more interested in watching Steve's mushroom cockhead slowly emerging from its embracing foreskin in his hand.

"Probably Buck—you remember him? He was on the rodeo circuit for a while with us. Bought a spread over the hill there. Got himself a nice wife, too."

Steve watched his buddy stroking him, enjoying the masculine touch of the work-roughened fist that knew just how to pleasure a man, and the intimate, complete understanding the two men shared. He turned toward Brad and took his rising tool in his hand. It wasn't quite as large as his, but more than just a hefty handful. Steve was known far and wide for his "monster dick."

"Sometimes I like to nibble on a foreskin. Like now, for instance." He stirred himself to switch to a sixty-nine position. The bucolic atmosphere slowed all their actions; there was no hurry, noone to impress or dominate, only themselves to please and they knew exactly how to do it. The nearby horses occasionally snorted softly, but otherwise there was a sleepy silence in the valley.

Brad wasn't completely hard yet, so it was easy to pull down the almost transparent covering to cap the blossoming cockhead completely. The foreskin pouted, waiting for the man's tongue and lips to spread it and explore its creases. The cowboy watched as his buddy admired it and then set to service it.

The warm tongue-tip intruded on the opening and swirled inside it, teasing the piss-slit before searching deeper under the skin and around the cockhead. Steve thought he could still taste the sweet creek water bubbling from hidden springs, mixed with masculine flesh with all its potency. Brad squirmed and groaned as his buddy's worship brought them even closer together, but he merely watched, knowing that his turn would come. Then Steve, as he had promised, began to nibble on the loose covering, catching the sensitive tissues between upper teeth and tongue, and Brad's groans grew louder as his cock throbbed with increasing demand.

The power in that rigid rod transmitted itself to Steve's hand; the cockhead demanded it be acknowledged, serviced, soothed. Almost reluctantly Steve allowed it to assert itself. As he released it from its entrapment, the head burst forth, the pink velvet helmet thrusting into his mouth and diving for his throat to be swallowed up greedily, leaving sweet trails of precum over his lashing tongue. Both men groaned heartily, welcoming the invariable force inherent in that virile vertex symbolic of man's primeval potency. It was right for man to service man as a sharing of power and as love for that power, a direct connection, a blending of minds and bodies.

To perfect the union, Brad attacked Steve's cockhead with equal fervor. He lapped and tongued the broad, swollen head, so thick, so potent. Gratefully it loosed some of its precious juices to tease its worshipper, promising more. But it too needed its warm, moist haven, and quickly Brad's throat opened to receive it, pulsating there in its demanding mode, matching its counterpart as the men clutched together, sharing the ultimate intimacy only men can achieve.

"A pretty sight if ever I saw one."

The voice, husky and deep, seemed to come from a distance but still a part of their union. Both men looked up at the grinning native-American standing closely over them.

Even the horses had not signalled his arrival.

"Buck, you son-of-a-gun," Steve grunted. "How'd you sneak up on us like that?"

Buck's brilliant teeth shone through the mouth-slit of his ruddy face. "Stalkin' was always one of our successes, back when the white man was the minority," he said with a grunt. "How ya doin', Brad? It's been a while."

Steve and Brad sat up, their bobbing pricks temporarily abandoned but still insistent. They glanced at each other and then simultaneously seized a leg of the intruder.

"The rule of the house is, if you bust in on a scene you get to participate," Steve growled, beginning to pull off the new man's levi's. Buck didn't resist very much, but pretended to be shocked by the avarice of his friends. In a minute his pants were in a heap to one side and his lengthening cock was free for the taking.

Brad was admiring the merchandise. "Shit, it's been a long time since I swung on that meat," he recalled. "Get that shirt off so you're not so overdressed." Buck didn't resist that invitation either, and soon was sprawled, as naked as his buddies, between them. Steve and Brad began to work on the tawny, trim body with their tongues and lips, bringing him up to speed by nibbling his tits and working their way down his broad, hairless chest to the thick mat of wiry black hair at his crotch.

Buck moaned appreciatively, his arms around the shoulders of his buddies as they stoked his fires. "You guys haven't changed a bit—still horny as a stallion and built the same."

Brad and Steve shared the towering prick for a while, their tongues lapping, intertwining, and surrounding the pulsing shaft and slurping at the swelling cockhead. While Steve concentrated on the swelling and oozing head, Brad was slurping the heavy, hairy balls into his mouth, his tongue admiring their size and potency. Then they shifted roles; there was more than enough to go around for both of them.

Such dual attention brought a muscle-snapping rigidity to the long, lean body stretched out for their pleasure. Buck groped for his buddies' tools, gripping them hard as his own dick began to ooze.

"As usual, you palefaces are excludin' the poor Indian – I got nothin' to suck on!" he complained. "Come here, Brad – let me start on you!"

There was a moment of confusion and rearrangement, but an orderly daisy-chain was quickly developed, Buck on Brad, Brad returning to Steve's offering, and Steve reacquainting himself with the long, stiff prick of his neighboring rancher. Three cocks disappeared down as many throats, and three voices murmured their satisfaction with the triangular arrangement.

"Big prick–"

"Fuckin' pretty balls–"

"Sweet meat–"

The three mens' mouths worked swiftly, almost ferociously, their heads moving up and down, lips drawing and clasping, tongues darting and twisting, savoring the sweet pre-cum starting to leak from each overheated prod. Their fingers closed around the heavy balls that promised their nectar on demand.

Steve proceeded onward to caress Buck's rounded butt-globes, He had always loved that ass, and between those perfect buns. . . His finger teased, circled, and probed, and soon began to enter the channel he found. At first there was resistance, but eventually the muscles relaxed, seeming to welcome him into their inner sanctum. Buck moaned at the enhanced connection. As the digit entered he pushed against it, and then raised Brad's upper leg to expose his partner's portal, also.

"Oh, shit, yeah," Brad breathed as he felt the Indian's

tongue probing his asshole. "Gimme your ass, Steve! I want to eat your fuckin' asshole!"

No argument there. Steve raised his leg and began to tongue his partner's hole, the daisy-chain becoming a rear-guard action times 3. They began to stroke the cock closest to them as they devoured each other in their most intimate zones.

"Hot ass–"

"Sweet hole–"

"Rimmin' you out, man!"

There's nothing so sensual, so erotic as a man's asshole. Anyone who's licked it, lapped it, tongue-twirled it knows that. It's as critical as a woman's clitoris, or maybe a bit more. At least with the men in action here, a tongue probing there was tantamount to twisting the horns of a bull; the mighty was about to fall, or shoot, or cum, and there was no denying that.

Afraid he would miss the cascade, Steve shifted back to the throbbing dick in his hand, and the others followed suit. He replaced his tongue with his finger, shoved all the way in and pressing against that sensitive seat of passion inside. Already he could feel the gland swelling and tensing, and the pre-cum flooding his taste buds confirmed the imminence of the main event. Brad followed suit as did Buck, so the finger-fucking, cock-slurping contest was underway in all three rings.

All bars were down; the time for lazy loving was over. They gobbled the thick pricks avidly, their fingers moving ferociously, pressing and demanding the maximum from their fervent partners. They scaled the slopes of the valley surrounding them, their muscles locked in ardent coupling, and their rigid bodies melted together in one massive, sensual mating of animals built for power and bred for lust.

The crest came all too soon – up and over they soared, the forces bursting under pressure and spewing liquid gold into the welcoming recesses. Thick spurts of creamy nectar bathed hot and yearning mouths that gulped hungrily, voraciously for the virile essence boiling there. No one heard their groans of joy in that remote canyon except a lonely bird circling overhead. Controlled from within, their balls opened their gates and gave up their magic potion freely and lovingly in gushing pearls of love.

The men took it greedily, tasting the manhood they shared, until the flood diminished to a trickle. Eventually their need for air became uppermost and they pulled back, sighing, wishing for more. Gently they milked the softening shafts, catching another drop or two on their tongue, and sighed, smiling.

All was quiet again in the valley. The horses still grazed contentedly, the hawks still circled lazily, and the men lay together, entwined in peaceful comradeship. Finally Buck broke the silence.

"I could invite you to the ranch, but I suppose you guys will have to be getting back to the wives soon, eh?"

Steve cleared his throat, still a little breathless. "Yeah, I guess, although not too soon. We don't want to walk in before they're ready. If I know them, they are doin' some powerful pussy-lappin' right about now! The real event comes later. Why don't you bring your wife over after supper and join us?"

"Sounds like a good plan. I didn't even get a taste of your monster cock today, so I get first crack next time, OK?"

They knew there would be a next time, but that's another story.

COUNTRY CARRYINGS-ON

Reid Dennis

I live smack dab in the middle of nowhere, what my old junior college pals and gals would have called "Bum Fuck Egypt." Years ago I was the Big Man on Campus in what was the big city where I really had built up quite a reputation as a ladies' man.

But those were the good old days when I was a big city slicker. Now I'm a good ol' country boy. Let me explain. My employer, a computer company, transferred me to this one-horse hick town way out in the country, selling computers and software to a thriving, new market—wealthy but low-tech ranch owners wanting to get high-tech. Oh, sure, I was thrilled that my salary almost doubled, but it was at the expense of my sex life, which practically disappeared. I say practically, because one day something curious occurred, one of those milestone events that was to change my entire social situation.

Just days before that I had been sitting, planted on my usual bar stool at the only saloon in this one-horse town, bitching to the bartender that I couldn't seem to find any decent looking women and get to "lay some pipe" as I delicately put it. I was feeling starved for pussy and hornier than the damned horny toads that seemed to overrun this town. But then that fateful day.

It was just before dusk, and as was my thing now that I'd moved to the country, I was settin' out on my back porch watching the sun go down, whittling a dowel of wood, thinkin' 'bout how the wrist action was a whole lot like jacking off, getting hornier by the minute, and fixin' on going up to my bedroom loft, as usual, with my stack of dirty girlie magazines to see me through the night. But I just happened to look over next door at the farm and noticed the barn door was open. That wasn't surprising, considering the owner was probably too busy tending his cows to be responsible and shut the gawd damn door. I thought I'd be right neighborly and go over and shut it for him.

What *was* surprising, when I reached the door, was to peer through the door and see a particularly well built and handsome young dark-haired farmer-type, the fly of his overalls completely unbuttoned, with a big ol' boner plumb ready to pop out of his drawers, right there near the open door. "I noticed your barn door was open," I said, utterly embarrassed, greatly flustered and frantically trying to somehow make conversation, but unable to stifle a laugh at the accidental pun. He made no attempt to zip up but instead approached me with a big, shit-eatin' grin on his face. "Well, I guess ya better come in and close the barn door before the horse gets out," he said, slyly pulling the fly of his underwear open and allowing his huge horse-dick to fly out and stand upright like a fuckin' flagpole. "Whoops, too late, looks like the horse got free," he said, the grin getting all the bigger. "Think you can catch that stallion, podner? 'Cause if you rope it, you can ride it."

Well, of course my first reaction was to turn away in embarrassment at such an intimate sight, since it had been so long since I'd seen so long a dick, and hell, that was only in those girlie show skin-flicks I used to go see when I lived in the city – shit, it had been so long since I'd seen *any* genitals other than my own I was plumb sex-crazed; so my second thought was to just keep staring in sheer amazement and curiosity (and, let's face it – horniness).

"Go ahead and let your horse run free, too," the country cock-teaser coaxed. "I can see by that big bulge in your slacks that you're interested," he added, grabbing his hard pole and jerking it while slyly winking at me and then giving my crotch area a friendly pat. Well now, I up and panicked. No guy had ever done that to me, and I wanted to turn around and head straight for the hills with fear and shame, but the ranch dude was absolutely right, since by now my dick had totally betrayed me, forming a big ol' tent in my pants. There was no going back now, I decided, and considering the alternative – paper pussies in a bunch of dog-eared porn magazines back home – I took a deep breath, pulled down my zipper, anxiously reached into my fly, and fished out my rapidly stiffening cock. I gave it a few strokes to bring it to maximum length and hardness. "Shoot," I thought to myself, "there's no harm in a couple of studs getting off until we can find some cunt."

By now my "country cousin" had pushed the restraining denim straps from his shoulders, unbuttoned the overalls, and thrust them down to his ankles, revealing his massive, hairless chest, his smooth, flat belly, his firm, stocky legs liberally decked with dark hair, and (dare I even think about it?) his entire cock. The pink rays of the setting sun were dancing lasciviously over his big, bountiful, beautiful cock (I'd never thought of a dick as being beautiful before, but there it was – surprisingly enough a gorgeous sight to behold) which throbbed ever so slightly in the twilight's gleam, while the bullfrogs began croaking in the nearby pond and the crickets started rubbing their legs to signal the evening was upon us. Mother nature had given us a cloak of darkness, and I suddenly felt a special permission to just let go and sow my wild oats in the dusky shadows.

He must have felt the same country magic because all at once he pushed his pelvis forward and rotated his hips with a down-home, down and dirty movement so that his cock vibrated and his big ol' hairy bull balls slapped against the inside of his thighs. I got so fuckin' excited I almost lost it right then and there, shooting all over the barn! As it was, I was dripping long strings of pre-cum onto the ground. The hotter I got over this wild and wooly interaction, the bolder I became. Especially when he made motions for me to play with myself and then said right out loud, "Do it, you know you want to touch that thick prick of yours. Go ahead, guy. Do it."

That was all the permission I needed to drop my drawers. Even though it was downright daring and dangerous to be jacking off in the open right by the adjacent bunk house, baring all barely after dusk, and especially in front of another guy, I was in a kind of sexual trance—like those hypnotism tapes with frogs croaking and crickets chirping while the soft, low, throaty voice of the narrator encourages you to 'just relax and let go, let your mind wander and enjoy the surroundings and just let go.' But this was the real thing, not a studio-recorded sound effect, and all nature seemed to be telling me it was perfectly natural to feel so turned on at the sight of this hot, hunky guy.

"Now hold on a minute here," I again rationalized to myself. "You're not excited by this guy; no, it's just that you're both horny and there's no broads around." So I just willingly obeyed his command, proudly playing with my pecker. All the while he was unabashedly yanking on his own big, hard, dripping tool, and then he started going on about what a nice piece of meat I had and what he wanted to do with it. God, I was so fuckin' hot and bothered, I'm tellin' ya I just about creamed right out there in the open. And I had to admit to myself that I was fantasizing not about chicks but dicks—in particular this ranch boy's bodacious boner.

Now what the hell was I, always a het before, doing getting so het up over a homo? Why was I all jacked up about another man jacking off? What was so hard core about his hard-on? I was beginning to talk myself out of my sexual reverie, starting to come out of my trance and pull up my pants, but damn if those frog and cricket sounds didn't get louder and louder and I just got looser and looser (well, I needed some kind of excuse, didn't I?). Suddenly it just didn't seem to matter any more, so that all at once, what the fuck, dropping the pretense and ignoring all sense of propriety, my only thought became this obsession to get as close as humanly possible to this hot, fuckin' farmboy, thrusting my body smack against his, two male bodies (yes, MALE, damn it all!) pressed together, all the while frantically pulling my pud to the same beat of his beating off.

He whispered in my ear, "My name is Chet, and I'm shore glad to meet ya!" I hugged him closer but chose to remain anonymous, replying, "Me too, Chet," revelling in the virgin sensory experience of feeling and smelling two men locked in sweaty embrace. In the midst of all this sexual near-oblivion, something caught my eye. I glanced over to the little ranchhouse on the other side of Chet's and saw, much to my shock and amazement, someone's curtains moving slightly aside as a pair of prurient eyes peered out at our illicit goings-on.

My first reaction was to pull up my pants and skedaddle, but, when I told him what I had seen, Chet assured me there was nothing to "worry your li'l old head about," while stroking my body in a calming, soothing, oh so sexy manner. Meanwhile the mysterious figure behind the curtains next door became increasingly bolder to periodically, briefly reveal himself in the window touching his upper thigh with his big, brawny hands and slowly travelling up to the burgeoning crotch of his longjohns, then he'd dart back out of view for a while, then give a momentary teasing glimpse of his body while caressing it invitingly, but again retreating and finally getting so bold as to begin stroking his massive cock beneath his union suit for a moment. When he knew we were hooked, he coyly disappeared, only to soon reappear with his prized prick proudly displayed poking through the fly. At last the figure abandoned all pretended attempts of propriety, dramatically pulling the curtains back and the long underwear open completely to display his very hairy, nearly nude body. He was so furry I thought of him as a big ol' country bear like you see in those nature films; well, more like a polar bear with all that light blond, almost snow-white fur. He was probably in his early thirties, and by now his longjohns were gaping widely and hanging off his body, topped off by a ten-gallon hat with a ten-inch (at least by my rough estimate) hard-on.

I would have paid more attention to that wondrous window show, were it not for the fact that my pal Chet had now dropped to his knees, worshipping my rod with gentle tongue laps carefully applied to the swollen mushroom head of my throbbing cock. I thought I'd go out of my mind! My heart was racing, my dick was pulsating, and my nuts were leaping in their sacks. My God, it felt incredible. Every hair on my body stood erect. Never ever had I felt such tingly, goose-bumpy, crazy-making sensations. His warm mouth engulfed the swollen head of my cock and gobbled down the free-flowing pre-cum. No woman had ever done me so well, that's for sure. And the frog and cricket chorus in the background seemed to say, "What do you need a female for?"

So with just a very little coaxing of my hands cradling his head and pulling ever so slightly, the country wonder swallowed my big cock right down to the wiry hairs of my crotch and sucked for dear life. I'd never been so deep into a mouth before! I was in heaven!! Then he reached down to his own tool and began whacking the sucker off, at first slowly, then a mite faster, and then in a sudden, stepped-up frenzy of full-tilt hand-frigging. I could tell that he was about to blow his load, so I sped up my face-fucking action in time to simultaneously send my steaming ejaculate shooting out my prick right down Chet's warm and willing throat, load after load of cooped-up cum. He eagerly gobbled down every drop, gagging slightly on the huge payload, and quickly followed my shot with his series of ribbons of hot, thick, white man-cream streaming out his pulsating dick, landing on the hay-strewn ground below.

I almost passed out panting, but recovered enough to pull

out from his mouth eventually and pull myself together, shaking the last bit of dew from my dick and fully expecting the sex to be over and done with. I mean, what could possibly top such sheer ecstasy? I never had such a pull-out-the-stops orgasm in all my citified days of boinking the broads, and lately my country sojourn had become, up until now, a sad tale of unwilling celibacy. Jeez, I felt I could die and go to heaven now, except for the fact that I'd already been to heaven in Chet's mouth!

But to my surprise, that cowboy country bear voyeur, having watched our whole scene intently from his window, motioned for us to come next door. I had thought I was satisfied with my manly encounter with Chet, but suddenly country bear's offer sounded somewhat tantalizing, my having decided by now that man-to-man sex was at least one way to go. And I also realized I was by no means satiated at that point (in fact I was amazingly even hornier than when I first spied that provincial but prodigious pecker poking out from behind Chet's neighbor's curtains). I nodded in agreement, asking Chet, my cock-sucker cohort, if he wanted to join us. "Oh hell, that's jus' Jake, the hired hand, and he's shorely got the best hand in town; so, yeah, let's go, guy." Moments later we stood at the blond bear's lair, pulling the little leather thong at his front door to engage the clapper on the cowbell, immediately hearing his deep voice boom out from behind the door, "Come on in." Coming. It was precisely what I had in mind.

No longer sporting his cowboy hat but still wearing those sexy long-johns and a pair of scuffed-up Tony Lamas, he introduced himself as Jake as he slammed the door behind us. I saw that he was even more good-looking up close. His body was hefty yet toned, just what you'd expect of a hard-working, hard-loving ranch-hand. You could tell he got that muscular build pitching hay, putting up fences, dogging dogies and futzing around the farm, but certainly not hanging out with the yuppies and guppies in a gym doing free weights (yeah, right—like they even HAD a gym in this cow town).

Jake had emerald green eyes framed by heavy sun-bleached eyebrows and eyelashes, accented by his golden mustache and sandy blond hair. There was a thick blond carpet covering just about all his sun-bronzed upper body and arms, and the top part of his chest and up the neck to his Adam's apple was even more hirsute. The blond hairs on his tanned legs and arms were bleached almost white from the sun, and the tan line indicated that he must have been working long days in the fields in nothing but very, very short cut-off jeans—his covered crotch a thick bush of light brown pubes, un-bleached, untouched by the sun, and the flesh of his unexposed pubic area a pure, porcelain white. His mammoth cock stuck out and up at a sharp angle, beckoning us to his body; we naturally complied, and as he hugged our three bodies close together, I felt his hard dick digging into my belly. I opened my shirt for more intimate contact.

"Why don't we all get nekkid?" the blond bear drawled, as he quickly undid my slacks and removed my shirt. Chet, my country fuck-buddy, gladly following suit, shedding his denim skin, so our three bodies could better press together firmly, unhindered by clothing. The sensuous feel of the cotton material being peeled from my skin while Jake's and Chet's firm flesh crushed against mine gave me a gradually stiffer and stiffer cock. As I lifted my arms so Jake could pull the shirt over my head, he tongued my armpit with long, slow strokes, gently biting on the pit hairs and playfully nuzzling my underarm with his knowing nose. Then he made a path with his hot, wet tongue, traveling from under my arms to the center of my chest, randomly nipping on my chest hairs and then settling on a nipple, rolling it softly between his teeth and sucking on it until it was fully hard and erect in his mouth.

By now my pecker was raging hard and throbbing, which he immediately noticed.

"Hey, looks like your ol' tits are connected right to your dadburned cock," he pointed out. "I better take care of that big ol' boner for ya." Jake sank down to his knees, furiously lapping at the head of my dripping wet, rock-hard cock, mixing his hot saliva with the sticky pre-cum on my distended dickhead.

"Ohhhhhhhmigod," I moaned as this expert, muthafucking, cocksucking cowhand skillfully swirled my big, throbbing, purple head inside his talented and very moist mouth. Even better than Chet! But it just made me all the greedier for his deep throat. I begged, "Can you take any more, cowboy? Come on, I know you can," while Chet looked on, choking his chicken like crazy, puffing and panting and jacking up a storm.

Blond bear responded to my plea by plunging his mouth all the way down the trembling shaft right to my bush, gobbling up every last inch of my grateful cock and intermingling his light blond mustache hairs with my dark brown crotch fur. While my prick was totally buried in his hot mouth all the way to his tonsils, he began alternately contracting-loosening-contracting his throat muscles to give a marvelous effect, like he must have learned milking Old Bossy the cow, except this was his hot mouth instead of his steady hands, and the cream he was going for was not the bovine variety. Whatever he was doing was absolutely driving me fucking mad, and it obviously had a similar effect on Chet, who was watching enraptured while practically pulling his pud right off.

"Go, Chet, go!" I cheered and then began pumping big bear's mouth faster and faster until I could fairly feel the cum welling up in my heavy balls and getting ready to spurt. Could I cum a second time so soon? It sure felt like it! And Jake could tell I was teetering right on the edge, so to send me over, he reached up and grabbed both my stiffened tits with his rough fingers, pinching them until I started shaking uncontrollably and shooting what felt like about a gallon of hot jism down his thirsty throat. I looked down in the midst of my sexual daze and noticed that Jake was cumming right along with me, and although he never took his mouth from my cock or his hands from my nipples, his swollen dick was pumping out stream after stream of thick, white spunk, spraying his grade A country cream, shooting up to my crotch and then dripping down my legs. Chet seemed utterly mesmerized but unwilling to squirt his contribution just yet.

We three finally collapsed in an exhausted but satisfied clump on the floor, the musty smells of man-sex and farm animals crudely but somehow appealingly intermingling. About twenty minutes of this utter bliss passed as we lay there contentedly wrapped in each other's warm embrace. I thought there could be no possible better feeling, until Jake tapped my shoulder and brought me out of my reverie. "Hey, are you up for something really kinky?" he asked.

"What in the world could be kinkier than this?" I wondered to myself, having just completed my very first sexual experience with not one but two other men – two very hot country fuckin' folks. I looked over at Chet, whose excited eyes signalled approval. I accordingly replied in the affirmative, trusting my new farmer fuck-buddy, and Jake suggested we all move out to the back porch for the last of the twilight sun. It may have been too late for some afternoon delight, but a little early evening friskiness on the farmland was evidently in order.

"What? Out there in plain view?" I questioned his ultra-bold attitude. "Where all the ranch-hands bunking across the way can see us?"

"Well, shore, why not?" Jake said with this hard-to-resist country boy innocence. "We three were pretty dang open when we were carryin' on in front of the glass doors of my ranch house and, well, heck, you musta seen all them eyes a-staring and a-watching us from the bunk house out back, so just think of what we'll attract when the three of us are out there on the back porch in full view of a bunch of horny country boys, making wild and woolly love together? Come on, now, don't ya wanna sorta show it off for them?"

I must say I was pretty shocked. I had naively assumed our three-way was only between us three, and during the heat of our encounter I was just completely unaware of that window which Jake or Chet must have exposed by pulling back the curtains; I honestly had no idea there were additional onlookers at our orgy. But I had to admit, Jake was definitely appealing to my newly developed, prurient exhibitionistic tendencies. That and a shot of Jake's homemade zillion-proof white lightning loosened me up a bit. "Ahhh, hell, you're on!" I finally piped up. "But we're still staying inside."

We started out with kind of an appetizer, as I described it, before the main course was to be served to our naughty neighbors' feasting eyes. We stood in front of the chintz-curtained sliding glass doors that opened out onto the porch. We three passionately kissed in front of the tightly drawn curtains (closed at my request, since I wasn't quite ready for that much openness just yet) which Jake had made sure were properly backlit by a kerosene lantern to provide a teasing, tantalizing sexual silhouette for all the voyeurs outside, as the sun was now completely set and the sky was at its very darkest. We got into deeper kissing, roughly hugged, smacked butts and rubbed right up against one another as the flickering flame from the oil lamp projected our sexy shadow show against the flimsy curtains.

Eventually Jake pulled the cord to draw the thin material back – as if we were on stage and the curtain was now going up. Sure enough, we could see drapes and blinds starting to move and open across the way in the bunk house. I made a mental note that I was in fact in no way the only horny guy in this countryside. To my delight our audience appeared to be ready and eager for the coming performance. I even spied a few binoculars trained on our "stage." I was amazed at the sophistication of what I once mistakenly labeled a hick town. Well, at least it was sexually sophisticated. Correction: these were gen-u-ine, full-fledged, all-out voyeurs and exhibitionists, with no holds barred! So what if this was out in the sticks?! These were hip, fuckin' hicks!!!

At his suggestion, I slipped into a pair of Jake's brown pigskin cowboy chaps. Then Jake pulled off Chet's overalls while Chet removed Jake's longjohns. We three were standing against the glass of the exposed doors, mostly naked with raging hard-ons throbbing and getting all the harder just knowing that we were being watched so intently by this captivated country congregation. Chet bent over and mouthed my cock, wetting it down real good, so I could then rub my slippery dick up and down the pane of glass, smearing it all over and leaving sexy little trails of pre-cum and spit.

Those two big pricks pointed at me by my new buddies started to get the better of me. Should I do it, give in to the ultimate urges that were buzzing in my brain? Again the country magic goaded me on. I got down on my knees and tasted Jake's monster meat.

It was the first time I'd had a cock in my mouth. My God, what a sensation! It felt so strange and yet somehow so natural. That big, thick, warm shaft lodged in my mouth, resting between the roof of my mouth and my tongue and growing even larger inside me. His cock was coated with dried cum from that last session, tasting slightly salty with a musty, heady scent that drove me wild. I wanted to just suck his prong all night long, but he suddenly pulled away, turned around and pressed the front of his body against the glass, reaching around behind him and opening up his blessed buttcheeks for me.

Well, I sure didn't need an engraved invitation! I got right up off my knees and leaned against him – my hard, wet cock twitching anxiously at his hot hole. I'd never been in an asshole before but I was sure willing to try this new experience on top of all the other firsts I'd had that day. He spread his legs wide apart and my slippery dick slithered right into his willing and ready ass, while Chet slapped us both on the butts. Jake and I just stayed in that heavenly position, my dickhead squeezed and held tight by Jake's trembling sphincter muscle, and we gazed out the window to see venetian blinds rattling like crazy as guys stared from across the way in that bunk house. We could even see a few dudes working on their dicks, which just spurred us all on even more.

I felt my ramrod growing bigger inside Jake and inched it deeper and deeper into him, until I had reached as far as I could go, my nuts to his butt. His bare bear ass. Then I very, very slowly pulled back and out so I could feel the walls of his ass tightly gripping my cock on the way out. He reached around for my dick and pulled it right back into his hungry hole. I got the message all right. He wanted me to stay inside him. My reply was: "No problem, my blond bear buddy."

I immediately plunged my slick, stiff dick right back into his hot, wet, wriggling, tight ass, and then started ramming it home, back and forth, hot and heavy, in and out, faster and faster, over and over. With each slam into him, he bumped against the glass door and his slick and quivering prick slammed up against the glass pane, "painting" strokes of pre-cum like an artist would on a canvas – only his stiff brush was far sexier than any available at an art supply store. And let me assure you this was no Norman Rockwell American-family kind of painting!

Meanwhile Chet was licking any and all organs and orifices available, spurring us all on in our unbridled lust. Mid-fuck,

I glanced out the window to see every one of the bunk house windows with blinds now fully open, the ranch hands' hands jacking off their cocks or else frantically pumping their buddies' excited pricks while I pumped Jake with an equal enthusiasm and Chet kept licking and jacking and puffing and panting. The thought of all this totally open sexuality right out there in this god-forsaken, bum-fuck bumpkin countryside only drove me into more of a frenzy, and I picked up speed to fuck Jake double-time, poking this cowpoke with my fuckpole.

His body was literally quivering against the glass pane when I heard him shout out loud in a long, sustained shout: "Ohhhhhhhhhhhhhhh . . . unhhhhhhhhhhhhhhhh . . . ahhhhhhhhhhhh . . . jeeeeeeeeeesus!!!" The inner walls of his ass quivered around my cock; he was bearing down on my dick with his asscheeks, pulling me tighter and tighter inside him, with his throbbing cock, pressed firmly against the glass doors, squirting out jets of jism that shot right up to the top of the sliding glass doors, stuck there momentarily, and then dribbled down in long, thin, white rivulets. Chet slurped them up while adding his own hot cum to the glass. I could just imagine the reaction of our audience, and although they may not have been applauding our performance, they were sure busy clapping those hands over cocks and balls in avid appreciation of the sexy show before them. I slid out of Jake's ass, still stiff and wanting more. I collapsed on the floor, my dick pointing at the moon that was now drenching the farmyard.

Chet knelt over me and kissed me deeply with that stubbly chin that was beginning to turn me on. Although I couldn't see him, Jake was cleaning my throbbing dick with warm, wet cloths, or was it his mouth that kept me up there?

Sliding the glass doors open, Chet and Jake pulled me erect again and took me by the hand (and prick) to lead me outside. I protested but they kept pulling me by my dick out to the porch and told me to get into a sixty-nine position, dragging a bed roll out and laying it beneath us. Sure enough, as soon as Chet lowered his soft, fat pecker into my mouth and I tasted that salty, musky, slippery cock of his between my lips, I felt my slumping peter once again stiffen. Chet took it into his mouth and just sucked on that mushroom head until it began to really throb. His cock was now stiff and thick inside my mouth, so I sucked furiously on his dick, bobbing my mouth quickly up and down while he worked on me underneath.

It was the first time I had sixty-nined with a man and it was yet another new and delightful sexual sensation for me – having the double treat of feeling his expert mouthmanship on my grateful dick while my lips were clenched around his throbbing rod. The more he sucked on me, the more turned on I got to suck him back even better, and the cycle continued until we were both engaged in this wild, crazy race to make the other come first. And now it was Jake's turn to watch and whack off. The way Chet was puffing and panting and squirming below me, I could have sworn I would win the cumming contest.

But then Chet took unfair advantage of me. He had already earlier discovered the magic, invisible connection running from my nipples to my cock, the ability to render me totally in someone's power by just simultaneously tweaking my tits while sucking my dick into a harder, longer, fatter state than before. So before I knew it, I felt Chet's rough hands brushing against my belly and making their way up my stomach toward my chest, where they began making large circles around my pectoral muscles; finally both hands landed, one on each tit, at first gently pinching each nipple but then pressing harder and harder. All this was happening at the same time that his lips increased pressure on my cock as I dipped it in and out of his mouth like an oil derrick. At last he craned his neck up and swallowed me whole, right to the base, sucking with a vacuum-like action until I could feel my nuts tingling with anticipation.

By now I had become quite familiar with the signs of oncoming orgasm and I knew it was just about all over now. I had lost the "contest" – but so what? I gave up willingly and let the cum shoot out of my cock like a cannonball fired from a cannon. As his mouth filled and overflowed with the last of my warm jizz, his own engorged dick suddenly exploded into my mouth and erupted hot, molten lava of cum right to the very back of my throat. And the whole time country Joe (Jake, oh, whatever the hell his name was–I was too far gone by now to observe such formalities) was frantically jerking his gherkin until he shot a major meteor shower of sperm all over the two of us.

Completely weak from sexual satiety and unable to stay with Chet any longer, I collapsed, falling to his side, and he rolled into my arms. We were both absolutely exhausted and didn't even have the energy to speak, but Jake tapped my shoulder and pointed out a sight I will never forget. Every one of the rustic, peering neighbors had by now come out onto their balconies or just hung out their windows, all ecstatically releasing their pent-up loads in unison–a sort of standing, shooting ovation for our show. We three heartily laughed loudly as we realized that Jake, Chet and I had offered some cultural (well – sexual) entertainment to the cowboys out in the sticks, relieving all our poor neighbors' sexual tensions at once while providing some rather stimulating, shall we say, outdoor country theater. And at the same time this ol' city boy had been initiated into the magical world of male-male sex in the country!

Next time maybe we could include a few of those other cowboys. . .

CAVE BEAR !

Lee Dennegar

I found the cave on the third day of my solo hiking vacation. I'm not going to tell you where it is, but somewhere in one of our larger National Parks a limestone cliff rises above a secluded mountain lake. Above and below the layer of limestone are harder rocks, so the erosion of the softer limestone has produced a kind of roofed shelf. It's semicircular in floor plan, and as you go toward the back the floor rises and the roof descends until they meet. It's sort of like a giant clam shell cut vertically in half.

The front edge of this rock shelter forms a cliff and is a spectacular place to dive from. The way the base rock slopes backwards produces a deep pool perfectly safe for diving. A nearby slope makes it easy to climb back up and dive again. In spite of the fact that the summer heat had prompted me to remove my shirt long before, I was covered with sweat, so I shucked my boots and cutoffs and dived right in. The surface layer of water had been heated by the sun, but the depths were still icy as a mountain spring. As I swam, I stirred up alternating waves of luxurious warmth and bracing cold. It was like the ice-cold plunge after a sauna, repeated again and again.

When I felt refreshed, I lay for a while on the edge of the cliff in the sun. I was enjoying the prickly, tickling feeling you get when wet chest hairs that have been plastered to your skin slowly dry and spring upright, when I noticed the opening in the back wall. It was too dark and deep to be a mere niche in the rock, so I decided to investigate. I squeezed the last of the water from my beard and went to see what exactly it was.

Sure enough, an honest-to-God natural tunnel followed the slight upward slope of the underlying bedrock into the hillside. It was relatively straight, so the daylight lasted a while, but it did get gradually darker. Then the floor levelled off and got wetter too. I was just about to go back and get my boots and the flashlight from my backpack, when I stubbed my bare toe on a rock. I pitched forward on my face into muddy clay, and to my horror, found myself sliding face first down a steep slope, deeper into the cave.

The clay was slick as axle grease and I could catch nothing solid to hold on to. I picked up speed, descending into pitch-black darkness, until I shot off the edge of a cliff into empty space. I thought I was done for. I vividly imagined a forest of jagged rocks waiting for me below in the darkness. When instead of being crushed to atoms, I plunged into a deep pool of icy water, my relief amounted to shock.

When I could think again, I reasoned that I must have fallen into a pool linked by a subterranean connection to the lake outside. This underground lake had broken my fall and saved my life. I was shaken, but unhurt. Now all I had to do was get out.

That wasn't easy to do in complete darkness. I picked a direction at random, and swam slowly forward. After a while, my hand struck what seemed to be a sheer rock wall that arched backwards over my head. I couldn't find any hand- or foot-holds at all. There was no way up from here. Treading water, I moved to my right, following the wall as it curved around the perimeter of the pool. I had no idea how large the pool was and couldn't tell if I was going in circles, but what else could I do? I was not about to try to find the underwater passage out to the lake. Even if it were large enough to enter, it had to be much too far to swim on one breath. If I were going to get out, I'd have to walk, not swim.

I tried not to think of what would happen if I were at the bottom of a smooth, unclimbable well. I'd found no place shallow enough to stand up in. If I couldn't get out, sooner or later I'd tire and drown. I was on the brink of panic when the vertical wall began to recede, and my feet squished into a sloping floor of mud.

With trembling knees, I ascended this underground mudbank and collapsed onto my back, staring up into the impenetrable blackness above me. The mud was cold and slimy but it felt like heaven to me. I struggled to catch my breath, and to stop shaking with cold and fear.

When I felt a bit more confident, I began to search for a way out. Afraid to stand up in case the blackness concealed a low ceiling, I crawled on hands and knees. The muddy beach continued to rise slowly, but I found no sign of a wall. I tried shouting, and sure enough, the echo was that of a very large space. I was glad because I wasn't trapped yet, but as the last of the echoes slowly died, I realized with a sinking feeling in my chest how very alone I was. The distance I had travelled into the hillside guaranteed that no one in the sunlit world outside could possibly hear me, even if there were anyone out there in the wilderness to begin with.

I clamped down on that depressing train of thought before it could go very far. Concentrate on the positive, I told myself. You're in a large cavern; in such a large chamber, there has to be a passage leading upward. All you have to do is find it.

I didn't get a chance. Out of nowhere, a darker-than-dark blackness fell on me, smashing me face down into the mud. I let out a yell of pure terror. It wasn't a rockslide; it seemed to be some kind of animal, and it was furiously strong. It flipped me on my back and lay on top of me, pinning me into the muddy floor of the cave. I could feel coarse fur against my skin and hot breath against my face. Images of prehistoric cave bears flashed through my mind. I'd been a heavyweight wrestler in school, but I couldn't even move beneath the crushing weight and incredible strength of my invisible attacker.

My fear turned to shock when I felt the creature grope between my legs and grab hold of my balls. Fear and cold water had shrunk them up in their sack; this invisible attacker was forcibly yanking them back down. It was painful at first, but then it started feeling terrific. I was much too scared to feel sexy, but my cock had different ideas. I could feel it stirring to life between my legs.

In my struggles to free myself, my hands began to provide

me with a mental picture of my assailant. It was shaped pretty much like a man, but it was huge. I'm six foot four and two hundred forty, but this hulk seemed twice my size. Long coarse hair hung past its shoulders, and its face was covered in bristly, wiry hair. Its whole body was covered with coarse hair thicker that what I had on my own chest. Its forearms and even its biceps were furry. Its ass felt like a two muscular bowling balls in a raccoon coat. The body hair was so thick I couldn't believe it was human. Maybe it was a bear after all.

Whatever it was, it was turning me on in spite of myself. The way it was squeezing and crushing my balls in its powerful paw made my flaccid dick stiffen of its own accord, and slowly the last of my fear was overwhelmed by arousal. Apparently, this beast had something besides dinner on its mind.

When it felt my prick responding, the cave beast shifted its head down to my crotch and slurped up my dick in its mouth. Its hot, juicy mouth slurped on my schlong hungrily. It took my roaring erection down its throat without hesitation, and sealed its throat muscles around the shaft. Then it tried to inhale my cock, creating a powerful vacuum around it. The beast alternately blew and sucked, so my cock alternately expanded and relaxed with the changes in pressure. It was like a living vacuum pump.

Without letting go of my cock, the enormous mass of hairy flesh shifted until I felt its crotch covering my face. A fur-covered scrotum the size of a softball dangled over my mouth, and a funky, animal-like smell of stale crotchsweat filled my nostrils. Trembling with fear, I stuck out my tongue and touched the tip to the hairy nutbag. I expected a certain amount of raunch, but not the clumps of moist clay that clung to the coarse ballhairs. I licked these off and spit them out as best I could. Then I sucked one of the huge nuts into my mouth and wet down the dense, bushy nutfur with my spit.

The beast on top of me gave a deep bass moan of appreciation that echoed through the cavern like a small earthquake, but after a while it grunted impatiently at me. From its urgent hip-bucking, it seemed to be urging me to suck its other ball. I had to let the first one go; they were too big to do at once. But that did not please the beast. It growled menacingly and pressed its razor-sharp teeth to my cock in warning. Frantically I sucked as hard as I could while using both hands to cram the entire huge, hairy scrotum into my mouth.

Finally I made it. Both of the enormous beastballs were inside me. I could hardly breathe around them, but I kept sucking. I was not about to antagonize this powerful creature that had the power to bite off my prick in an instant. I was shaking like a leaf, but I couldn't tell whether it was fear or lust that was electrifying me.

The monster seemed to be satisfied for the time being. It pulled its mouth off my cock and sucked my own nuts into its hairy face. It worked them forcefully around in its mouth and stretched them painfully far from my body. When my balls were thoroughly stretched out, the hungry monster actually swallowed them. I felt throat muscles contract repeatedly as they attempted to send my nuts down to the voracious animal's gut.

The brute rocked me back and forth until it could get both beefy, furry arms around my waist. It pulled my butt out of the mud with an obscene sucking sound, and to my amazement, stood up with me still clasped tightly to its hairy, muddy body. I was upside down in midair with an enormous animal's testicles stuffed in my face and my own balls literally down the beast's throat. The powerful monster lumbered forward through the knee-deep mud until I was pressed against a cold stone wall, pinned there by its massive, furry belly. I continued to clamp my lips around its balls, holding on for dear life. It sucked my nuts even harder, then let go of my waist. It grabbed my arms and pulled them from around its own waist as well, holding them immobile with its huge hairy paws. I was hanging upside down with no connection at all but the mouth-holds we had on each other's fucking balls!

The big, hairy brute crushed me even harder against the

rocky wall, but then it released my balls. Immediately, its tongue entered my asshole. I could feel the thick, bristly face hair scratching my asscheeks as it noisily ate me out. It made loud slurping sounds and contented growling noises as it reamed out my shithole. It sealed its lips around my bunghole and gave me the vacuum treatment again, then blew its hot, steamy breath into my ass. Its tongue was so far up inside me I discovered that it's possible for a rectum to be ticklish.

Then it pulled its face away and I could feel its fingertips at my hole. When it roughly shoved one finger in me, I cried out in agony. Its one hairy finger was thicker than most men's cocks! While it was screwing this tremendous digit into my shithole, it pulled its ballsack out of my mouth, but the pressure of its furry belly kept me pinned to the wall. I sucked air greedily into my screaming lungs as spit drooled helplessly out of my inverted mouth.

I didn't have long to catch my breath before it pressed its cock against my face. I grasped the animal's huge schlong with both hands. Shit, it was fucking enormous! It was so thick I couldn't even close my fingers around it. When I slid my hands to explore its length, I could feel that like the rest of him, it was hairy as hell! My God, I thought, it's even got hair on its fucking prick! What kind of animal is it?

The beast was thrusting its massive hips insistently. The blunt, wet tip of its schlong pried my lips open, then invaded my overstretched mouth. The huge, foreskin-sheathed head alone filled my mouth completely; there was still more than a foot to go! Before it was too late, I filled my lungs to the maximum.

I was overstuffed as the enormous hunk of flesh impaled me. It felt like an organic baseball bat was being shoved down my esophagus by force. I could feel my neck bulging as the bulky meat stretched out my throat. In one slow, powerful thrust, the huge beastcock plowed all the way into me.

Once the enormous cock was all the way in me, and the huge hairy beastballs were pressed against my face, the bestial rapist started getting more and more excited. It pumped its furry hips violently, driving its huge hairy cock in and out of me in a fury of lust. With every powerful stroke, my head bounced off the rocky wall. There was no escape from the brutal mouthrape. All the time it was raping my face, the starving animal was gobbling my own stiff cock ferociously.

I don't know how much time went by, but finally the man-beast stopped its assault. Wrapping its arms around me again, it backed off from the wall of the cave. The Herculean beast carried me, still upside down, through the blackness. If my mouth hadn't been full of its rock-hard prick, I would have screamed as, for the second time today, I found myself falling blindly through space.

I hadn't fallen far before I landed on my back, with the huge weight of my bestial rapist slamming down on top of me. Fortunately, the surface I fell on was soft. It felt like a fur blanket spread over several feet of straw. Now that we were in a more secure position, the beast could redouble its attack. Its massive hips slammed down on me as it ruthlessly rammed its bearcock down my throat. The creature's massive hairy bulk slammed into me repeatedly as its enormous cock reamed me out like a clogged sewer.

I was getting seriously short of oxygen. Multi-colored points of light seemed to float through the inky blackness. I felt like I was floating in space, and I thought I was going to pass out. At the last minute, I felt the enormous schlong slithering out of my ravaged throat.

I gasped and wheezed gratefully once the monster obstruction was withdrawn. I was so relieved I didn't even wonder what the brute had in mind for me next. I found out. Two powerful paws gripped my ankles, and hauled them into the air. I felt a hot, moist pressure in my buttcrack as its hairy bearcock searched for my hole. I tried to relax my sphincter to ease the pain I knew was coming, but strangely, I felt no fear. I was too dizzy and too relieved that I was no longer suffocating to even care.

Even so, the pain was profound. I expected the entry to hurt and it did. What I didn't expect was that every inch of the furious penetration would hurt so much. It was a tearing, ripping feeling, and it was powerful and prolonged. My screams echoed throughout the cave, and once again, I thought I was going to faint. The beast drove its meat into me in one long, slow, but brutal shove. The pressure it exerted against my resisting ass threatened to break my spine. I could feel my guts being pushed up into my chest as my bowels were distended by this mutant monster meat.

Finally the gigantic cock was in to the root. I felt a sensation like steel wool as a pubic forest pressed against my asscheeks. Then it was gone as half a foot or so of bearprick withdrew from my shitter. Slam! It crashed back into me like a Mack truck. Another slow withdrawal, and Bam! An enormous weight slammed me into the silky fur rug. A mouth surrounded by coarse bristles smothered mine in a furious slurping kiss, and I felt sharp teeth chewing on my lips. Sour-tasting drool dripped into my mouth, choking me, but powerful arms kept me immobile. I could not escape from the beast's crushing, muddy, reeking, raping embrace.

Every time its massive body smashed into me, I felt the thick fur on its chest and belly being crushed flat between us, and wet clay mud squeezed out. The movement of its hips made its scratchy pubes stroke my cock with every cruel impalement. It was like being jerked off by a giant Brillo pad while there was a phone pole up your ass!

The darkness and the violence of the assault had me totally disoriented. I no longer knew which way was up, where I was, nor what was happening to me. All I knew was that my body felt like nothing on earth. My head was whirling; I felt dizzily drunk. Then I was floating weightlessly in an infinite black void, lightyears from Earth. And the whole time, this huge piece of beastmeat was sawing in and out of my ass. I've been fucked before, but I had no idea it was possible to feel like this and live!

The entire cosmos contracted to a tiny point inside my balls, and exploded outward again. It felt like someone was pulling a string of sausages out of my dick as what seemed a gallon of thick, viscous semen blasted out of me and saturated my own body. I could feel it dripping off my stomach and into my armpits. There was enough spunk to completely cover both of us. The feel of the beast's chest went from muddy but still scratchy fur to something like a sponge soaked in cream. Obscene squishing noises echoed through the cave as pounding fuckthrusts squirted my sperm out into the darkness.

The living mountain raping me had long been grunting like a locomotive in heat. Now its grunts became growls, growls became roars. Finally, it bellowed, like a thousand contrabass wolves cannonading off the stone walls. The incredible noise shook me like an earthquake. I swear to you I actually felt the monster's already-huge cock expand before it blasted its scalding, slimy, sloppy beast-spunk into me. I felt it blast an almost solid slug of semen up my digestive canal, and I felt more animal-cum seeping backwards past the thick plug of hard hairy flesh in my ass until it oozed out and dripped slimily off my upturned butt.

Slowly my mind came back to earth, but I was still so high that when the beast removed its enormous prong from my ass, it didn't hurt a bit. The beast crashed down next to me, panting, one massive, hairy forelimb across my heaving chest.

We lay like that for I don't know how long. I could have been underground for days as far as I could tell. I felt more dreamily satisfied than any sex had ever made me before, but still that nagging question was bugging me: what was the thing that had so satisfyingly raped me?

My question was answered when an ultra-deep bass rumble came out of the blackness. "I hope you enjoyed that as much as I did."

PENDULUM

Bill Lee

From a novel in progress.

Randolph II came home from college during spring break that year and did not return.

Even as he climbed the broad, white steps and passed between the ornate columns to the front door, he began to feel the cobwebs growing and closing around his feet like silver strands of intricate design, lions' claws and paired, pendulous peaches intermingled in chain links, half-forgotten remnants of repetitive dreams. Peeled white paint chips had collected on the floor of the veranda from the columns and the walls of the mansion. At the door he hesitated and then swung around, gazing through the towering elms and sycamores that bordered the sweeping driveway, as if reviewing what he had left behind and listening for the sounds of another world which still resonated in his brain. The massive shadow of his father's house almost reached the gargoyle fountain now nearly choked with ignored leaves from last year's autumn. Nothing moved on the distant highway. No motors or telephones or clicks of computer keys would dare to interrupt his father's rustic isolation.

He had not been older than ten or eleven when he had helped his fragile mother plant the border of rhododendrons now dropping ruby petals from blooms past their prime. The scrawny branches seemed to beg for succor, perhaps a more appropriate setting; their planting had been another example of his mother's failures to adjust to the way things must be. The box hedge at the edge of the driveway seemed healthy enough, although those bushes were generations old.

Green shoots of new grass were peering through the old growth of lawn left uncut the previous fall. Brown leaves, dry and twisted, shifted restlessly in the sporadic breeze, rearranging their drifts around the base of the fountain, in the knurled trunks of the rhododendrons, and against the foundations of the house.

Returning to the heavy door, Randy extracted the heavy old-fashioned door key from his pocket where he always kept it, a weighty token that he sometimes pressed against his leg surreptitiously in moments of pain and question. It was too much to ask that it could unlock the dungeons of conflict that he reasoned he must have built for himself. He turned the key in the lock and the mechanism turned as reluctantly as his hand.

The vaulted entrance hall, with its polished hardwood floor stretching to the graceful staircase, was empty, but he heard the familiar bell, activated by opening the front door, peal briefly in the distant kitchen. Almost immediately Mr. and Mrs. Rutledge appeared at the kitchen door at the far end of the large room, their black and white uniforms spotless and formal as usual. They contemplated the young man with the suitcase somberly for a moment, their aging faces expressionless, murmured "Sir" almost in unison, and then returned to the kitchen, closing the door quietly. He knew their concerns were confined to the master of the house; Randy's presence merely meant an additional mouth to feed and a room to clean. He was home.

A creaking floor board caused him to look up, meeting the eyes of the housekeeper descending the stairs. Again he was forcibly struck by the sensuality of the man's muscular, compact form. A product of New Orleans' bayous, Lucien carried with him an aura of decadence and suppressed violence with his rigidly erect posture and catlike movements. As always he was dressed in a tight, black silk jumpsuit, as dark and lustrous as his skin and closely-cropped hair; only the hair showed traces of white. His unusually small feet were encased in black boots that made no sound on the polished floor.

Without greeting, Lucien came to the important point. "Does your father expect you?" The voice was soft and carried a southern slur which, Randy knew, could become menacing without warning.

"No," he answered, his eyes shifting to the left, down the hall to his father's study. He had caught a glimpse of movement behind the delicate panes of the french doors to the study while approaching the house, and knew that his father was aware of his presence. As he peered down the hall, he saw the door of his father's study open but the man did not appear. The open door was his only acknowledgement.

Instead Randy moved to the stairs. Lucien made no move to assist him, but appraised the trim, athletic body, its long, tapered muscles moving easily under the nondescript clothing, as the young man climbed the stairs, suitcase in hand. "I'll freshen up first," Randy said without looking back, awkward as usual in the presence of the housekeeper. As he made the turn in the curving staircase, he saw Lucien gliding silently down the hall toward the open door.

His room, although unchanged and spotless, seemed foreign, almost hostile after his sojourn at school. He lived in a series of furnished apartments, solitary by preference, while at the university; each month his rent was paid by the trustee of his account, and he seldom sought the company of the other tenants or students in his classes. His yearnings, he had come to realize, could not be satisfied there. Reacting to the ghosts in his room, he did not linger to unpack but threw his suitcase on the high, old-fashioned bed and went downstairs. Rather than make his appearance at his father's study, he turned away and emerged on the back veranda, the sunny side of the house.

The difference was striking. Here the grass was mown smoothly and stretched its velvet carpet to the creek at the bottom of the long, gentle slope. Rose and delphinium and peony splashed the bright white of the house, and ancient magnolias greeted the sun with pink-white blooms at both sides of the flagstone patio. Not far down the slope was the neat, two-storied house of Lucien and his son, newly-painted, restored slave quarters from one hundred-fifty years ago. Now it was blue clapboard with lavender trim, and shone like a sapphire in the brilliant sunshine. A large picture window had been added to the present living room, bringing light to what had been a dark and foreboding dwelling. The expansive lawns now appeared as grounds, settings, for a second but smaller manor house.

Kneeling at work in the flowerbeds of the blue house was a figure, stripped to the waist, his back and shoulder muscles rippling and gleaming in the sun. Lucien's son was not as dark as his father but taller, in his early twenties. Louis had joined his father here only recently after his mother remarried in New Orleans, he had heard. Randy had seen him the previous Christmas, but only at a distance. Was Louis responsible for the transformation of the back garden?

With a sigh, knowing he could postpone it no longer, he turned back to the house and down the hall to his father's study.

Randolph Senior was bent over his tilt-table, carefully inscribing his latest project. Although the scion of an old established, wealthy family with extensive holdings and investments, he had chosen to make a career for himself in architecture and was now much sought-after, renowned for his designs of impressive buildings across the country. Few of his "customers" had even seen him, however, since he was also known as a recluse. He refused to visit sites or oversee construction and rarely returned telephone calls, but the meticulous drawings, showing every aspect in excruciating detail and flawlessly reflecting the beauty and purpose and function of the buildings he designed, left little need for communication. He left his home only rarely. His study was almost the extent of his world, even for sleeping at times. Randy had stood at the door for several minutes before his father interrupted his work.

"Ah, Randolph," he smiled tightly, as if he had to concentrate to remember how to smile. "School year's not over yet, is it?"

"No, it's spring break," Randy ventured into the room but remained standing. He suddenly realized what that mysterious quality about his father's face was, a quality he had always noticed but could not define; his clear, blue eyes were startlingly innocent, almost child-like. "What are you working on?"

"A new museum in San Francisco," his father responded with a shrug. "They have been talking about it for twenty years, and it is finally going to be built. Perhaps you will see it one day. . ." he broke off vaguely. For the first time, Randy thought he detected a hint of emotional involvement in a project, a wish to be a part of and perhaps even see one of his designs after completion. The room was suddenly silent, neither knowing how to communicate or even if they wished to communicate. They avoided each other's eyes.

"And your studies, how are they progressing?" It wasn't really a change of subject.

"OK, yes, OK," Randy responded uneasily but then continued. "Your work is part of the curriculum this semester."

"Really?" The older man did not seem pleased but somewhat puzzled. "Why?"

"Father, you must know that your design of that midwest municipal center has become known as a classical masterpiece." He didn't mention that the library and convention center on the west coast were required study for every budding architect in all major schools.

"I had no idea. . ." His father stared out of the window at the gently waving trees and the forsaken fountain for a moment, then ran his fingers through his wavy, gray hair. At that moment he looked curiously like his son; they were approximately the same height, the same slim, skeletal features, the same sensitive face structures. But Randy's hair and eyes were brown, like his mother's, and now the eyes were guarded, almost angry.

"It's a problem," he blurted out.

"What? Why?" The older man was not accustomed to problems brought to him for solution. He had never wanted to become a father, or even a husband. Problems were to be handled by someone else, an employee hired to insulate him from such importunities. He stared down at his partially completed drawing, his face tense.

"Your name. . . the same as mine. Other students see that now famous signature, 'Randolph P. Gilman,' and look at me with envy and even hatred in their eyes." Randy's fists were clenched, his face flushed. He hated his father and all he stood for, all he had accomplished. But then, unexpectedly, tears came to his eyes. "Some students seem to be friendly, even invite me to fraternities or bull sessions, but eventually it becomes obvious that they only want favors, a leg-up when they finish the course, knowing that I have my future cut out for me."

As quickly as his anger seized him, it was gone. He slumped in a chair, his voice almost a whisper. "I love architecture. Being your son has nearly ruined it for me."

In the silence that followed, Randy stared about the room as if memorizing it. For the first time he noticed two iron rings mounted securely to the wall, alone in the center of a long wall. They barely registered in his brain that was trying to sort itself out, now that he had brought *it* to the surface. As soon as he had said it, he was no longer sure that his famous father was his problem. It not, what was the real problem? He couldn't mention the other thing, the defect, the private dungeon that he secretly struggled with daily. . . He stared at his father who remained silent, almost cringing at the display of emotion by this stranger in his house.

"Father—why did Mother die? So young. . . what was wrong with her?"

The older man's head swung around to stare at the young man. Was this a change of subject or was there a connection?

"Why do you ask after all these years?" When there was no immediate response, he swung around again to stare out the window, his mouth working silently. Outside the light was beginning to fade.

Randy stared at the floor, at the nearly black rug that set off the white furniture in startling contrast. "I don't know," he said slowly. "I just wondered."

Carefully the older man's lips moved. "She was never strong. . . diabetic, anemic. . . but she wanted so much, more than I could give. . ."

"Did you love her?" Randy was insistent.

"I suppose so. . . in my way."

There came a discrete cough from the open doorway where Rutledge stood, a dark sentry.

"Dinner at six, sir? Cocktails in the library?" The confrontation was over. The chains were drawing tighter.

* * * * * *

Randy stood at his bedroom window in his shorts, staring out at the grounds in their shadowed disrepair. There had been no more opportunity to talk to his father at dinner. Lucien was the controlling presence at the table, giving subtle instructions to Rutledge about the service and practically forbidding his father from having brandy following the meal. The older man went directly to his study after dinner, closing the door, incommunicado. For many years it had been understood in that house that Lucien was the only one who would be admitted at night. Randy had finally unpacked and showered, although he knew he would not be able to sleep if he went to bed. The elm trees were casting pale shadows and he could hear the distant hoots of owls as night closed in on the estate.

When he looked down at the box hedge he caught a movement, a darker shadow among lighter ones. A figure stood almost in the hedge, parting the branches and peering at the house. In some alarm and without much thought, Randy slipped on his shoes and descended the stairs, slipping out the side door so he could approach the figure from the rear. Fortunately the night was balmy, warm for the season, since Randy had not thought to add any clothes beyond his undershorts. Keeping close, in the shadow of the hedge, he glided quietly to the spot where he had seen the intruder. He calculated that the figure had been near the french doors to his father's study, but he found no one.

He noticed faint, flickering light visible through the french doors, and was about to investigate further when he was seized from the rear, one strong arm around his neck. He started to cry out, but a second hand was clapped over his mouth.

"Shhh," came the whispered admonition. "Shut your face. Just watch."

A muffled snapping sound could be heard from the study as Randy tried to pull away. Even as he struggled he discerned that the light was emitted by several candles and there was movement inside. As his eyes grew more adjusted to the darkness, he could see his father's nude, white form stretched against the wall. He stopped struggling, his mind whirling with questions.

"You going to behave now?" the husky voice inquired softly from behind. Randy nodded, and the hand over his mouth was removed.

"Who are you?" he asked with difficulty, the throat hold still restricting his breathing. He realized that he was pressed backward against a bare chest, skin satin-smooth and hairless.

Again the muffled snap, and this time a second figure was clearly defined in the study. It was Lucien, wielding a leather whip in repetitive slashes across the back of Randy's father. Randy almost yelled again, but the hand clapped over his mouth again, almost strangling him.

"Keep still, fool! Can't you see they're digging it?"

Enjoying it? How could anyone – but then as he watched he began to sense the trust, the profound intimacy that seemed to pervade the strange scene in the study. He was not prepared –

Again the hand was removed and Randy wrenched his body around to see his tormentor. He was a tall, muscular black man whose handsome face was set off by eyes that seemed almost white in the shadows—that seemed to penetrate to his soul. Short, dark hair clung to his forehead and crept down over his neck in back. His naked shoulders and chest gleamed dully, the muscular ridges casting darker shadows. He wore mud-stained Levis and construction boots.

A series of whip slashes pulled Randy's attention back to the room. He could clearly see the stripes of the whip on his father's back and rear now, but he did not seem to be resisting or trying to escape. His movements seemed instead to welcome the whip, and his ass weaved and bobbed excitedly; his wrists were tethered to the iron rings in the wall by broad leather straps. Lucien still wore his black silk jumpsuit, but now it was open all the way to his crotch where his thick, stiff cock protruded obscenely.

Randy turned questioningly to the man beside him. "Are you Louis?" he asked when his brain had steadied somewhat. The handsome man nodded but his eyes were fixed on the couple in the room, their fathers in their private rituals. Without shifting his concentration, he asked gruffly, "Do you always wander around out doors at night in your jockey shorts?" Randy flushed but turned back to the two lovers. "Do you always invade people's privacy, peeping through their windows?" It was a stalemate.

Lucien had discarded the whip at last. Randolph the Senior quivered in his bonds as his lover/housekeeper smoothed the raw welts with his fingertips and then reached around to twist the concealed nipples. The older man stiffened and jerked, his actions even more frantic as his lover's hands dropped to his crotch; the rough treatment he was receiving was obvious from the rapid and twisting movements of Lucien's arms. Then he brought his hands to the man's hips, soothing and caressing the narrow hips and down the older man's thighs. Randy watched spellbound but suddenly jumped as he felt a calloused hand on his neck; it caressed gently, almost hypnotically, and after a moment he felt himself ease back against the shoulder, the broad chest of the powerful man at his side. But the dungeon yawned, beckoning and deep, and he pulled away.

Lucien had suddenly become gentle, his lips kissing and coursing along the welts and then along the spine of his lover. It appeared that this shift in approach was more stressful than the whip had been; Randolph twisted and thrust in agony and desire, but Lucien was relentless, almost methodically covering the tossing, bruised surface with kisses. At times, Randolph's head was thrown back as if screaming to the sky, his graying hair tossing fitfully, his eyes closed, his own fantasies overwhelming. Louis' arm slowly encircled Randy's chest and their cheeks touched. The dungeon's claws reached out once more, threatening damnation, but this time Randy surrendered to his instincts and moved into the embrace. He reveled in the warmth of the firm chest, the bulging pectoral with its tense nipple against his back, the short beard stubble against his cheek.

Lucien had changed tactics. His hand was probing between the older man's buttocks, first one finger and then two, three – moving in and out, rotating, penetrating. Randolph pressed back, eager, libidinous. Then the fingers were replaced by the thick stalk, the black root of the housekeeper, pressing in slowly at first and then thrust abruptly to the maximum. Randy cringed involuntarily, his father's violation perceived as his own, but the arm about his chest tightened reassuringly. Randy realized in the recesses of his mind that for the first time he could identify to a degree with his stranger-father. He felt Louis' lips against his ear and then his tongue teasing.

He turned slightly toward Louis to welcome the caress, but could not shift his gaze away from the room.

Lucien moved in and out, rhythmically, forcefully, fixing his subject in place with black fists on white hips. Randolph was relatively quiet now, welcoming each thrust and preparing for the next, his face tilted upward, smiling. Louis gathered Randy closer to him, his dark hand gripping Randy's tumescence encased in his jockey shorts. For the first time Randy realized that he was erect; Louis' touch compounded it, painfully stretching, massively throbbing. . . Louis began to move and weave slightly behind him, and he could feel his thick, pulsating erection, still confined in the faded Levis, pressing against him.

The scene was changing in the room, at first subtly, Lucien reaching around with both hands to grasp Randolph's cock, and gradually more aggressively. The black master's thrusts became more erratic, more penetrating. Even in the dim candlelight, Randy could see that his silk was soaked with sweat, the black becoming blacker, and the bulging muscles were quivering in anticipation. Randolph's upturned smile became a grimace, almost a death-mask, but when Lucien cried out in joyful agony, sperm spilling in spurts deeply buried, his smile broadened, radiant with his own fulfillment.

Randy stood transfixed – and suddenly he was alone. Confusedly he turned, seeking, but only the pale moon was watching and only the dry leaves, victims of the fitful breeze, were moving in the darkness. Too embarrassed now to continue his vigil of the lovers in the study, he retraced his steps to his bedroom, shaking and alone. The spectacle of his father being whipped and sodomized by the housekeeper loomed huge and perplexing in his mind, but, strangely, he was more sensually stimulated than horrified, he realized. In fact the confusing contact with the housekeeper's son was more upsetting and, he could admit to himself, profoundly evocative. That night he could not deny his need, a practice he had avoided since leaving his adolescence, but his fantasies were much more complicated now.

* * * * * *

When Randy appeared for breakfast the next morning, his father's door was closed and Mrs. Rutledge said he had breakfasted earlier. As usual, Randy ate only a flaky croissant and coffee. Randy returned to his room as soon as he had finished, alienated by the remote servants. Immediately he drew the curtains widely and opened his windows, restless and suddenly frustrated by the closed atmosphere which he supposed he had always taken for granted before.

As he looked down on the front grounds he was somewhat surprised to see Louis at work, collecting leaves from the forlorn fountain and the rhododendron beds. He watched for a moment, reproducing in his mind some of the events of the previous night – the satin touch of his bare chest, again glowing with masculinity in the morning sunlight; his lips, tender and mysterious against his neck; his rigid erection, demanding, confusing. . . On impulse he pulled on an old pair of slacks; he went downstairs and to the front lawn.

"Good morning," he said brightly as he approached.

Louis did not look up from his work. "Mo'nin', Massah," was his eventual response.

"Uh – what?" Randy responded uncertainly.

"Jus' sweepin' up de leaves. Winter done lef' a mess hyar."

Randy stared at the broad back, the dark neck with a trace of perspiration at the edge of the short hair, the calloused hands which seemed so familiar. They belonged to a stranger. Had he dreamed last night's traumatic experience?

He was just turning to leave when Louis turned around, looking at him squarely with a trace of hostility. His lips were tight, his expression studiedly blank, but what was most striking was the eyes that had seemed almost white the night before; they were blue—like chips of ice, piercing, withdrawn. Their gaze held for a moment and then Louis returned to his work.

Randy stumbled back to the house, his brain fuddled. He remained in his room for the remainder of the day, deep in thought. His father's door remained closed.

Dinner was awkward, chilly. His father falteringly attempted communication, but Lucien's presence, at usual, seemed to inhibit all attempts father and son made to touch on important subjects.

Later, after the moon had climbed above the roof top, Randy watched from his window for the dark figure to appear again near the french doors, but it did not. Eventually Randy slipped downstairs and out the side door, approaching the spot near his father's study with trepidation. No one waited in the shadows, but he could see his father and Lucien inside, talking intimately. This time Randy did not linger. He walked around the side of the house to the blue renovated slave quarters at the rear where a yellow light glowed dimly. Frogs croaked sleepily in the creek below, and dew was already settling on the neatly trimmed grass. He knocked on the door.

Louis did not seem surprised to see him, nor did he seem particularly welcoming. He nodded and returned to his chair where apparently he had been reading, leaving the door open. Randy entered and stood accusingly near him, his anger rising.

"Why did you treat me like that this morning?" he demanded.

Louis looked at him silently, his expression solemn, guarded. Then he asked, "Don't you know?" No trace of the uneducated patois remained in his speech. When there was no reaction from Randy, Louis looked away, his shoulders hunching protectively. "You are the son of the owner, the white 'massah'. Look around you. This was the slaves' quarters. Oh, sure, it has been modernized, renovated with your father's designs, his money, his paint. . . but look at the wall. We preserved the iron rings mounted there, and the worn, bleached floor boards the women scrubbed with rag mops, where naked children with no hope for the future played, the blackened fireplace where pots of hamhocks and greens once bubbled, even the dangling bell that was controlled by a long rope to the manor house when 'service' was required. . ." He looked around the room and cocked his head as if listening to ghosts of the past. "My father transplanted a pair of slave rings to your father's study, you know. . . Actually I've become quite fond of these reminders. I won't let him make any more changes."

Randy followed his gaze around the room. The furniture seemed rather old and traditional except for a leather recliner next to the reading lamp and a pile of large colorful cushions filling one corner. He tried to reconstitute the past from remnants left intact, a stranger in his own environment. He had grown up here, played his juvenile games in and around the cottage, a southern child of the 1970s with no thought of history. The civil war had been over for more than a hundred years, a time span incomprehensible to a child. Slaves were pictures in books – a cause of cultural and political guilt but of no particular consequence to a white youth with a bright future. Certainly he had never been exposed to thoughts of discrimination from his parents. His eyes returned to Louis, confused and questioning.

"You still don't understand, do you?" His pale eyes were almost green in the yellow light of the reading lamp. "I guess I shouldn't expect a white man. . . I am neither – do you understand that?" When Randy's confusion did not clear, he continued. "I can't even claim to be one with the slaves. My mother, with her china-blue eyes and yellow hair, is white. I am mulatto. A fuckin' half-breed."

It took a moment for Randy to grasp the significance, the anguish streaming from the man who had inexplicably become so important to him. He had no experience to guide him. No one had ever asked him for support, for understanding before. No one had ever expected anything from him before, not even his father. How could he be of any use to anyone when he understood so little about himself? But he did understand, in a way –

He dropped to his knees between Louis' legs, his eyes brimming, his lips working. "But–I am, too! A half-breed! I know now that – I can never – never marry – never have children – never. . . I can no longer pretend that I am a man, in the usual sense of the word. I long suspected it – it was a pit that I avoided, stepping around it fearfully. . . And last night you touched me – and I discovered my father. . . I am a half-man, a degenerate, a failure." His voice tapered off in misery.

Louis stared at him, not sure he grasped the pain that showed so clearly in the young man's face. Then he tipped his head back and roared with laughter, his robust basso ringing through the small cottage in mirth that must have seemed out of place to the spirits that seemed to hover there only a few minutes before. Randy stared at him, shocked and hurt by the apparent frivolity that greeted the confession wrung from him at such pain. His injured expression finally penetrated Louis' brain, and he sobered with some difficulty.

"So you think you are the only man who loves men? Is that it? Is that your huge problem?" His eyes softened, and he took Randy's face between his hands.

"I was born and raised in New Orleans, you know, where gay men are everywhere. They practically manage the French Quarter. In my circle of friends, even in my landscape architecture class in college, perhaps half my friends were gay. I have known since I was thirteen that I am gay. There's no 'half-breed' there!" He hesitated and then added quietly, "And my father is also gay, as you know."

"Yes." Randy realized too late that he had possibly brought more pain to Louis through his clumsy but honest attempt to counter his anguish. How could he have been so stupid? Even with the best of intentions, he had failed.

"Did you know – last night – that I am – gay?" The question came unbidden to his lips but he had thought about it all day. It was the first time he had ever put his guilty secret into words.

Louis searched his eyes, his face now soft and caring. "I assumed you were," he answered simply.

"Then why did you – go away, leave me last night? I needed you – wanted you. . ."

Louis answered quietly, patiently. "I didn't think you were ready then. Are you – ready, now?"

"You mean – with whips and torture?"

Louis' eyes smiled again, knowingy. "I'm sure you're not ready for that, not at all. That would be a difficult way to begin. But making love, man to man. . ."

Louis' soft eyes held him, the first sincerely caring look he could remember receiving since his Mother's demise. Randy returned his gaze steadily, drawn beyond his depth but gaining confidence in a way he never thought he could. This man was one of the most beautiful, one of the most masculine men he had ever met, and he was proposing. . .

His eyes dropped to the mound in the tight crotch that had subliminally intruded on his consciousness since the previous night, and especially potent when so close. . . Slowly he reached forward to grasp it gently, the worn, faded Levis barely concealing the thick shaft, the bulging head. "May I?" he asked hesitantly. Louis smiled but did not move. As he gazed in awe, the bulge assumed a life of its own in his hand, strengthening and lengthening, consenting.

Louis was clearly uncertain what he could do for his friend. Tentatively he rose but Randy gripped his legs. "Please," Randy pleaded, looking up from the floor. "Let me – please. I have thought about this moment for so long. . ."

Shaking fingers unbuttoned the Levis while Louis stood

passively, hands at his sides. Crisp, black hair crept through the fly as it was opened, but the pants did not fall, held in place by the swelling tenting the left leg. Randy took an anticipatory breath and pulled downward on both pants legs, but was not prepared for the massive, virile flesh, thick and stiff and potent, that sprang outward inches away from his face. He gasped and stared as the deep-red mushroom head was unleashed, gliding from its black cape to throb proudly, enticingly for his admiration.

Slowly he grasped the beautiful organ in both hands, thrilling to the velvet texture, the vein-etched skin that moved majestically at his touch. His gaze shifted for a moment to the blue eyes beaming down, showing the beginnings of yearning, of desire for – him? The giant lurched in his hands but – now that the moment had arrived, that moment he had dreamed of for so long, he was unprepared, uncertain about how to proceed.

Louis reached down and lifted him to a standing position, his offering left unattended for the moment. "It takes two, you know," he murmured, eyes brimming with unaccustomed tenderness. "Put your arms around my neck."

Randy obeyed. Of course one should start with a kiss, he supposed. Why hadn't he thought of that? But Louis did not pull him close. Instead, locking Randy's brown eyes with his own, he unbuttoned the young man's slacks and extracted the nearly-matching flesh, pressing the two manly tools together in an intimate grip. Randy cried out and lurched forward, pressing against the muscular form and taking possession of the full lips that beckoned so strongly.

Louis clasped their joined manhoods with one hand and clutched the straining body to him with the other arm. Tongues met and entwined, lips teased and sucked and tortured, beings blended, excluding the outside world around them and even the intrusive spirits. Muscle and masculinity matched and converged with their counterparts.

There were no longer questions of practicalities, of technique or protocol. Within minutes their clothes were removed, discarded, and their bodies were totally exposed, opened to the other's eyes and hands and lips. And when they sank together on the pillows and consumed each other in total abandon, the only spirits that remained announced the triumphs of man with man, to take and give and share equally and unequivocally.

* * * * * *

The Rutledges were shocked in the morning when Randy bounded into the breakfast room, dressed in disreputable T-shirt and faded Levis, demanding a huge breakfast of eggs and bacon and biscuits. "Lots of work to do today," he explained mysteriously, with a huge smile.

He caused further consternation when he strode down the hall and opened (opened!) his father's study door and proclaimed "Good morning!" to his father bent over his work table. Immediately he closed the door without waiting for a response and strode out of the front door, joining Louis who was busy raking leaves under the trees along the driveway.

Rutledge watched suspiciously from the kitchen window as the two young men greeted each other with smiles. He watched them looking closely at each other, talking quietly, and then Randy retrieved a rake from the cart containing gardening equipment and actually began to rake leaves in concert with the gardener. From time to time they would stop and smile at each other, talk for a few minutes, and then bend to their tasks, side by side. Both removed their shirts; Rutledge snorted at Randy's paleness, anticipating that he would soon develop a sunburn in the beaming, spring sun. Of course it didn't matter with Louis, he thought.

Soon they had accumulated a huge pile of dry, brown leaves which tended to scatter in the morning breeze. One would collect the errant remnants, sweeping them back to the pile, and then the other would retrieve others blowing in a different direction. It became a game with them, Rutledge could tell, seeing them laughing like children as their project seemed in danger of faltering. And then he clearly saw Louis make a grab for the young master, Randy not really trying to evade him, and then they fell together in a heap in the pile of leaves, laughing and – kissing.

"What are they doing out there?" Mrs. Rutledge asked from the pantry door.

"Nothing much, just raking leaves," her husband sniffed, turning away from the window. "Like father, like son," he muttered.

Randy was not thinking about his father at that moment. He was astride, smiling down into the eyes, of the most desirable person on earth. Then he bent to kiss the dark nipple that seemed to tense whenever he touched it. Hungrily he tongued it and then nipped at it with his teeth.

"Hey, didn't you have breakfast this morning?" Louis grinned, pretending to be in pain.

"Not enough," Randy answered promptly, one hand cupping the enlarging swelling in Louis' crotch. They smiled into each other's eyes for a long moment.

"You kind of like to be on top, don't you?" Louis observed curiously.

Randy smiled and began to twist and grind his rigidity against his partner. "Yeah, I guess so," he smiled. He gripped Louis' wrists playfully and stretched them out above his head.

"Hmmm," Louis responded. "I guess I sort of like being on the bottom, too. . ."

Neither noticed, down the long drive at the manor house, the face at the french doors nor its enigmatic expression.

* * * * * *

The next two weeks flashed by, it seemed to Randy. Sunny days were spent with Louis, working side by side in the fragrant loam, mowing lawns and laughing – Randy laughed more in those two weeks than he had ever laughed in his life before. Their rainy days were usually spent in the cottage talking, sharing private thoughts, sharing their bodies when the urge struck, which happened frequently.

Gradually he learned about what it meant to be gay from Louis. Most people did not care one way or another, Louis maintained, and there were advantages sometimes. He had many comical tales to tell about queens and their more masculine counterparts in the French Quarter, and Randy began to feel more comfortable about the burden that he had carried for so long in fearful, humiliated isolation. It was possible to be gay and to be happy, it seemed. He did not ask the critical questions about the master and slave relationship of their fathers, and Louis did not elucidate. Perhaps he did not really understand it, either. In his philosophy, everyone was free to choose his own path and to follow his own rules, as long as they did not hurt others.

Randy's love grew steadily and he began to acquire more confidence in himself as a man, in control of his own destiny, and as a lover. He rarely saw his father except at dinner, which was still awkward and strained with Lucien at the foot of the table. He frequently caught his father's eyes observing him, apparently curious about the more effervescent personality that was obviously developing, but he did not ask questions. Finally Randy brought up a subject that was troubling him.

"Why don't we have Louis join us at dinner?" he asked one night of his father, with a side glance at Lucien. His father looked flustered.

"Well, Mrs. Rutledge always fixes something for him in the kitchen. . ."

"I know, and that's pretty strange as well as being more trouble for Mrs. Rutledge. He's not just a gardener, a servant."

His father did not answer, perhaps expecting Lucien to make the decision, but Lucien was also silent.

"By the way," his father finally said, changing the subject, "since it looks like you will be home for a while, would you like to help with some of the design projects that are being submitted? I haven't seen any of your work but, uh, perhaps I could contribute something to your education. . ."

Randy brightened. He had not put pencil to paper since he had arrived, and realized at that moment that he missed the challenge. "Great!" he said enthusiastically. "Father, have you ever considered using Computer Assisted Design computer systems for your drawings? I could teach you, if – if you wish."

His father stared at him in disbelief. "Computers for designing buildings? No, I have no idea – I've never done that – and probably would never – but if you wish, we could buy a computer for you to play around with. . ."

"Sure. I know just the one we should have. I'll bring you the information tomorrow."

Lucien ventured a comment. "Louis was trained in computer design for his landscaping as well."

"Well, then it's settled." His father seemed relieved to conclude the conversation.

Randy rose to leave the table but turned back at the door. "I'll mention to Louis that he can join us for dinner from now on." Without waiting for a response, he hurried to his room to shower for his evening with his lover.

His relationship with Lucien remained cool but it had become more complicated. Twice, as he headed for the cottage in the evenings, he encountered Lucien on his way to join Randolph. They merely nodded and passed on, too involved in their own thoughts, perhaps, to recognize the irony of the situation.

It surprised Randy that Louis was not enthusiastic about taking his place at the long, polished dinner table. It had also become apparent that Louis and Lucien were not on the best of terms. Louis did not feel comfortable in the manor house where his father was *major domo,* and certainly Randy now thought of the cottage as his and Louis'. After a few awkward evenings, Randy moved Louis' plate next to his own at one end of the table, leaving Randolph and Lucien at the other end. The result was actually two pairs of people dining together, and the young lovers could communicate in their own ways while their fathers were usually silent.

That summer the number of design projects accepted and the work produced almost doubled. Although father and son never seemed to communicate easily on ordinary subjects, there was intuitive understanding on aspects of architecture, and the new computer and printer occupied a significant corner of the study. The teacher role switched frequently from father to son and back to the father; ideas that could benefit from investigation could be designed on the computer screen before acceptance and even produced in print without laborious hours over the drawing board. Randolph remained in awe of this advancement in his traditional science so easily managed by his relatively inexperienced son, but together their work thrived far beyond his expectations. All the plots and drawings carried proudly the name, *Randolph P. Gilman.* Now the name stood for father and son.

It was soon after the first frost, when the leaves had begun to turn their myriad colors and the evening air was crisp, that Louis presented Randy with a gift wrapped in foil.

"It is your birthday, isn't it?" he responded to the question on Randy's face as he sprawled on the floor in front of the cottage's crackling fireplace. Its flickering light was the only illumination in the room.

"Yes, but – " Randy had not received a birthday present

since his Mother died.

When he unwrapped the gift, he found a wooden box with a sliding lid, and inside the box was a package containing a black leather cat-o-nine-tails. Randy looked up questioningly.

Louis smiled uncertainly. "In a way it's really a present for me – but for you to use."

Randy understood. He removed the whip from its box and held it closely to him, stroking it, absorbing its texture, its symbolism. "How did you know I've been thinking about –"

Louis' blue eyes became mischievous. "If'n a slave don' know what the Massah wants b'fo' Massah do, he ain't no good slave, no how."

Randy's eyes crinkled in beginning amusement, but then grew stern. "That's a smart-ass response, boy; and I know a good way to make your ass smart in return." Louis' eyes glowed in anticipation.

"If you look further in the box, you'll find another package of some leather straps for – whatever you decide to use them for, sir."

"Yes, I see."

There was no levity now. Instead there was an instinctive realization that a turning point had been reached in their relationship, a direction that must be carefully explored.

Randy could only proceed by instinct as well.

"Stand up and strip," he ordered gruffly.

Immediately Louis rose and stripped off his t-shirt. Randy's pulse increased as it always did when his lover's broad chest, muscular shoulders and arms, and sculptured torso were revealed, but his face remained controlled, stony.

"Your Levis, too. Don't stop there!" he barked.

In a flash the narrow hips, the swelling thighs and their intervening treasure were exposed. Randy resolved to postpone temporarily their full enjoyment.

"Turn around," he ordered, his crotch painfully constricted by his Levis.

Louis' buttocks shone dully in the flickering light, rounded, proud, inviting. His muscular back and shoulders, powerful and expansive, seemed to bear cultural memory both of menial toil and graceful, Mediterranean sculpture. Randy's thoughts reverberated with these ironic elements, his eyes remaining fixed on his lover as he quickly removed his own clothes.

"I am going to tie you to the rings in the wall," he said huskily, "and punish you for your insolence, do you understand?"

"Yes, sir," was the prompt answer.

"Move over here and stretch your arms up to the rings." There was no hesitation; Louis moved into position, his face to the wall.

Clumsily Randy used the leather straps from the package to tether Randy's wrists loosely to the rings. When he finished his work he discovered that the tall man was not stretched as tightly as his predecessors; apparently the men had been shorter when the rings had been installed and served their original purpose.

"Spread your legs wide," he commanded. When Louis obeyed his heavy balls were visible between his thighs in the shadows, as were the coarse, curly black hairs that lined his cleavage and clustered around the opening. Both men were trembling, recognizing the steps they were taking were not retractable but were inevitable. Louis stood stiffly erect, his head proudly high.

"You belong to me." Randy was merely voicing his thoughts.

"Yes, sir."

"My – slave."

It seemed that the spirits in the cottage stirred, an almost audible groan, memories suppressed for over a century recalled.

"Yes, sir."

"Your body, your mind, your heart, your – love, are mine."

"Oh, yes, sir!"

It was the first time the word "love" had been spoken by either of them. The word echoed as if foreign in the setting, but then faded away. . .

Louis was becoming impatient. Randy could sense this but was unsure of himself. He stroked the handle of the cat, responding to the texture, the aroma, the symbolism of the leather whip. The lashes draped themselves downward over his rigidity.

"What up? Massah gon' keep me hangin' hyar all night? Mebbe he jus' lak lookin' at my black ass?"

The whip slashed the broad back with authority, each strand finding its own course, leaving its individual trail of pain. Louis had expected it, of course, but the speed and violence were surprising.

"Uh, yes! Yes, master," he cried.

The spirits in the former slaves' quarters immediately set up a clamor, shouts and curses, masculine roars and women's screams, echoing over and over, slowly fading. The very air seemed heavy with resentment and suspicion and hatred, memories of previous beatings, floggings. . .

Again the whip slashed the quivering body, this time including the licorice mounds. Louis' head snapped back, his body pressed against the wall, fighting for breath.

Again the distant voices close in their ears, shouting, screaming, cursing, but they tapered off more quickly.

"I love you – sir!"

The third blow was no longer painful. Louis smiled although he trembled still, perhaps more because of his excitement than discomfort. "Oh, yes, sir!" he exclaimed.

The voices began again, faintly, but abruptly died away, banished; the exorcism seemed complete.

Randy dropped the whip, shocked at the vehemence of his sadistic reaction but sexually excited, almost swept away by the depth of sensuality of the experience. He lunged forward to press against the trembling form of his lover; his copious chest hair, which Louis admired and coveted, imposed its prickly and sensuous presence between their skins. Randy kissed the muscle ridges and tender valleys of the streaming back, his lips soothing the welts rising on his beloved's skin. Long, parallel, reddened trails as might have been left by animal claws – like lions' claws as in his recurrent dreams. No time for those thoughts now. Quickly he worked his way down the muscled back and along the spine, setting up shivers of delight in both of them. He paused at the base of the spine.

"Yes," he said firmly, "'Massah' does like your black ass, boy! I'm goin' to show you how much I like it, boy! And tied up like that, you're not going to be able to do a damn thing about it!"

Quickly he burrowed his face between the two dark cushions, tonguing the crease and the dark hairs downward until reaching the nirvana he had coveted for months but never dared approach. His tongue probed deeply at the puckered opening, and Louis gasped his surprise and pleasure. Involuntarily he pushed back, yanking on his bindings and silently pleading for more, and Randy gripped his hips, pulling his lover to his face to press ever deeper, even to his very core.

"Chocolate ass, my favorite flavor, slave!" he growled between forays, his ardor overflowing. "Open that hole, boy!" Louis groaned loudly, his brain whirling with mixed memories of the pain of the whip and the sensations in his ass and the love for his man.

Abruptly Randy stopped and grew quiet. He needed his lover's face, needed to look into his eyes at that moment. "Turn around," he ordered.

It took a moment for Louis to register the new order and respond. Randy drew back as Louis turned, the tethered wrists crossing over his head in the new position. His cock jutted out rigidly, bobbing excitedly; the flickering firelight was reflected by their sweaty bodies, their glowing, embracing eyes. Randy adored openly.

"I know now why your eyes are blue," he said quietly, only inches away. "Those beautiful blue eyes are to mark you as mine, my lover, my man – my slave, if I wish it." He kissed the eyes, one at a time. "And your cock, your bone-hard prick seeping sweet nectar, is for me, also," stooping to kiss the throbbing length, setting up even more demanding clamor. "Your dark balls are two delicious, paired peaches–" *Of course! In my dreams!* He knelt to kiss them, but that was not enough; he sucked them into his mouth greedily, internalizing his fantasy for all time as he stroked the thick shaft above.

After a moment he rose. "I need your arms around me," he said, releasing the bonds with trembling fingers. He stepped back for a moment and then, again taking up the whip, returned to his lover's embrace. He gripped their cocks together, as Louis had done that first night, and wrapped them in the thongs of the whip, the leather bestowing its warm-rough strength, binding them together as Louis's arms closed around him.

As he began to move his hand, the velvet skin of their manhoods creased by the leather, their kiss became a muscle-snapping connection that defied time and space and separation. Only moments later they crested simultaneously, their juices spurting, gushing, flowing together, indistinguishable, white. The leather binding them together was flooded with their masculinity, softened but as strong as ever.

* * * * * *

Lucien, returning to the cottage that night, had observed some of their activity and brought Randolph out to join him. Outside on the fading lawn, crackling with frost that had already ended summer blooms, Randolph and Lucien, each with an arm about the other's waist, had watched the last few minutes of the scene unfold through the picture window of the cottage. They smiled at each other, comfortable in their long-term comradeship and love that they could never admit or explain.

"And the pendulum swings, father to son, colorblind. . ." Randolph murmured.

"And the truth shall set you free," Lucien finished.

THE CIRCLE Q

Denis Hunter

It wasn't my best day, or at least it didn't start out that way. But sometimes it's just when things hit rock bottom that they bounce right back. Anyway that's the way it happened for me one hot, sweaty day in Durango.

The temperature had finally died down enough for me to leave the old motor court outside of town. There was an air conditioner in the $10 a day room, but it didn't do much good, though I guess it was better than nothing at all. So I drove my old Ford pickup to a MacDonald's, since I hadn't eaten since yesterday, and then into Durango to take in the sights. At that time of year, the place is filled with rich tourists having a good time, spending money and looking beautiful. I must have looked like a sore thumb; I sure felt like one. There was one place in town, though, where the tourists apparently never went, just drifters and ranch hands – Durango's old Central Saloon.

Nothing to do but drink beer and smoke and feel sorry for myself. And I had a lot to be sorry for, as I thought it over. I guess I was lucky they reduced that DUI charge back in Chicago so I didn't lose my license, but I sure had to earn that reduction, sucking off the arresting officer's fat dick in an alley. Yetch! I don't know which smelled worse, him or the garbage cans. Anyway, I got him off, so he had no call to piss on me afterwards as well. But the bastard wasn't as bad as that goddamned sergeant who had fucked me over in the Army.

Sgt. Poltesky, sir!! Just because he caught me once getting sucked off by one of those North Carolina boys in a men's room off base, he thought he could blackmail me into servicing him regular. And he thought right, come to think of it. He was always calling me into his office and pulling the blinds down. If I had a dollar for every ounce of his goddamned cum I swallowed I wouldn't be sitting in this dive today.

And now I was just about out of cigarettes. Shit!

I ordered another beer, my fourth, and looked around. The bar was starting to fill up, especially around the pool tables in the back. Latinos, Indians, anglos, each one as grungy as the next, played, watched, bet, and drank till they could hardly stand up. The smoke made the air hazy, and the low buzz of conversations in strange languages and accents made the atmosphere even hazier. I swivelled back around to face the bar and hunched over my beer.

I was so absorbed in my thoughts that it was a few minutes before I noticed someone had come in and was standing next to me at the bar. The guy had carefully spread the local newspaper out on the bar and was reading it methodically, page by page. What I first noticed were his hands resting on the edge of the bar. Thick, gnarled fingers, rough, weathered skin, and light brown hair fanning out on the backs of his hands.

It made me uncomfortable that I was attracted by those rough, masculine hands. I was straight, after all, wasn't I? That sergeant had given me a taste for dick, sure, but that's not what I really wanted.

I was still hunched over my beer, but I turned my head slightly to get a better look. His thick, brown hair was cropped close against his head, and he sported a thick, brown moustache that wrapped around the sides of his mouth down to his jaw. A red bandanna was tied around his neck, and a blue plaid, cotton shirt, carefully pressed, with the cuffs reaching just to the end of his wrists, outlined his lean, muscular chest. A black leather belt with a big silver buckle defined his narrow waist and drew my eyes down to his fresh, neat blue jeans. He stood perfectly straight at what I guessed to be six-foot-two, yet seemed perfectly relaxed, content to read his paper and drink his beer-and-whiskey.

God knows what I must have looked like to him! My clothes were dirty, I hadn't shaved in three days, and that last time I looked in the mirror there was more red in my eyes than white. Just thinking about what I must look like made me even more miserable.

When he finished his paper, he ordered another beer and walked away from the bar to a table in the corner. I couldn't help but watch him. He moved so easily, so smoothly, like he wasn't moving at all. He didn't seem to have a worry in the world, like he just couldn't be bothered with hassles of any kind. I couldn't take my eyes off his butt as he walked to the table. The jeans hugged those mounds so tightly you could see the muscles contract and relax as he moved.

What am I looking at? I thought in alarm. I turned back to the bar angry at myself for staring at a man, but I couldn't get him out of my mind. I tried to turn my head oh-so-discreetly down and to the side to get a better look at him, but then I noticed that I could just see the top of his head in the streaked, mahogany-framed mirror that spanned the back of the bar. I lifted myself from the barstool to get a better look, and when I did, I was startled to see him looking back at me, laughing slightly as if he knew what I was trying to do. He raised his beer bottle as an acknowledgment when our eyes met. I was so embarrassed I didn't know whether to acknowledge him in return or slowly sit back down as if I hadn't noticed. Before I could decide, he waved me over to him. Still embarrassed, I slid off the bar stool and walked toward him, rather hunched over like I was trying to hide myself.

"Been drinkin' awhile?" he said in a broad western accent.

"Yeah, about a month, I guess."

"You sure look it." The tone of his voice did not seem disapproving, as I thought it would be. He just seemed open and friendly. "Take a load off," he added, and I slumped into a chair next to him.

"Things haven't been too good for me lately," I said, staring at the curly brown hair in the triangle of his shirt opening.

"Well, it happens to everyone some time or another. Here, let me buy you another beer."

He stood up to go to the bar so I had to look him right in the crotch as he passed me. I didn't know what he was hiding in those jeans, but it sure seemed too big to be a dick! He moved to the bar and back again as gracefully as a cat.

"What's your name?" he said when he returned with the beers.

"Will."

"They call me Pete," he said.

We shook hands, and he asked me to tell him about myself. I went through the miserable recital, leaving some parts out for obvious reasons. He listened without expression, but I thought he listened deeply. When I finished, he said he was sure I had left some things out but that was all right, for now anyway. Already it seemed like he owned me.

"I could use some more help on the ranch right about now," he said, "if you're interested in earning a little money."

"Sure, but I don't know much about ranching."

"You don't have to. We're just repairing things right now, after the winter. If you're interested, come by tomorrow. The Circle Q Ranch, out on Old Mesa Road. Just ask anyone." He got up as soon as he finished talking and walked out. I was so dumbfounded, I couldn't speak, even to say good-bye or ask directions.

The next morning I washed myself up as well as I could and packed up what few possessions I had left. I didn't know what I was getting myself in for, but I needed the money and that man sure caught my fancy.

It took some time, and a few wrong turns, but I finally found Old Mesa Road, a good twenty miles out of town. It looked like it threaded its way through a long, winding canyon. No really spectacular colors there, but vast, endless, empty space. After about ten miles, the road narrowed and became less well surfaced. Eventually, it gave out into just dirt and rock. I knew I was passing into real country when I drove over cattle guards and heard the trilling sound the tires made when they rode over them. The Ford bounced along, sometimes pushing my stomach into my throat when it hit the really rough spots.

Finally, just as I crossed a small creek that ran through the middle of the canyon, I saw a big wooden circle on top of a gate and the letter "Q" in the middle of it. My eyes followed the drive through the open gate to a large, dark log cabin set back near the canyon wall. The gate was open so I drove through to the cabin. I couldn't see anyone or hear anything but the car motor. I had barely gotten out of the car when I heard horses hooves beating the ground and could smell the dust they kicked up. The sun was behind him, but as I shaded my eyes I could just make out Pete, with a big cowboy hat and no shirt, astride a stallion. When he rode up next to me and I thought I would choke on the dust.

"So, boy, you did come!"

I was speechless. His bare chest was lean and muscular, shoulders clearly defined and pecs like twin, round rocks, and not an ounce of fat on his stomach. Light brown hair swirled around his pecs and cascaded down a line to his belt.

"Well, aren't ya goin' to say something?"

"Uh, yeah, well, I mean, I need work so I thought I'd come on out."

My tongue must have been hanging out or something. Pete laughed, twisted and flexed his torso to survey his spread. "I think you like what you see."

"Yeah, it's beautiful out here." My gaze never left his hairy chest.

He jumped off his horse in one smooth movement and put a sweaty arm around my shoulder, the hair of his deep armpit brushing against me. It sort of embarrassed me to be so close, but Pete acted like it was just natural.

"I want you to meet a couple of the boys, and then you and I got some business."

He steered me around the side of the house toward the

stables. Two shirtless men were coming out of a shed, carrying fence posts to load into a pickup truck. The real beefy one was introduced as Big John, the foreman. The slimmer, more trimly muscular one was Dutch.

"You'll be seeing a lot of Dutch and Big John while you're here. They met here a few years ago, and just won't leave!"

"Hey, we like it here," boomed Big John. He and Dutch hoisted some posts into the pickup and then he threw his arm around Dutch just as Pete had done to me. "Anyway, you need a couple of reliable guys to keep this place goin'."

"Just kiddin', boys. You two are a real pair."

"You mean, they're . . . " I couldn't say it.

"Yup, that's just what I mean. Can't keep those two apart. They work hard and they fuck hard. You'll see. You're beddin' down in the bunkhouse with 'em."

I looked around as the three of them discussed some ranch business. Circle Q property spread out north and west from where we were standing. The land seemed to rise gently out of the canyon onto a mesa where the grass grew thicker. Here in the canyon it was mostly dust and sagebrush and gray scrub. The bunkhouse was behind the stable near the canyon wall.

Pete steered me into the cabin, scraping his boots on a mat on the porch. "My Dad bought this ranch when he was young, but the old house burned soon after he died about ten years ago. At first I thought I would sell the place, but then I realized how much I loved it out here. More privacy, no one to bother you and tell you what to do. So I built this cabin for myself."

The red cedar walls, the Indian rugs, the big kiva-style fireplace, and the deep leather chairs gave it a firmly masculine appearance, like the owner. He poured himself a whiskey and selected a fat cigar.

"Tomorrow you'll start helping the boys inspect the fences," he said as he lit his cigar. "You'll have to repair some, maybe even put some new posts in. Right now, you got another post to deal with."

The rich warmth of the room and of Pete's voice completely encompassed me. My dick was straining against my jeans. I knew what was coming, and for some reason, I wanted it this time. This wasn't like that horny sergeant or the nasty cop. This was a real man, who wanted real pleasure. As Pete took his boots off, he stared straight at me, cigar in his mouth. Finally, he unbuttoned his jeans and slid them down his legs in one smooth movement. He straightened up, erect and naked, looking as natural as if it was supposed to be this way.

He took his place in one of the high-backed, leather wing chairs, looking like a naked, reigning monarch. A long, thick hunk of meat hung from his hairy crotch. His legs were outstretched, and his smooth, muscular thighs joined as an impressive setting for his kingly dick. He downed his whiskey and commanded me to come toward him with a wave of his hand.

"I'm going to show you how to put a post in a hole. You're the hole."

He never lost eye contact. My legs wobbled as I approached and knelt down. His free hand guided my head to its goal. I brushed my beard against his mantool and buried my face in his balls. His dick was cut, but the skin was very loose around the head, and as he hardened, the head emerged from the skin. I took it into my mouth and slowly working down to the base until I could feel the brown fur of his crotch and smell his manliness. That musky aroma mixed with the odor of the rich cigar, reinforcing the defiantly masculine ritual of cocksucking.

As I deep-throated him, his hips began to thrust, forcing his dick deeper into me. I kept it up for almost twenty minutes, pulling back whenever he seemed about to cum or whenever I was close to choking on his nine inches. I could sense the sweat breaking out on his body as I worked that stallion into a real lather.

"Oh, man, big fuckin' mouth's just right for my dick." His voice was deep and almost hypnotic.

I drew back from his dick and looked him straight in the eye. "Blow smoke in my face, Daddy," I growled. He pulled my head back by the hair, leaned down, and, forming his lips into a circle, enveloped me in a cloud of rich cigar smoke.

Then I went all the way down on him again and stayed there, the masculine smoke ringing my brain. Almost immediately he seemed almost totally consumed with animal lust, and he gushed what seemed like gallons of his rich, warm male juice into my mouth, down my throat, and, when I had to pull up, over my face and head. That dick must have shuddered for five minutes before it finally became quiet.

"I think you've done this before, boy."

"Never like this, sir."

"You'll get along just fine here."

I whispered to myself, "Thank you, Sarge!"

* * * * * *

The next few days I rode the fences, getting the lay of the land and spotting places where major repairs were needed. I restrung some of the barbed wire myself with the supply I brought along every day. I hadn't ridden a horse for years, but it didn't take long to pick it up again. I had forgotten how good it felt to spread your legs over leather and straddle a powerful animal. The lazy, natural rhythm of a horse sure beats the endless hum of driving superhighways.

The land was still and vast. No noise from people or machines, just a few birds circling overhead. The haughty, granite canyon walls seemed to make the passage of time irrelevant, as if they were planned to outlast history itself. Strange, but I didn't feel lonely; in fact I enjoyed the indifferent company of their monumental beauty and they made me think of myself as part of the west. Or maybe it was the slow, warm massage my cock and balls got from the leather moving with the horse under my crotch. Sometimes when I was alone, I'd unbutton my jeans all the way down, lean back in the saddle, and let my dick rise in the sun. Man, there's nothing like cuming out there all alone—just you and the sky and the open land. You can hoot and shout all you want, and only the canyons and sagebrush can hear you.

The strange beauty of the country, the untroubled sleep, the abundant food, and the work all began to bring me back to life. Sucking Pete's big dick every night helped, too.

Life in the bunkhouse wasn't dull, either. Big John and Dutch regularly put on a fuck show for me and the other two ranch hands, Cal and Vern. They usually got involved in the action too, one way or another, but they really got off on watching me pump loads down Dutch's throat while Big John plowed his butt.

No matter what had happened the night before, every morning Dutch would bring the pickup around and we would load fence posts and shovels and postmauls for the day's work. We'd stand about eight feet apart and each of us would dig a hole, drop a post in and pound it deep and solid, re-fill with dirt, and then go eight feet further on. Monotonous work in the hot sun, but Dutch made a game of it.

"Come, on, Will, slam that shovel in deep, pretend you're fucking butt, now you know how it's done." I guess he was referring to the action I'd been watching in the bunkhouse. I was getting hot, but I couldn't tell if it was the work or if I was getting horny from Dutch's talk. Pretty soon I was almost as fast as he was.

* * * * * *

"Big John tells me that you've come up to speed real quick. You're working as fast as Dutch and you've only been here a short time." Pete and I had walked into the main room to leave the other hands to clean up after supper.

"Thank you, sir."

He put his arm around me and led me to the bedroom, where I had never been before. Moonlight streamed in through the skylight and the big windows to reveal a colorful Indian rug on the floor and a large, four-poster bed. Large hooks and rings hung from each of the sturdy posters, and a mirror was positioned overhead.

"Strip," he said.

He smoked a cigar as he watched me fumbling around nervously. "Something wrong?" He looked a little puzzled. "Hell, I'm not used to being watched while I take my clothes off. It makes me feel funny." He still looked puzzled as if he didn't understand why anyone would be embarrassed to be naked.

I got my clothes off, though pretty awkwardly, not like the graceful way Pete strips in front of men. When I stood up straight in front of him, he seemed to mumble approvingly and puff a little harder on his cigar.

"You know, you look a lot better than you did that day at the Central Saloon. Hard work must agree with you."

I was also aware of the changes. My face had a darker, more rugged appearance, and the spare tire around my waist was almost gone. He moved close to me and began examining my body in detail, feeling me all over like a stud horse.

"Real nice. I've always had a weakness for dirty-blond types, especially those with hairy chests and muscular legs like you."

I buried my head against his chest, inhaling the aroma of his body. His rich, natural odor made me want him even more. He told me to lie down on the square bed. I watched his dick grow to its full nine inches as I looked at his reflection in the mirror over the bed. Maybe I could watch us have sex together. He was naked when he climbed in between my legs. He ran his rough hands over my body, manipulating my tits and pulling on my balls. He raised my legs over his shoulders and greased up a couple of fingers before starting to probe my butt hole.

"I guess I should have known this was going to happen," I said to myself a little nervously. He continued to puff on his cigar and look at me steadily.

"Virgin hole, huh?"

He pushed his fingers in further, turning them, giving me even more new sensations. I liked the smooth feeling of the lubricant, and I also liked having his fingers probing inside me, but this had never happened to me before.

"You got a good, old-fashioned cowboy fuck coming tonight."

He pulled himself upright enough so I could get a good look at his outsized manhood. I wanted to get my mouth around that nine-inch fucker again, but he just held it and waved it at me as he enveloped both of us in a cloud of cigar smoke. Then he inserted it into me slowly, but it still hurt. I wiggled my butt to try to accommodate the dick better, but my hole just seemed to get sorer. He began thrusting in and out and pushing a little bit deeper each time. I was getting more and more uncomfortable and tossed my head, thinking "No, I can't do this," but he just kept pushing deeper.

The pain was getting so bad I thought I was going to split, and I was ready to ask him to stop, but before I could, he hauled off and slapped my cheek hard with the palm of his right hand, so hard I was stunned for a moment. He took the cigar out of his mouth and gave me a look I can never forget. In that one expression, he seemed to say so many things.

"Take it like a man."

"This is the way it's supposed to be."

"I own you lock, stock, and barrel."

"I'm the hunter; you're the prey."

"Stop resisting if you want the pain to stop."

"Let your butt appreciate what a man's doing for you."

As his communications seared into me, the fear, the reluctance, the pain, the past, all disappeared. He and his dick took control of me and it felt good just to be lost in the moment. Now the real fucking started.

"Open your hole for me, Will. Let me all the way in."

I spread my legs for him as far as I could and watched his narrow, muscular butt in the mirror, thrusting up and down between my legs. I don't know how much time passed, but it seemed forever until he spewed his cum deep inside my gut. And I started cuming at the same time he did! I didn't realize it was going to happen, but gobs of my balljuice spurted up, landing on his face and chest. The man had literally fucked the cum out of me!

We both lay exhausted, still coupled, not wanting the moment to end. When he did finally pull out of me, it felt like my insides were being ripped out. And the fucker's dick was still hard! My whole body felt electric, and my hole ached for his dick.

I could hear my voice, low and desperate, as I lifted up to clasp his sweaty body. "I want you, Pete. I want you in me all the time." He pushed me down gently, smiling slightly, and massaged the cum into the skin of my chest and belly. "I own you, Will. I can do anything I want with you. There's only one more thing you have to do to get it all, but you're not quite ready."

He penetrated me again, this time from behind. We didn't fuck, though. He just stuck his dick in me, and we curled up and slept for hours.

* * * * * *

I worked hard all day and fucked hard by night. Most nights, anyway. I hardly knew where I was anymore. Pete would fuck me up one side and down the other – standing up, lying down; on my back, on my belly; tied up, strapped down; on the bed, on the floor, and once lashed to a corral fence post. After he was finished with me I was sent to the bunkhouse, where the other hands usually wanted me to tell them what had happened.

"He's got a reputation as a mean fucker in these parts," Dutch said one night. "Wait till the cowboys come back. They can tell you some stories!"

One night I made the mistake of telling Pete how I wanted to do it. I got the shit beat out of me for my trouble. I never forgot that lesson!

I had forgotten most everything about the past. Well, maybe not forgotten, but I wasn't thinking about it all the time now, so I had more energy for work. My only problem was that my clothes were getting too tight because the muscles in my thighs and chest and arms were thickening. Pretty soon I could even beat Dutch at setting up new posts, but we were about finished with the work on the fences.

"We'll be all done by noon today, Will," Big John said over breakfast. "Be sure to show up behind the bunkhouse this afternoon. We got a little party planned."

When I rode back to the bunkhouse that afternoon, I could hear ecstatic moans echoing around the canyon. I reined in the horse when I saw what was going on. There was Big John, strutting around naked in his boots like he was some sort of prize bull (he really was). Vern and Cal, the other cowboys, were standing naked with their hands pressed over their heads against the canyon wall, their legs spread and their butts pushed out. I already knew that Big John serviced them sometimes as well as Dutch. Big John had apparently been working on them for some time and they didn't even look up when I rode up. I leaned forward on my horse and watched Big John fuck one guy with his manly tool for awhile, then pull out and fuck the other guy. Dutch was squatting down against the canyon wall so he could suck their dicks while they were getting fucked, and watch them writhe as their butts were speared by his man's huge dick.

As I got down off my horse, I heard a horse approaching fast. I turned to see Pete riding toward us. Then, foolishly, I turned back again, fascinated by Big John and the boys. What I didn't notice was that Pete was bare-assed and carrying a coil of rope over his shoulder. I heard a whirring in the air, but it was too late to react. Before I knew it, Pete had a lasso around my chest and my arms were lashed to my body. He rode in a circle around me a few times, smiling and laughing, before dismounting. His big dick flopped up and down as he landed hard. He gave me a big bear hug and then walked me by the rope over to Big John.

"We're going to have some real ranch-hand fun now."

He brought another saddle from the stable and threw it over a sawhorse that Big John had thoughtfully provided. It was a special saddle, one that was sometimes put to use in the bunkhouse. The sight of that beautiful, muscular body gliding gracefully and naked in front of the gray canyon wall, slinging a saddle effortlessly over the sawhorse, transfixed me. As he bent over to strap it down, I watched his muscles working just as I had watched them through his jeans in the Central Saloon. He and Big John spent a few minutes fussing with the saddle but I couldn't see what they were doing.

After they finished, Pete looked steadily into my eyes as he pulled the rope off me. "Mount it, Will," he ordered gruffly. "Show off for the men."

When Pete reached into the saddle bag and retrieved the lube he liked to use, it started to sink in. I knew this was it. When Big John saw what was going to happen, he pulled out of Cal, and the four men, their hard dicks bobbing up and down, strode over to us, as I prepared to do what Pete wanted me to do. I stripped completely and Pete bent me over, greasing me up. Then I put one foot in the stirrup and hoisted myself up. I paused after I swung my other leg up, standing in the stirrups, proud to be Pete's lover, and then started to lower my butt.

"That's it, Will, go all the way down on it."

They all encouraged me as they watched the leather dildo, firmly stitched and anchored in the middle of the saddle, slowly disappear up my butt hole. After it was all in, I began to slide up and down on it, faster and faster. Pete slammed his worn Stetson onto my head to show his approval, and I rode that fuckin' sawhorse hell-bent for leather. Big John dragged Dutch to a big rock right in front of me and laid him spreadeagle over it, facing me. Big John fucked him from behind so both of them could watch me, and I could watch them. Pete motioned Cal and Vern in closer.

"Jack off on him, boys, give him a big, ranch hand welcome!" He shoved his big, beautiful dick in my mouth and twisted my tits with his hard fingers. It wasn't long before I shot, and that brought Pete off, gushing his thick load in my throat, and then Cal and Vern shot too, one in my face, the other over my chest and stomach. Our cheers and hollers of triumph echoed down the canyon, and maybe all the way back to Durango.

* * * * * *

"Will, let's you and me go into town. We got to get you some clothes that fit, anyway."

Pete had moved me into the main house so I could "service him regular." He had also given orders to Big John to keep his hands off me since I was his property. Probably I'll get Big John's meat one of these days when it suits Pete, and that's the way I want it. But now we had to put on street clothes for a change and check out Durango.

We went by the Grand Hotel, where tourists were drinking and spending themselves blind, but that wasn't our kind of place. We strode into the Central Saloon together, where we had met. Pete began reading a newspaper at the bar, paying no attention to the bartender or customers. The bartender even addressed me as "Sir" this time. The place was pretty full as usual, mostly cowboys and ranchers, but through the cigarette haze, I could see more than a few of the guys positively drooling at us.

Thoroughly pleased with myself, I turned back to the bar and looked happily into the huge, old mirror behind it. Pete looked up and smiled at me in the reflection. But that smile wasn't the only thing that mirror showed me. That old, ornate piece of glass also reflected back an image of the thick, steel chain around my neck, clasped in front with a big silver lock fashioned in the shape of a Circle Q.

PICKUP

Bart Louis

Andrew piloted the gleaming, new pickup down the dusty, rutted road, uneasy that he really didn't know what gear the purring motor was in. Automatic transmissions were new and worrisome to him, but he was pretty sure driving the high-slung monster on the four-lane highway would have the effect he was looking for. At least the shifting lever wasn't in the way anymore, and if he wanted to, he could move the steering wheel up by activating the Tilt Steering and Speed Control Group, whatever that was.

He had been almost superstitiously reluctant to sell the old truck for the memories it held. Even now he could tick off many delirious moments spent with the fragrant, young hitchhikers who had dropped their tattered jeans on the leaky floor of the old Dodge and spurted hot, young juice into his avid mouth after his fumbling approaches. That was the scene for his own first youthful experiences with a man, and so it was natural that it became his method when he became the hunter.

Of course it had been over forty years ago that the old farmer from the next county had stopped his V-8 on Highway 41 for the gangly farmer kid in the worn jeans with his thumb out. The truck cabs in those days barely accommodated two grown men, so it was pretty easy for the old farmer to grope the kid's bare knee protruding through the hole in his pants while the old guy talked about sexy things. All the tract homes hadn't been built along the highway in those days, so it wasn't hard to find a place to pull off in the bushes when Andrew had sported a boner and the farmer drooled all over his jeans before he finally extracted the young prick and went down on it. It had taken Andrew about thirty seconds before he came down that gulping throat the first time, and about three more minutes before he repeated the favor.

After that he hitchhiked regularly and frequently got "taken care of." Sometimes he had to take the initiative a little to make it clear he was available; after a few experiences his conversation frequently turned to sex as soon as he had settled himself, and the rest was pretty predictable. He learned to cut his ride short if the driver didn't seem the type, so he could try again. After loosing a couple of loads, he would hitchhike back, dropping a couple more loads when he was lucky. He remembered that day when he was picked up by a guy barely older but a lot more experienced than Andrew; the young man had taken out his own dick and waved it at Andrew. At first Andrew thought he could suck it a little to start things going, but quickly learned that he had missed a lot from his passive role. That's when he started to pick up a certain amount of versatility.

By this time his mother and father were getting nervous about his apparent lack of interest in dating, and before long his mother had selected a proper girl for him. Mariann was the daughter of another dairy farmer near by, also a member of the Grange, and soon the two families were planning a wedding with little consultation with the bride or groom. Andrew didn't really object, knowing that was the thing everyone did, and thinking, hoping Mariann might be an adequate substitute for hitchhiking, but after they were married she made it very clear that it just wasn't proper to suck his cock, no way. She would only do "it" in the missionary position with the lights off, and she never actually touched his cock in all their years of marriage.

But there was always that smell, the sour, yeasty smell strongest between Mariann's legs, that soon pervaded the bedroom and eventually the whole house, it seemed. His cock, that reared high and hard when a man touched him, seemed almost impervious to his wife's entreaties, but when he thought of one of his highway escapades he could usually function. And that's how the kids came along, Roseann and Loriann, before he decided that wife-fucking just wasn't worth bothering with anymore, and Mariann didn't care, either. Andrew heard her tell her friends in Ladies Aid that she'd "done her duty" by bearing two children and that was all that was necessary. With three women in the house, the sickly sour odor was even more prominent, and he spent most of his time in the barn. The smell of cow shit was better.

He had learned many years ago that newborn calves gave the best blowjobs in the world! You had to get them before they grew teeth. It was easy, with the just-dropped calf teetering on spindly legs but with a voracious appetite, to dip his two fingers in the thick, clobbered milk of the mother and allow the calf to get a taste. Then he could easily substitute his rampant cock for his fingers and lean back, enthralled by the rough tongue and the terrific suction. After he came, which never took more than a minute of that ferocious action, he switched the calf back to the milk. They needed feeding twice a day. He made sure to breed the cows so that calves were available almost every month of the year. And he still had occasional opportunities to pick up hitchhikers.

Recently the Farm 'N Feed store had taken on the Dodge franchise, and when he took his ancient pickup in for service and found that it needed a new motor, it was pretty easy for the young salesman to talk him into buying a new truck. His salesmanship did not falter when the two drove a new model—the "Magnum V10 and Cummins Intercooled Turbo Diesel"—out on the back roads for a test drive, his sales-order clipboard on his knee. He was able to add several expensive luxury items, like "Mirrors—6"x9" Dual Power, Remote-Bright" and "Premium AM/FM Stereo with Cassette and Clock, Six Infinity Speakers," while a ravenous Andrew was nibbling on the salesman's thick, luxurious foreskin, preparatory to taking the entire stiffness to the root.

But this was Andrew's first foray for hitchhikers in the new truck on the highway. As he turned onto the 4-lane highway, he noticed that the other side of the cab looked very far away, and he hoped his subject wouldn't huddle against the far door so he couldn't reach him. Hitchhikers weren't so common anymore. It seemed like most of the young men had cars of their own now, and were frequently getting drunk and wrapping themselves around a pole or something. At least out here in God's country it wasn't like the horrendous TV pictures of New York and Los Angeles and even Chicago, where kids were taking drugs and firing automatic rifles into crowds and the like.

He could barely hear the engine as he drove southward slowly in the outside lane, alert for a lonely figure needing a lift. An observer would have wondered about the cautious progress of the flashy vehicle built for speed and power. The day was becoming hotter, but Andrew did not think to turn on the air conditioner, even if he had known how. The highway stretched out shimmering, straight ahead of him. Sharp-eyed hawks soared and glided in circles, searching for their breakfast of darting field mice in the grassy plain.

His wrinkled, chambray shirt was starting to stick to his chest when he got his first glimpse of a figure ahead. He prided himself on his far vision, although he needed glasses to read the newspaper. As he drew nearer his pulse quickened; it was a young man showing a broad expanse of bare, tanned chest and wearing only droopy cut-offs and black boots laced high around his ankles. Andrew hated the loose pants that were the preferred style for youth these days because they showed no indication of cock size. Strapped to his shoulders was a backpack, apparently his only luggage. Andrew stopped the truck along side the boy with a jerk, not used to the 4-Wheel ABS Antilock Hydraulic Brakes.

The hitchhiker immediately tried to open the door, but Andrew had forgotten to unlock it. He struggled to reach across the vast expanse of Heavy-Duty Vinyl Bench With Integral Headrests to release the lock, accidentally releasing pressure on the brake and allowing the truck to creep forward in his confusion. Finally the boy climbed in, bringing with him that intoxicating fragrance of young, sweaty, male flesh that Andrew had missed so acutely. Without any conversation, the youth shrugged out of his backpack, depositing it on the floor at his feet. He looked quickly around the shiny cab.

"Bitchin' wheels, pop," he commented then with a direct smile. His voice was low, almost guttural. For a moment Andrew was speechless, first because he had no idea what the boy meant with his comment and also because of the impact of bright blue eyes and the longest eyelashes he had ever seen on a boy. He was taller and rangier and more muscular, but Andrew's first impression was a memory of James Dean who had captivated him back in 1954. To cover his uncertainty, he released the brake and managed to ease out onto the highway without mishap.

"Yo, tape player! Got any metal?" Without waiting for an answer, the boy opened the dashboard compartment but found only the Users Manual. He fumbled for a moment in his backpack and came up with a tape that he inserted in the tape player. When he turned it on the cab was immediately engulfed with what Andrew could only describe as wails and clangs and thumps from all six speakers at a decibel level close to the maximum for the equipment. Andrew's hair stood on end but the boy leaned back into the seatback, stretching out luxuriously, listening with a beatific smile on his James-Dean face.

This wasn't what Andrew had been hoping for, exactly; he was especially startled when the boy started drumming on the dashboard in an erratic rhythm which may or may not have been in time with the "music." He relaxed a little when the boy ceased his drumming and stretched out further, eyes closed and his hands behind his head. He fiddled with a short pony tail of his golden hair, although there seemed to be a hint of bright blue in it for some reason. There wasn't a hair on his broad chest, but his football-player legs were matted with crisp, curly strands bleached almost white by the sun. But then Andrew almost swerved off the road when he spotted the boy's cock head creeping out from the leg of his cutoffs. The music was turning him on.

Whatever the source of inspiration, Andrew knew how to take advantage of the situation. He slowly, carefully, slyly reached across the seat and fondled the broad cockhead. It was hot and lurched a little in his grasp. There was no reaction from the boy at first (not a bad sign), but then, without opening his eyes or changing expression, he unbuttoned his shorts and abruptly shoved them down to the Heavy-Duty Black Rubber Mat. He gripped his entire equipment in both hands, two huge balls and a still-lengthening prick, and began to shake them rhythmically, his smile broadening as he lay back in his apparent reverie.

Andrew had to get off the highway before his palpitations overcame him. He was not aware that in his confusion the truck was rocketing along at an easy 90 mph. He tried to watch for a place to exit, but could not keep his gaze from the towering, swaying prick and furry balls. It was one of those cocks that Andrew categorized as "spade-like," meaning that it was broader than it was deep and curved gently downward, just right to fill the throat of an expert cocksucker positioned between the boy's legs. Also, it was almost as long as the spade he sometimes used in the garden.

With great relief, Andrew saw a sign **TURN OUT – FOR EMERGENCY USE ONLY**. God knew this was an emergency. Saved by those Antilock Hydraulic Brakes, he managed to swerve into the space just in time and came to a shuddering halt. He turned off the motor, killing the sound that was blasting the confined space. For the first time the boy stirred. He reached over and calmly flipped the ignition switch to the third position, and the Six Infinity Speakers took up their task again with scarcely a beat lost. He returned to flipping his own equipment which now towered high and handsome but quickly engulfed by Andrew's mouth as he leaned across the seat.

"Mmmmm," was the response, with no sign of surprise, even when Andrew managed to cram almost all that tool into his throat (he was an expert after all those years). He backed off and took a deep breath before starting up-and-down suction of his favorite joy-stick. After several swipes he pushed the boy's hands away from his balls to lap and suck them, one at a time (again eliciting an "Mmmmm") and then returned to his major task. The boy stiffened under the pressure, his cock lengthening even more and beginning to seep sweetness onto Andrew's tongue.

Suddenly the boy pulled back and Andrew reluctantly released his prize. But then, leaving his shorts on the floor, the boy doubled up on the seat on hands and knees, his dusty boots smearing the Heavy-Duty Vinyl and his asshole inches away from Andrew's face. The older man quaked, eyes popping, as he stared at the forbidden treasure. Quickly he fished his overheated hardon out of his fly (it was threatening to destroy his overalls) and then set to work.

His tongue slurped and circled and then dove straight in, the moist heat and masculine musk setting up whirlpools of lust in his brain. As he probed and lapped, he was rewarded by an occasional gasp, forthright appreciation of his expertise. The opening relaxed somewhat under his onslaught, making more and more of the boy available for the deserved worship. The hairy balls hugged nearby, and the thick prick jerked repeatedly between the furry legs.

Just as suddenly as he had assumed the crouching position, the boy flipped over on his back, knees bent and spread, his cock pointing straight up. Andrew sighted up, over the flat, ridged belly and heaving chest, to that almost-familiar face. The incredible eyelashes were flat on his cheeks, the eyes still closed. He knew the time was now; this boy couldn't take much of his expert treatment without dropping a load; he was right. Quickly he slid down over the broad head, streaked with precum and threatening to explode, and hadn't even struck bottom yet when he was met with a viscous flood of sweet-salty cum straight from those luscious orbs below. Over and over the flow gushed, and Andrew almost followed suit without a touch, his own eyes closed in gratitude. Great spurts of honeyed juice splashed his throat and coated his tongue. It is understandable that he was too occupied to notice a highway patrol car drawing up behind the pickup.

The hitchhiker was the first to recover, and he caught a glimpse of a uniformed officer alighting from his car to the rear. Quickly he swung around and pulled his shorts up, stuffing his still-rampant cock inside with difficulty. Andrew, unaware of the visitor, grabbed his own cock while staring at the boy, jerking it excitedly, on the verge himself. By the time the officer peered into the cab, the hitchhiker was fairly well composed, but not so Andrew.

"What's goin' on here?" the officer boomed, his eyes taking in the situation and focusing on Andrew's crotch. Andrew jumped and swung around to face the arm (and accusing scowl) of the law. Dark glasses concealed the officer's eyes, but his mouth was stern. His beefy chest was nearly bursting through the natty uniform shirt and there also seemed to be unusual tension in the crotch of the matching pants.

The boy was calm. "This gentleman was kind enough to give me a lift, Officer," he said in an unexpectedly polite, well-modulated voice. Considerately he turned down the volume on the tape player and got out of the car, taking his backpack with him. An experienced eye could have detected an enormous bulge in his shorts, but that was mostly hidden as he towered over the truck in all his nearly naked, muscular glory.

At that moment another car pulled into the turn-off, a raspberry Mercedes convertible driven by a young woman with long, flowing hair. She looked over her shoulder at the hitchhiker, obviously liking what she saw.

"I guess that's my ride, now," the boy mumbled and sauntered over to the convertible. She beckoned him in and they immediately sped away, spewing dust on Andrew and the officer who looked after them enviously. His attention returned to Andrew and the drooping, moist dick in his fist.

"I guess there's nothing to do this time," he intoned sternly, "but I advise you not to harass hitchhikers, you old fart. I catch you again and it's the pokey for you." Reluctantly he returned to his patrol car and sped away.

Andrew sat alone, staring after the officer, trembling from the multiple shocks he had had in the last few minutes. The hawks still circled silently, the cicadas droned monotonously, and the police car disappeared in the distance. Finally he removed the keys from the ignition and, leaving the pickup behind, staggered across the highway to the lanes leading home. Somehow he had known he would regret selling the old truck. He stuck out his thumb as he heard the sound of an approaching motor.